To Irene, who made me feel alive again.

A TANGLED WEB

Vallance stopped in the doorway of the kitchen. The body was sprawled across the kitchen table and had dripped a pool of blood on the polished floor. Its arms were flung back over the sides of the table. Two policemen, the second ambulance man and an unidentified woman were arranged around the table, chatting quietly.

One of the PCs turned and saw Vallance. He straightened instantly. 'He's dead, sir,' he reported stiffly.

'I didn't think he was having a nap,' Vallance responded.

CRIME & PASSION

A MOMENT OF MADNESS
A Fairfax and Vallance mystery

DEADLY AFFAIRS
A John Anderson mystery

INTIMATE ENEMIES
A John Anderson mystery

A TANGLED WEB
A Fairfax and Vallance mystery

A TANGLED WEB

by
Pan Pantziarka
A Fairfax and Vallance mystery

CRIME & PASSION

First published in Great Britain in 1997 by
Crime & Passion
an imprint of Virgin Publishing Ltd
332 Ladbroke Grove
London W10 5AH

Crime & Passion series editor: Pan Pantziarka

ISBN 0 7535 0156 2

Typeset by Avon Dataset Ltd, Bidford on Avon, B50 4JH
Printed and bound in Great Britain by
Mackays of Chatham PLC, Chatham, Kent

Part One
October

ONE
Friday 4th October

She was late.

Michael glanced at his watch. Again.

It was already after eight o'clock. Jenny was still not home from work.

The room was shrouded in darkness and only the glare from the television cast shadows on the walls. For a moment he was distracted by the scenes of death and destruction on the screen. A disaster somewhere; dead bodies ferried on makeshift stretchers; horror and shock etched in the vivid expressions on people's faces. The TV was on mute and the full colour carnage played on in the silence, a lurid silent movie from some distant part of the globe.

Light flashed through the room, twin beams slicing through the darkness as a car turned onto the estate from the road. Automatically he stood and walked to the window to draw back the net curtains. The car had already turned off and was heading away, the rear tail lights blurred by the rain that had started to cascade down the window.

She was still late. He inhaled sharply, letting the anger surge through him. The bitch. How many times did she have to rub his nose in it? How many bloody times did she have to do this?

The red lights of the car grew brighter for a moment as the car slowed and then stopped at one of the houses at the other end of the estate. The rain was growing heavier, beating against the window in waves driven by sharp gusts of wind. A car door slammed and he watched the driver make a dash for the front door of a house.

Michael let go of the curtain and turned back to the room. The electric light from the TV danced across the furniture and onto the walls. He stared at it for a few seconds then walked across the room to turn the light on. The darkness just served to remind him how long he'd been waiting for Jenny to get home. He glanced back over his shoulder at the room, which now seemed warm and cosy, a shelter from the wind and the rain outside.

Should he call her at work? The last time they'd rowed he'd promised not to keep checking up on her. That was what he'd agreed, even though he knew it was letting her off the hook. And what if he did call? What would he feel to find out that she'd left the office two hours previously?

He walked to the kitchen and clicked a switch. The fluorescent strip flickered hesitantly before shedding a sterile light. The work-tops gleamed white, stealing any warmth that should have been there. He consciously avoided glancing at the clock on the wall, even though its heavy, electronic tick paced him as he walked. She was late. And getting later.

He poured himself a glass of wine from the open bottle on one of the counters. Vodka would have been better, he decided, downing a mouthful. Half a bottle of that and nothing would matter. At least not until he'd sobered up the next day.

The flash of headlights was reflected in the green bottle and when he turned he heard the car pulling up outside. She was back. The bitch.

She fumbled for her keys and then the front door opened and she came in. Her shiny black plastic coat glistened with jewels of rain and her hair was dappled with water. She looked at him directly, the soft green of her eyes meeting his own.

'Don't say a word, Mike,' she warned, slipping her coat off as she entered the kitchen.

There was no way she was going to get off lightly. Not after all that waiting. 'Where the fuck have you been?' he demanded.

4

She threw her wet coat across the table and looked at him. 'You know very well where I've been,' she said.

'No, I don't. Tell me.'

She exhaled slowly, closing her eyes as though trying to keep calm. 'I don't want an argument,' she told him. 'Please.'

He poured himself more of the wine, his fingers gripping the glass so that his knuckles turned white. 'Why shouldn't we have an argument? Why should tonight be any different from any other bloody night?'

She shook her head sadly. 'What time is it?' she asked, glancing up at the clock on the wall.

The cry came to his lips suddenly, a roar that tore from his throat even as the glass spun from his hand. In slow motion the wine arced towards her, a dark red splash of colour that moved through the white light as though its path had been carved into the air. The glass tumbled over and over, catching the light as it chased the red fluid.

Jenny watched the glass move towards her, the graceful parabola aimed directly at her. And then she moved, instinctively stepping aside so that she was showered by the wine while the glass shattered spectacularly on the wall behind her.

'Satisfied?' she asked, looking down at her wine-spattered dress.

He looked at her silently. The wall was dripping with wine and the floor glittered with shards of glass. Her light-coloured dress was ruined and her face and hair were flecked with dark red. It could have been blood. Her blood. The bloody bitch had brought him to this.

'Well?' she demanded, her hands outstretched so that the wine ran down her arms.

He could have killed her.

'I'm sorry,' he whispered.

'Don't just stand there,' she snapped, 'help me clear this mess up.'

He reached for a towel but his fingers refused to work properly. His breathing was laboured and he was shaking. She stepped forward and slapped his hand away impatiently.

'Look, I'm sorry,' he said, his voice a whisper that begged forgiveness. He had been angry, he hadn't meant to throw the glass. It was just — just that sometimes things were so hard to take.

She wiped the wine from her face and arms. 'Are you happy now?' she asked and he couldn't tell whether she were angry or sorry.

'I didn't mean to,' he said. He reached out to take her by the waist but she slapped his hand away again. 'It just slipped,' he added.

'We don't have time for this now,' she said quietly. 'I need to get dressed and everything.'

She wasn't angry. It was so stupid, he knew, but he felt relieved that there wasn't going to be a blazing row after all. It *had* been an accident, at least she understood that. He couldn't help it. 'I only wanted to know where you'd been,' he said.

She looked at him calmly and then handed him the towel. 'You know where I've been,' she said. 'I've been working. I've explained it a dozen times, Mike. Graham's got a big order on and we're all working late to keep up. All of us. Me, him, Bev, everyone.'

'Then why didn't you call to let me know?' he asked. 'All it takes is one phone call.'

She shook her head. 'All it takes is a bit of trust. That's all.'

Trust? How could he trust her after what she'd done? How could he ever trust her again. For a second the anger threatened to become real again, but she looked at him with wide green eyes and he felt ashamed. 'I'm sorry,' he whispered softly.

'Clear this mess up while I go and get dressed,' she suggested.

He reached across to her but she stepped away. 'Not now,' she said, 'we don't have time.'

From the back there was no sign of the shower of wine that had drenched her. The dress was unsoiled and her reddish hair sparkled with droplets of rain. He listened to her heels on the stairs and then he turned to look at the puddle of wine and the splintered glass that lay like entrails across the tiled floor.

Michael was glad that the rain had eased off. It seemed to

6

make the silence in the car less heavy to bear. Jenny had spoken just once since they had left home, and that was only to ask him what wine they were taking. He'd chosen a bottle of Chateauneuf du Pape, but the information elicited no response from her. It was an expensive bottle too, one they'd promised to keep for a special occasion, but she merely accepted the news without comment.

He hated it when she was so quiet. It sometimes felt better to be arguing then not talking. But there was no point in trying to force the issue. He'd said he was sorry, what more could he say?

Jenny was out of the car even before he'd opened his door. Rosemary was already there to greet them, as though she'd been at the window waiting for them to arrive. He glanced at his watch. They were late but not outrageously so.

'I'm sorry, Rosemary,' he heard Jenny say as he stepped out of the car, 'I hope we haven't spoiled anything.'

He watched the two women embrace warmly. They were old friends and they always seemed so pleased to see each other. 'No, you haven't spoiled anything,' Rosemary said, 'we were just getting worried, that's all. Hello, Mike,' she added, turning towards him.

'Sorry we're late,' he said, forcing a smile. Had Jenny made up a story that he'd missed? 'Perhaps this'll make up for it,' he added, handing over the bottle of wine.

Rosemary took the bottle without even glancing at it. 'Come on in, we're all starving.'

He waited for Jenny to go in before following her. Patrick was waiting inside, a pleasant smile already on his face as he pecked Jenny on the cheek. 'It's been ages,' he said.

'I know,' she said, 'I keep telling Mike that we ought to have you round but you know how things slip.'

It was a bare-faced lie of course. Jenny hated Patrick, though the feeling never got in the way of her friendship with Rosemary. They all walked into the front room. The other couple were already there, sitting on the sofa, glasses of wine to hand. Patrick strode to the centre of the room to handle introductions.

'Mike and Jenny this is Minesh and Cleo. Minesh is one of

the new registrars at the hospital,' he added.

Mike stretched across the room to shake a proffered hand. 'Pleased to meet you, Minesh,' he said.

'And Cleo's currently enjoying housewife status,' Patrick continued, laughing at his own joke.

Mike swapped a quick 'hi' with the young woman. She smiled a perfunctory sort of smile, one that suggested she was already bored with the evening.

'Mike's our finance man,' Patrick explained. 'He makes sure we're kept on the straight and narrow.'

Mike's smile became even more forced. He hated the way Patrick spoke about his work. 'There's actually more to it than that,' he said.

Patrick laughed pleasantly. 'Of course there is,' he agreed condescendingly. 'And Jenny works for an electronics company.'

Jenny flashed Minesh and Cleo a smile that seemed warmer than anything Mike had been treated to. At least she wasn't going to be a bitch in front of company. That would have been too hard to take. He knew that she was more than capable of being a prime bitch in front of people.

Rosemary came in from the dining room at just the right moment to rescue them all from the post-introduction silence. 'It's ready,' she announced.

They sat around the mahogany dining table in Patrick's pre-arranged order. Jenny was sitting between Rosemary and Minesh, Mike between Minesh and Cleo. It was the sort of upside-down order that Patrick always excelled at. He liked to think of it as being quirky or original. The fact that no one else saw it that way meant nothing to him.

'No talking shop,' Jenny warned, half way through the first course.

It was no surprise that Patrick tried to laugh it off. The whole point of the evening was to talk shop. 'There's nothing wrong with a bit of shop talk now and then,' he said, casting around the table for support.

'She's right,' Cleo said, 'you two have been talking about nothing else since we got here.'

Minesh smiled sheepishly. 'They've got a point, don't you think?'

8

'Come on, Pat,' Rosemary agreed. 'I'm sure you and Minesh are going to have plenty of time to talk about the charity later on.'

Michael could see that Patrick didn't want to let go. 'I agree,' he said, 'I'm sure there'll be time later.'

Patrick looked from Rosemary to Mike and then back again. The smile was still on his face but there was something about his eyes that betrayed his annoyance. 'Later then,' he conceded, 'though to be honest I can't see that it would have done any harm.'

Mike caught Jenny's eye but she looked away, refusing to acknowledge his smile. He hoped that no one else had noticed, nor that he and his wife had not exchanged a single word since sitting down.

For a while everyone seemed to concentrate on food. Without shop talk there was nothing to animate the conversation. Sometimes, Mike realised, it was possible to imagine that Patrick was still motivated by the best of reasons. He and Rosemary had set up an appeal fund for the local hospital six years previously. Back then they were driven by a sense of anger after Rosemary's mother died needlessly because the hospital was lacking the equipment to keep her alive.

Six years on the appeal fund had switched focus and had become a registered charity that raised money for all kinds of good causes in the local area. Patrick was its director, Rosemary head of fund-raising and Michael had recently been taken on as accountant. He had expected things to be very different. In moving from a prosperous manufacturing company to a small charity he had been prepared to face all kinds of culture shock but it never came. To all intents and purposes Good Neighbours was just another business, with cash flow, ledgers, accounts and all the rest.

'What were you doing before you moved down here?' Jenny asked Cleo as Rosemary and Patrick cleared the table after the first course.

'I worked as a buyer for one of the book chains,' she replied, her voice carrying the slight trace of a northern accent. 'But I had to give that up when Minesh was posted to the General.

It was just too far for me to travel back up to Oxford every day.'

'Have you tried any of the shops in town?' Michael suggested, pouring himself another glass of wine. There was no sign of the bottle he had brought, but he hoped that Patrick would do the decent thing and serve it with the next course.

'Sure, but none of them need a buyer.'

Minesh smiled. 'I'm sure that something'll turn up soon.'

'If you've got lots of time on your hands then I'm sure we can find something to occupy you,' Patrick said, sitting back at the table.

'Are you talking about a job?' Cleo responded. She was looking at him dubiously, as though she couldn't work out what he was on about.

'It is a job,' Patrick beamed, 'but probably not in the sense that you mean it.'

'He means doing some voluntary work,' Jenny explained, her cold voice cutting through Patrick's smile.

'You make it sound so bad,' he said. He was still annoyed but as always the smile was fixed on his face. Sometimes Michael longed to see the smile wiped clean away.

'I was hoping for something that paid,' Cleo replied. Minesh smiled sympathetically.

'She means money,' Michael said, knowing what Patrick's next line was going to be.

This time there was no way that Patrick could hide his irritation. 'I was well aware that Cleo was talking about a salary,' he snapped. 'It's just that there are other rewards apart from the financial ones in this life.'

'But they're not the ones that pay the bills,' Cleo said.

'Perhaps not,' Patrick agreed, 'but sometimes one has to think beyond that.'

'Here we go again,' Jenny muttered, loud enough so that everyone around the table heard it.

'That looks good!' Minesh said immediately, even before Rosemary had placed the casserole dish on he able.

'Yes, that looks wonderful,' Cleo agreed, her voice, like her husband's, just that bit too loud to sound relaxed.

Patrick glared silently at Jenny but she ignored him completely. He deserved it of course. His holier-than-thou attitude was hard to take at the best of times.

There was a subdued angry silence for a long while as everybody ate. Michael kept looking to Jenny but she ignored him as resolutely as she ignored Patrick. If it had been anyone else then Michael would have sympathised with him, but he could not bring himself to side with Patrick no matter what he felt about Jenny.

Another couple of bottles of wine were opened during the course of the meal but the bottle of Chateauneuf du Pape seemed to have disappeared from view. It irked. It was an expensive bottle and Michael had been looking forward to it all evening. Rosemary knew next to nothing about wine. Patrick was the one who would have recognised it for what it was. The pious bastard was probably saving it for himself.

The conversation kept flickering back to life but it never lasted long. Each time it fizzled for a few minutes before lapsing into an awkward silence. Patrick was seething. He'd been thwarted, robbed of the chance to preach to someone new. Minesh was probably a Hindu. Did Patrick really imagine that he'd make a convert to Christianity?

Rosemary had picked up on the atmosphere. She had been in the kitchen when Patrick had been put in his place but she could probably work out what had happened. How did she put up with it? Michael would watch them working together in the office and he'd ask himself the question again and again. Patrick saw himself as the idealistic visionary and she was supposedly the practical one. In truth she was the one closer to saintliness. She needed the patience of a saint to put up with her husband's constant preaching.

It was only when coffee was served that Patrick decided to pick up where he'd left off. Michael canned his smile when he saw Cleo raise her eyes to heaven. She had already worked Patrick out. Minesh had probably worked him out too, Michael realised, but then he seemed more obliged to smile and listen.

'Good Neighbours is about more than dispensing cash to the less fortunate,' Patrick said, putting his coffee cup down.

He was leaning forward across the table, his watery blue eyes fixed on Cleo in a vain effort to communicate goodness.

'Minesh has told me all about it,' she countered, no doubt hoping that she could forestall the ten-minute spiel that Michael knew by heart.

Patrick ignored her. He wasn't talking to her, he was talking through her. 'It's about promoting the best qualities in all of us. There's more to charity than the simple act of giving. In a sense it's an affirmation.'

Jenny laughed. 'Come on, Patrick, it's about running a business.'

'Why is it? Tell me that?'

The look on Rosemary's face was one of pure panic. 'We don't need to talk about this now,' she said quietly. The poor cow. She needed to placate her husband and to salvage the evening as best she could.

'Jenny's right though,' Michael said, deciding that Patrick deserved it. 'There's no difference between running a small company and running a charity. Is there?'

'No shop talk, remember,' Cleo said quietly.

'Cleo's right,' Minesh agreed instantly. The two of them were trapped and they clearly wanted to get out and go home.

Patrick's gracious smile did not extend to his eyes. He was seething. Michael could see the rage that boiled inside him. 'This isn't shop talk. We're talking about something more important than that. I'm talking about basic, human decency, which some people are inclined to –'

'Please,' Rosemary said, putting her hand on Patrick's shoulder, 'I'm sure that we can have this discussion another time.'

'Are you?' Patrick demanded angrily. 'Why is it that we can't have it now? What is it, exactly, that seems so terrible? Is there something wrong in having belief?'

'There is if you shove it down people's throats,' Jenny responded calmly.

'Jenny, please,' Rosemary whispered.

Patrick stood up. He suddenly seemed bigger and taller, his lean frame puffed out with self-righteous anger. 'I'll not rise to the bait,' he said, his voice ice cold. 'I'm sorry if I've offended any of you, but I make no apologies for spreading the word. I'm not quoting scriptures, I'm not haranguing anyone in the street, all I'm doing is attempting an honest discussion. If that's too much then –'

'Perhaps we ought to get going,' Minesh said.

Cleo nodded emphatically. 'It's been a lovely meal, Rosemary, thank you.'

Rosemary looked to Patrick but he ignored her. His anger was directed completely at Jenny. 'Perhaps we ought to get going too,' Michael suggested.

'You know, Jenny,' Patrick said, 'I just wish you'd tell me what the problem is. Why is it that you take such offence when I talk about our work?'

'But I don't,' Jenny said, smiling. 'I've no objection to you talking about your work. None at all, Patrick.'

'We really had better be going,' Minesh repeated, standing up finally.

'Jenny's not having a go at you,' Michael added, ignoring Minesh and Cleo.

Jenny finally turned and smiled at Michael. 'We ought to get going too,' she said.

At last. Michael felt the relief flood through him. A truce. 'Yes, thank you for a lovely meal,' he told Rosemary.

Patrick stood by the table watching everyone go. He made no attempt to be civil, and refused to see his guests to the door.

'I'm so sorry it turned out like this,' Rosemary whispered to Minesh and Cleo as they climbed into their car.

Michael put an arm around Jenny's waist and she let him hold her there. They watched Minesh and Cleo go before Rosemary turned to them. 'He's furious,' she said, as though it had escaped their attention.

'It'll soon be Sunday,' Jenny said. 'He'll have time to calm down when he's in church.'

Rosemary shrugged. 'Forgiveness is not his strongest point,' she admitted. 'The silly bugger's going to be sulking all week.'

Michael smiled. 'He'll be fine by Monday. Once we're back at the office doing good works he'll snap out of it.'

Jenny wriggled out of his arms. 'I really don't know which

of you two is the most cynical,' she said. 'Anyway, we'd better let you get back to him. I'll give you a call tomorrow,' she added.

'He'll be feeling neglected,' Rosemary said. 'We must meet up again soon,' she told Jenny. 'And I'll see you at work after the weekend,' she told Michael.

'Tell him to pray for me,' was Jenny's parting shot as she got into the car.

Michael started the car but waited for Rosemary to return to the house before he turned to Jenny. 'I haven't had too much to drink, have I?' he asked. It was a neutral sort of question. Now that they were alone he needed to see if the truce still held.

Jenny nodded. 'That reminds me, what happened to our wine?'

Michael felt relieved. 'Patrick's stashed it away somewhere. For all his holy words he likes a good drop of wine.'

'The bastard, if I'd noticed I would have said something.'

Michael backed the car from the drive onto the road. It was after midnight and there was no traffic to worry about. The road glistened, black pools of tar catching the soft orange glow from the street lights. 'If you'd said any more then Patrick would have exploded,' he said.

'Not like some people I know,' she said, twisting round in her seat to look at him as he drove.

'I said I'm sorry,' he said. How many times did she want him to apologise? She was the one who'd been home late. She was the one with the acid tongue. She was the one who liked to provoke.

'Sorry's just one little word.'

'It's a bloody big word,' he retorted. She was the one who should have been apologising, not him.

They drove in silence for a while. He was aware that she was watching him, studying the profile of his face as he steered the car along deserted suburban streets. At last, when they stopped at a red light, he turned to her.

'Am I forgiven?' he asked hopefully. He hated himself for asking, for being so pathetic, but he needed to hear her say it.

14

She leaned across and kissed him softly on the mouth. 'Yes,' she whispered, 'you're forgiven.'

The lights changed and he moved the car into gear.

'What did you think of Minesh and Cleo?'

'The poor bastards didn't know what hit them,' he said, laughing.

Michael stripped off quickly and slipped under the duvet. It had started to rain again and the patter of it on the bedroom window sounded good. Jenny loved to be inside when it was horrible outside, she always liked to cuddle up close, to curl under his arm and lie across his chest.

He lay back with his hands tucked under the back of his head, waiting for her to emerge from the bathroom. The questions were still there in the back of his head, and with them the anger that had flared earlier that evening. He knew it was pointless going over the same old ground but he couldn't always help it. If she had strayed once then what was to stop her doing it again?

'In bed already?' she asked, walking into the bedroom dressed only in her black bra and knickers. The lights were dimmed but her soft white skin contrasted with the black just the way he liked. She was still slim – as slim as she had been twelve years previously when they had first married – and her body had lost none of its allure.

'I was waiting for you,' he said, pulling back the duvet on her side of the bed.

She climbed into the bed slowly, her eyes looking into his, playfully. 'You've not had too much to drink then?' she whispered.

He took her hand and placed it on his erect cock. 'You tell me,' he replied before kissing her softly on the lips.

Her fingers closed around his cock as she responded to his kiss. Her skin felt warm and soft, her body moving closer to his. He kissed her harder, pushing his tongue between her lips forcefully.

'Shall I undress?' she asked when he released her.

She looked so good. Was it any wonder that men still fancied her like mad? He nodded and she sat back on her knees to unstrap her bra. Her breasts were small, pear-shaped and tipped with large nipples that were already starting to harden. He moved forward and kissed each nipple in turn, lashing at the fleshy nub with the tip of his tongue. She cradled his head in her arms as he sucked harder, closing his lips over one nipple and then the other.

As he continued to play with her nipples with his mouth he began to slide his hand between her thighs. She inched her thighs slightly apart so that his fingers could caress her pussy over the tightness of her lacy black knickers. He stopped sucking her breasts and began to kiss her on the mouth again, tracing the inside of her lips before pushing his tongue deeper.

She lay back on the bed and pulled her knickers off slowly. For a moment he imagined her stripping off for someone else and the anger coincided with the wave of desire that pulsed through him. His cock was so hard for her.

'Fuck me, now,' she whispered hotly, kissing him on the neck as he moved between her thighs.

His fingers pressed between her pussy lips, seeking the wetness that he wanted. She wanted him, there was no doubt about it. He put his pussy-soaked fingers to his lips and licked away the sweetness of her sex. She liked him doing that, he knew how much it excited her and that in turned excited him.

She took his cock in her hand and guided him to her pussy. He pushed down against her slowly, closing his eyes as his cock slid into the wet groove of her body. She felt so good under him, it felt so good to be inside her. He pushed away the image of another man's cock inside her, even though it aroused him even more. He was screwing her. There was no one else.

'That's it –' she sighed as he began to move inside her.

He fucked her slowly, enjoying the feel of his hardness entering the wet heat of her sex. She sighed and moved with him, matching his rhythm, pressing her clit against the base of his cock. She was close to orgasm, he could feel the tension in her body and in the way she clung to him, her nails digging into his back.

He fucked harder, harder, harder. The wordless sighs and

16

moans that escaped her lips spurred him on, making him hold back the pleasure of release until she began to cry out. He pushed himself into her, driving his cock deep into her body before crying out himself. She held onto him tightly as they orgasmed together.

He rolled to one side, sated. They were bathed in heat and sweat and the drumming of the rain on the windows had never sounded better.

TWO
Monday 7th October

There was no sign of Patrick's or Rosemary's car when Michael arrived for work on Monday morning. Not that it signified anything. Patrick and Rosemary still treated work as though it were a hobby. It was anything but that of course, but then some habits were too deeply ingrained to change easily.

The office was empty, and Michael wandered casually through it towards the coffee machine. He hated having to make the coffee, it was always better to come into the office when its aroma was still strong and fresh. He put in a fresh filter, poured in the coffee and then leant back against the wall as the water began to bubble through the machine.

It was after nine o'clock and he was still the only person there. The phone started to ring but he let it go until the answer-phone kicked in. If no one else could be bothered to turn up on time he didn't see why he should be bothered to answer calls. Besides, answering the phones was not part of his job. Nor was making the coffee.

He waited until enough coffee had filtered through to fill one mug and then swapped the jug quickly. A few stray drops of coffee fell on the hot plate and it sizzled and cooked nicely, the burning smell merging with the coffee aroma. He poured himself a cup and then swapped the jugs back again. It made a mess but it couldn't be helped. Barbara could clean it up later.

He walked back the way he had come. The office had been open-plan but he'd managed to talk Rosemary and Patrick into putting in new partition walls to create some private space. He needed his own office, there was no way he could cope with working with everyone else out in the pit. Back at AlarmIC he'd had an office which would have housed the entire staff of Good Neighbours. And his own secretary. Now he had room enough for a desk and a chair and had to make do with the services of Barbara when he wanted anything typed up. That was if Barbara was in a good enough mood to deign to do some work.

His own room was near the front of the office, with a good view of the car park and, beyond that, the back of the pub. An office at the back of the Coach and Horses was hardly the most prestigious in the world, but it was the best that Patrick had been able to come up with. That was one of the problems with working for a charity, you had to depend on other people for funding. It was a big come-down after working for a real company. A big come-down.

By ten everyone had come in apart from Patrick and Rosemary. Perhaps Sunday's visit to church had not been enough. Was Patrick still angry? Michael smiled at the thought. Patrick had a child's anger and there were times when he could sulk for days on end. It occasionally made life difficult at work, for Rosemary more than anyone else. At least, Michael reflected, his was not the only marriage going through a bad patch.

Most of the morning was taken up with telephone calls to the bank, invoices to chase up and the rest of the routine stuff. Thankfully it wasn't his turn to go over to the Coach to collect the sandwiches. That was another thing that rankled. Why the hell couldn't they get one of the office girls to get them every day? It was another of Patrick's half-baked ideas. Rotas for collecting sandwiches, rotas for buying the tea and coffee, every task had to be shared equally.

Rosemary arrived just as Jane got back with the tray full of food.

Michael grabbed his sandwiches and then walked over to

Rosemary's office. 'How are things?' he asked, poking his head round the door.

She smiled but she still looked harassed. 'You wouldn't believe how difficult things have been,' she admitted. 'Why don't you come in?'

He closed the door and sat down, carefully placing his sandwiches on the edge of her desk. 'Still sulking?'

She sighed wearily. 'Sulking isn't the word for it,' she said.

Michael looked at her. She was an attractive woman in many ways. Her dark brown hair was streaked with grey. Her eyes, ringed by spidery lines, looked tired and yet there was something very desirable about her. She wasn't obviously pretty in the same way that Jenny was, for example, but she was still very attractive. She looked after herself, that was the thing, he decided. And she still had a good figure which she worked to keep trim, and which she clothed well. He knew that if she had wanted to she could dress to turn heads as well as any woman half her age.

'I'm sorry if Jenny stirred things up,' he said, realising that he'd been staring.

'It's not your fault, and I've known Jenny long enough to know that she likes an argument now and then,' she assured him. 'Besides, I know that Patrick comes on a bit strong sometimes.'

'Do you mind if I ask you something?' he said quietly.

She looked at him expectantly, doubt clouding the soft brown of her eyes. 'Yes?'

He paused, ditched the obvious question and decided on something less contentious. 'How much of what he says do you agree with?'

The answer took a moment to arrive, as though she had never really thought about it. Or perhaps she was trying to gauge how candid she could be. 'Enough of it to make life liveable,' she said, finally.

It was a diplomatic answer but it didn't mean anything. 'I don't mean to pry, but what does that really mean?' he said.

'It means that I agree with the general principles even if he sometimes drives me to distraction,' she said, smiling.

'What about how things are run here? I've only been here

a couple of months but already I can see that –'

She stopped the conversation dead with a shake of her head. 'I'm sorry, Mike, but that's strictly *verboten*. Patrick's very keen that we run this place on Christian lines.'

'But what about all this sharing of jobs business, surely that's got nothing to do with –'

Again there was the shake of the head. 'I'm sorry, Mike, but you'll have to talk to Patrick about that. It's his department.'

Michael smiled. 'That's his department while yours is making sure things work. It hardly seems a fair division of labour.'

'What's not a fair division of labour?' Patrick demanded, marching straight into Rosemary's office unexpectedly. To have knocked first would have been too much.

'Nothing,' Rosemary said.

'You were talking about something,' Patrick insisted. 'What's not a fair division of labour?'

There was no way to back out gracefully, Michael realised. It was bad timing, he would have liked to have discussed things properly when Patrick was in a better mood but it was too late. 'I was just talking about the division of labour in the office,' he explained, changing things slightly. 'I mean things like the sandwich rota and so on.'

Patrick closed the door and leaned against it, arms crossed over his chest. He wasn't going to budge, his body said everything. 'How is that an unfair division of labour? If we share tasks equally then it's the fairest it can possibly be.'

'Come on,' Michael said, 'that's such a simplistic point of view, Patrick. You and I both know that our time is more valuable than Barbara's or Jane's. Doesn't it make more sense to let them get on with that sort of thing rather than us wasting our time?'

'Have you ever heard of the sin of pride?' Patrick asked.

Michael smiled. It was Monday and he didn't have the energy for an argument that would probably splutter on and off for the rest of the week. 'This isn't about pride,' he said quietly, 'it's about the best use of resources. I'm sure that the people who depend on us would rather we spent our time bringing in more money than in running across the car park to fetch sandwiches from the pub.'

'This is a charity not a business, there's a difference,' Patrick insisted. 'You're going to have to get used to that.'

'Why be so dogmatic about it? If you really think like that then why don't we share out our salaries equally too?'

Patrick smiled. 'I think you'll find that we could all earn a lot more working elsewhere,' he said.

What was he talking about? Michael had been through the accounts and knew what everyone there earned. 'This is a charity but you're earning a good commercial salary,' he stated bluntly.

Rosemary stood up suddenly. 'This is getting silly,' she said. 'I'm sure that there's no need for any of this bickering.'

'We're not bickering,' Patrick said, once more wearing the fixed smile that masked his true feelings.

'Michael,' Rosemary said, 'would you mind if we continued this discussion later? There's just a few things I need to sort out with Patrick.'

Michael drew a deep breath. She was telling him to get out of her office. 'Sure,' he mumbled, carefully picking up what was left of his lunch.

Back in his own office he felt the anger surge back. What the hell was wrong with Patrick? The self-righteousness, the dogmatism and the arrogance were growing harder and harder to take. Did he really think that Michael didn't know what he was earning? Or what Rosemary was earning? Between them they were earning salaries that most people would have envied. Far from being poorly paid charity workers they were highly paid executives.

Damn them both! Why the hell should they pretend to be any different? Good Neighbours raked in a small fortune in donations and from fund-raising events, it had a turnover that any small business would have been proud of. And its expenses were proportionately high. Pretending that they were actually working for a pittance for some noble, charitable reason was the worst kind of hypocrisy.

He tried to calm himself down for a while but the anger kept coming back. At last, unable to concentrate on anything else, he moved over to his PC. The figures were all there, they told the truth and Michael was determined that this was one argument with Patrick he was not going to lose.

The industrial estate looked even more run-down in the twilight of early evening than it did in the cold light of day. Most of the larger units were vacant and the few that were still occupied bristled with security cameras, alarms and heavy steel shutters over the doors and windows. The car park was almost empty but for a huddle of cars in one corner, as though the drivers thought there was safety in numbers.

Michael steered his car into a space near the entrance of Components International and switched the engine off. The graffiti that stained the walls of the industrial units added to the general feeling of neglect. The place was a pit, there was no other way of describing it. Could it be turned around? More and more units were being vacated, and each vacancy only made it harder to find new tenants. It wasn't the sort of place that anyone would go to through choice. It was cheap and that was the only point in its favour.

Components International occupied the unit closest to the perimeter wall that ringed most of the estate. There was a loading bay at the front, firmly shuttered, and an entrance up a single flight of steps to one side. Jenny worked in the office but when things were hectic she would help out by going down to the warehouse to help pack the orders.

He glanced at his watch. He was half an hour early. Her car was in for servicing and so he'd offered to pick her up. She agreed easily enough, though they both knew why he'd made the offer. He couldn't stand the idea of her accepting a lift from any of the men she worked with. It was why he'd bought her the car in the first place, even though after the collapse of AlarmIC they'd been short of money.

There was no point in waiting in the car. It was cold, and besides it wouldn't do any harm to drop by and say hello to Graham. He locked the car and primed the alarm before jogging up the steel steps to the reception area. The cramped little room consisted of nothing more than a deserted trade counter which was faced by a couple of battered wooden chairs and a wall decorated with posters of transistors and integrated circuits.

He rang the buzzer and sat down on the least rickety looking of the chairs to wait. The floor was filthy, stained by heavy footprints and dotted with stubbed-out cigarettes. A bin in the corner was overflowing with food wrappers and empty drink cans, the usual debris left behind by the army of motorcycle couriers that picked up the smaller orders. That at least had not changed by much, it had been the same with AlarmIC.

'Hello, Mike,' Graham said, appearing at the trade counter suddenly. He still looked like an engineer made good: black trousers, dark-coloured silk tie, an expensive white shirt which was ruined by rolled-up sleeves and the pens that poked from the top pocket.

'I thought I'd come down in the world,' Michael said, grinning. 'Looking after the trade counter yourself now, things must be tough.'

Graham shrugged his shoulders. 'I can't complain too much,' he said. 'I admit it's a real step down in the world but there are worse things in this life. Anyway, how are things with the born-agains?'

'Hard to take, mostly,' he admitted, not bothering to hide the bitterness. 'Sometimes I just want to – That sanctimonious bastard, Patrick, drives me up the wall sometimes.'

Graham nodded sympathetically. 'You know that you're only with them until you get something better. That can't be too far away, can it?'

Michael shrugged. He had accepted the job at Good Neighbours at a reduced salary with the intention of moving on to something better as soon as he could. But the fall-out from the collapse of AlarmIC had not yet settled and it looked like his tenure at the charity was going to be much longer than he'd anticipated.

'How's business with you?' he asked. 'Jenny says you're snowed under at the moment.'

Graham looked perplexed. 'Snowed under? I wouldn't call it that, exactly.'

'Wouldn't you? What about all the working late?'

'Working late?' Graham repeated. 'Oh yes,' he said, catching the look on Michael's face. 'We've had a few rush orders recently, that's all.'

It sounded like a load of rubbish. It sounded like someone trying to cover up. 'Rush orders? How many days would you say that you've had people staying in to help?'

Graham started to look flustered, his eyes darting nervously from place to place and the pale skin of his face beginning to flush. 'A few days,' he said vaguely. 'I'm sorry, Mike, but I need to get back to things. You know what it's like when the boss's back is turned.'

'Of course,' he said coldly.

'I'll tell Jenny that you're waiting,' was Graham's parting shot.

So she had been lying. There was no way the bitch had been working late. No bloody way. And if she hadn't been working late where had she been? And with whom?

He sat back down angrily. The anger raged through him. He wanted to smash something, to grab the chair to smash it to bits in an effort to vent the violence and the rage that burned inside him.

The bitch.

She had to have some other bloke.

She needed some other cock to satisfy her.

He stood up again and paced back and forth across the tiny space. He clenched and unclenched his fists, letting the adrenalin pump through his veins.

'You're early,' Jenny said, appearing suddenly behind the counter. She was smiling, as though she were genuinely pleased to see him. Dressed in a short, bright red skirt that contrasted with her black stockings and the tight checked sweater that was moulded to the curves of her body, she looked like she had walked into the drab surroundings from another planet.

'Why shouldn't I be early?' he demanded through gritted teeth.

She looked shocked by the violence in his voice. 'What's wrong this time?' she asked.

'Not working late tonight?'

She shook her head. 'No, you know I'm not.'

Michael grinned. 'The rush order finished? Or has your boyfriend got a little wife at home he has to see occasionally?'

For a second he did not know whether she was going to laugh in his face or launch into an argument. 'Stop it,' she whispered. 'I don't want you to embarrass me here.'

'Embarrass you? You? I bet those bastards down there are all wetting themselves laughing at me right now. They know about it, don't they? Am I the last one to know the bloody truth, again?'

'Stop it! For Christ's sake will you just stop it!' she cried, her voice rising above his. She was livid, shaking, her eyes wet with tears of anger.

He slumped back down on the seat and held his head in his hands. Jesus, why did it have to hurt so much? Why did it hurt? His breath felt like fire in his lungs and he knew that he was close to tears.

She waited for a second and then lifted the counter top and walked over towards him. His eyes were closed but he could feel her so close to him, he could breathe her scent and was aware of the warmth of her body. When her fingers touched his face he stifled the sobs of pain that threatened to burst from his throat.

'Please, Mike,' she whispered softly, 'let's not fight.'

He opened his eyes and she was there beside him, on her knees looking directly into his eyes. He could see the doubt and the anxiety, the vulnerability and the pain that she felt too. She was so beautiful, the tears that welled up only made her more so.

Her lips were slightly parted, sensual, sensitive lips that he adored. He inched forward and she kissed him softly, her lips meeting his in a fleeting touch that meant everything.

'I'm telling you the truth, Mike,' she promised, her eyes filled with the hope that he'd believe her. And could he? How could he believe her after the affair she'd had before? How could he ever trust her again?

'I wish I could believe you,' he whispered.

She took his hands and he realised that he was still shaking. 'Please believe me,' she begged. 'I made a mistake before. Please, you said that you've forgiven me but this – this is getting too hard to take.'

He stood up unsteadily. 'Let's go,' he said.

He hoped that no one else had overheard the argument. Especially not Graham. Nor anybody else that he and Jenny knew. It was hard enough to accept that she had been unfaithful. To have other people know would have made it totally unbearable.

Part Two
December

THREE
Sunday 8th December

Michael pushed his hands deeper into his pockets as the sharp gusts of wind whipped against him. It was cold enough for snow and the icy breeze that whistled through the woods had a Siberian feel to it. He stopped for a minute and considered trudging back home, the way he had come. It was getting too cold for early-morning walks, and even the thick scarf, boots and padded jacket were beginning to feel inadequate against the weather.

The breeze died down suddenly. It was cold but bracing, a good way to clear the brain before settling down with the Sunday papers. A few more minutes, he decided, setting off again along the well-trodden path through the woods. He had lost sight of the road but he could hear the passing of cars easily enough. His own was parked nearby, the only vehicle in the clearing that served as a car park. Early mornings were always the best, and with a sharp December wind there'd be even fewer people out walking dogs.

He followed the path through the trees, taking care to avoid the icy mud where possible. His boots were already coated with a thick layer of sludge but there was no point in making it worse. The wind picked up again suddenly, racing through the bare trees before settling back again. It was getting colder by the second, each blast of chill wind seemed to lower the temperature still more. It was bound to snow soon, no matter what the weather people predicted.

His face felt numb, locked rigidly into place by the repeated blasts of freezing air. The scarf around his face and neck had slipped slightly and the tips of his ears were burning. Suddenly being at home with the smell of the roast and a glass of red wine seemed like the perfect heaven. Jenny was good at doing a roast, and when he had left her she was getting the potatoes and parsnips ready.

As he neared the car park he saw that his car had been joined by a heavy black motorcycle. It was parked close to his car, though there was no sign of its rider. At least there was no question of someone with a dog to foul the paths.

He stopped at the car and pulled out his keys. The alarm was still armed and he pressed the key pad to switch it off. He would have preferred an alarm on the central locking, the way it had been with the company car at AlarmIC, but it was too expensive. The alarm beeped twice as it disarmed itself, he reached down to unlock the door and then heard a noise.

'It's a bit nippy,' he said, straightening up to face the motorcyclist. Dressed from head to foot in black leather, apart from the crash helmet, the biker made no reply.

Why didn't he answer? Michael glared at him angrily and then reached down to open the door.

He saw the motorcyclist move towards him suddenly and realised that something was wrong. He turned quickly, his eyes fixing on the stubby black object that the other man had started to raise.

A gun.

A bloody sawn-off shotgun.

'What the fuck —' Michael began to say as the muzzle of the gun exploded in a deafening roar of sound and flame.

FOUR
Sunday 8th December

The afternoon sky was streaked with dark bands of grey when Vallance arrived at the murder scene. The entrance to the car park had been cordoned off, which was lucky because if it hadn't been for the bright yellow tape he would have driven past it. He turned the car off the road and flashed his ID to a shivering uniformed PC, who lifted the tape so that Vallance could park his car next to the array of police vehicles already there.

The victim's car was being given the once-over by SOCO. The scene of crime officers were meticulously going over everything, taking prints, fibres, impressions of the tyres, footprints and anything else that caught their attention. The natural light was fading fast so arc lights were been used with the video cameras to record as much detail as possible. Vallance sat in his car and watched for a few minutes. The warmth of the car was better than the bitter cold which set people's teeth on edge. It was too cold for a crime of passion, he guessed. Too cold and the muddy, icy woods were not exactly conducive to the emotional extremes which lead to that kind of killing.

The body was on the other side of the car. It was hard to make out, but Vallance was sure that it was sprawled over the ground. The victim was on his back, arms outstretched, legs apart. He shifted to one side of the car to get a better look.

He really had to make a move, the light was fading fast and he needed to see as much as possible while the body was *in situ*. If only it wasn't so bloody cold. The woods were not the sort of place he liked to visit. Alien territory, like most of the countryside.

DC Anne Quinn was already on the scene. She was standing by the victim's car, talking with one of the uniformed PCs. She was wrapped up warm by the look of things. As he watched her she turned and looked towards him. She finished with the PC and then started to walk over. There was nothing for it, he'd have to brave the freezing temperature.

'How does it look?' he asked, getting out of the car as she approached. The sharp wind was like a kick in the teeth. He wasn't dressed for the cold. He never was.

'Like a good clean kill, sir,' she reported. Her face was flushed pink by the cold and her breath misted as she spoke.

He smiled. A good clean kill. There was almost a note of appreciation in her voice. 'And how many of those do you get in this neck of the woods?'

'Not many,' she admitted. 'But this one looks like the work of a pro.'

Vallance had no doubt that she was telling the truth. Gangland killings and contract deaths were not very common, even in the heart of South London where he had grown up and had first served as a detective. 'Let's take a look,' he said.

The car park was surrounded on three sides by trees, and the tarmac surface and clinker paths soon gave way to winding trails of well-trodden leaves and thick mud. The victim's car was at the far end, in a space bounded by trees at one side and the thick, mossy trunks that had been cut down and served as a barrier between the car park and the trees. As Vallance neared the car he got a proper look at the body. Most of the face had been blown away, and a chunk from the back of the skull looked like an exit wound. Thick dark blood merged with the stuff from the back of the head as it leaked onto the carpet of dead leaves and dirty mud.

'Do we know who the victim is?' he asked, stopping close to the car. The victim's boots were caked with mud and matted leaves. He'd already been out for his walk, that was immediately obvious.

Vallance and Quinn were joined by the new sergeant on the team, Jim Crawley. 'This used to be Michael Cunliffe,' he said. 'Aged 43, married and a resident of one of those expensive little executive estates not far from here.'

'No previous,' Quinn added, answering Vallance's next question before he had a chance to ask it. She was sharp, the way that Vallance liked all his team to be.

'Has anyone done the dirty on the wife yet?' he asked, hoping that some other poor bastard had been round to break the news.

'No, sir,' Crawley replied, 'we were waiting for orders on that, sir.'

It was the one duty that Vallance hated above all others. There was never an easy way of telling someone that a person they loved had been killed. And, despite what older hands had told him, it didn't get easier with time and experience.

He turned to Quinn. 'Have you got the address?' he asked, knowing full well that she had all the information he needed already.

'Yes, sir,' she replied. 'Shall I drive?'

Vallance hated driving, it was one of the first things that his subordinates got to learn about him. 'In a minute,' he agreed. 'Have SOCO come up with anything worth knowing?'

Crawley shrugged. 'It depends on what you mean, sir. They've got lots of footprints and tyre tracks so far, but I'm not sure they know what's what yet.'

'No eye witnesses,' Vallance guessed. Thick woods, icy weather and a Sunday morning meant that the place was probably deserted. In that sense it was the perfect place to kill someone. But the ice and the mud were also perfect for preserving evidence, which made it less than ideal unless you were incredibly lucky, incredibly stupid or very professional.

'None,' Crawley confirmed.

'The body was found about an hour ago,' Quinn said. 'An old boy walking his dog. Got the shock of his life.'

'What does the doc say about time of death?'

Crawley flicked over a page in his notepad but Quinn knew the answer already. 'Before lunch-time, perhaps as early as ten o'clock,' she said.

'That's right,' Crawley confirmed, reading from his notes.

Vallance turned away from the body and looked at the car. A basic family saloon, dark blue, no flashy extras and in good shape. As cars went it was pretty nondescript, not the sort of car that one associated with gangsters or the victims of gangsters.

He looked at the victim again. Dark green waxed jacket, heavy walking boots, sensible jeans, gloves – clothes as nondescript as the car. There was nothing fancy about the way Michael Cunliffe had been dressed. His face and neck had been protected by a thick woollen scarf which had been blown to bits by the shotgun blast.

'No chance that this was self-inflicted?' he asked, even though there was no sign of a gun near the body.

This time the Detective Sergeant was first with the information. 'There's no weapon at the scene and no obvious sign of powder burns on his gloves,' Crawley reported.

'You don't think someone's walked off with the gun, do you sir?' Quinn asked.

'No, only a bloody idiot would stumble across a dead body and then nick the gun,' Vallance said. 'But a gun's worth a few quid and people have done even stupider things for money before. It's not much of a possibility but we shouldn't discount it until ballistics give us more info. Now,' he added, 'I know he's got no previous, but is he known to us?'

Crawley shook his head. 'Nothing on file, sir. I've checked back at base and there's nothing on him at all.'

'What line of work was he in?'

'You don't have this then?' Crawley asked, a broad grin on his face as he showed Quinn a business card. 'There was a stack of them in the glove compartment of the car,' he added, passing the card to Vallance.

The card described Michael Cunliffe as Finance Director of Good Neighbours. The phone number and address were complemented by the slogan 'Good Neighbours – People That Care For The Community' and then the charity number.

'An accountant working for a charity,' Vallance said. He looked once more at the body lying on the ground, cold in more ways than one.

'Hardly seems the sort of person a professional hit man would be after,' Quinn remarked.

Crawley nodded his agreement. 'Unless it's a case of mistaken identity,' he added.

'You mean someone might have thought he was a big-time drugs dealer or something?' Vallance said, smiling. 'The boring accountant's uniform and a crap car were all part of a front?'

Crawley looked at Vallance strangely, as though he wasn't sure how to react. Was Vallance putting him down or was it a gag?

Quinn's complicit smile seemed to annoy Crawley even more. The last thing that Vallance needed was strife between members of his team. 'It was a joke, Sergeant,' he said. 'You're right. Cunliffe could have been in the wrong place at the wrong time. But for the moment I want as much background on the man as possible. Also I want you to get onto DCI Simpson at New Scotland Yard, tell him you're working for me. If this is as professional as it looks I want to know who's in the frame for it. An MO like this is like a fingerprint. Everyone works differently and I want to know who this one matches.'

Crawley looked mollified. He knew that a professional contract killer would have a particular trade mark, a *modus operandi* that was unique to him. 'Yes, sir. What about the body?'

Vallance shrugged. 'You can tell the docs that they can shift him to the mortuary once SOCO have finished. The poor bastard deserves to get out of this cold as much as we do.'

The call through to the car came almost as soon as DC Quinn was at the wheel. An anxious Jenny Cunliffe had called the police to report that her husband had not returned from his morning walk. He was late home for lunch, which was most unlike him. The details had been taken and she'd been told not to worry before the person taking the call had realised who he was talking to. Vallance hoped that nothing had been given away at the moment that realisation had dawned. He hoped that the officer had remained calm as he had repeated his advice not to worry.

Although it was still the middle of the afternoon the sky had lost the tint of daylight. The trees that lined both sides of the road were black outlines against the sky, shifting uneasily in the cold gusts which buffeted the car. It always seemed colder in the darkness.

'This really isn't your scene, is it, sir?' Quinn remarked, nodding towards the silhouetted trees.

Vallance looked out at the landscape in front of the car: thick woods, narrow country roads and an absence of people. It was hard to believe that they were still in an area covered by the Metropolitan Police, but they were, just.

'How far to Cunliffe's house?' he asked, as they pulled up at a T-junction. There wasn't much in the way of traffic but it was moving fast, as though people were in a rush to get in out of the cold.

'About two minutes,' Quinn said. She took a left, accelerating sharply. 'He lives at Fenton Close. It's one of those estates that went up in the 80s. You know, mock Georgian, box rooms and tiny lawns out front.'

'Very desirable,' Vallance said. Already he was trying to work out how to break the news.

Quinn was about to say something but she stopped herself. He was grateful. The last thing that he needed was inane conversation.

Fenton Close was not an easy place to find. It was a side turning off a side turning off a minor road in the middle of nowhere. Even Quinn, who seemed to know the area like the back of her hand, had had to double back to find it. A dozen houses were set around a long rectangle of grass and tarmac. Joyless under the dark sky, each detached house was set with a lawn, a garage and a tiny path running down one side. Identical units, the only thing that differentiated one house from the next was the car parked alongside.

'Very des res,' Vallance concluded.

'That's the one,' Quinn said, squinting hard to read the numbers on the doors.

The Cunliffes' home had lights on in the front room and in the hall, and, as Quinn slowed the car to a stop, Vallance saw a face peer at them from behind a curtain.

'I hate this,' Vallance said, inhaling sharply to give himself strength.

The door was open before he and Quinn were fully out of the car. Jenny Cunliffe was obviously younger than her husband. Vallance guessed that she was in her early 30s. Very attractive, with long reddish brown hair that was set off by her pale skin.

'Mrs Cunliffe? I'm Detective Chief Inspector —' Vallance began, but she was already shaking her head.

'It's Mike,' she said, her voice bordering on panic, 'what's happened? Where is he?'

There was no point going on with the introductions. 'We'd better go inside,' Vallance said, taking her arm gently.

'Is it an accident?' she continued, peering back over her shoulder at the unmarked police car in case her husband was in it.

Quinn came in last, shutting the front door behind her, and then followed on into the front room.

A gas fire was on, the blue flames licking around glowing lumps of pretend coal. It was warm at least, though Vallance could see that Mrs Cunliffe was almost shaking. She sat on the very edge of the sofa, her hands locked together tightly at her lap.

He sat beside her, trying desperately to find the right voice. 'I'm afraid that it's very bad news, Mrs Cunliffe,' he said softly.

She looked at him directly, her grey-green eyes staring into his. Was hope still burning there? All he could see was the fear and the vulnerability. He was going to hurt her. 'I'm afraid that your husband is dead,' he said, looking away at the last minute, unable to cope with the pain that was sure to be expressed in her large, clear eyes.

'No!' she cried. 'No, you're lying! It's not true, it's not!'

Vallance glanced at Quinn, whose eyes were sparkling with tears of sympathy. 'I'm sorry,' he whispered, 'I wish there were something I could say to —'

'Liar!' she screamed, her voice filled with hopeless rage.

'Would you like some tea,' Quinn suggested softly.

'I don't want tea I want my husband,' Mrs Cunliffe wailed and then she bent forward to hold her face in her hands. She began to sob, her body hunched over as she gasped for breath and the pain poured liquid from her eyes and sound from her lips.

Vallance put an arm around her. He felt useless, the way he always did. 'Get some tea,' he mouthed to Quinn.

Mrs Cunliffe sobbed and cried, rocking back and forth gently while Vallance had his arm around her shoulders. When Quinn returned she tried to offer her a mug of hot milky tea but it was ignored.

'Please,' Vallance told her gently, 'take the tea, it'll do you some good.'

Mrs Cunliffe shook her head emphatically. She looked up and wiped her tears on the back of her hand. 'How do you know it's him?' she asked, her voice a whisper.

She was clutching at straws, seeking hope where there was none. 'We found his credit cards and his driver's licence,' Vallance said. 'I'm sorry.'

'No, no, no,' she whispered, shaking her head as though she could shake the truth away.

'Is there someone we can call to stay with you?' Vallance asked her.

'A neighbour?' Quinn suggested when there was no reply.

'I want my mum,' Mrs Cunliffe said, and it sounded pathetically human.

'We'll send a car round for her,' Vallance said, indicating to Quinn that it should be arranged quickly.

Mention of a car triggered something inside her. 'Was it the car?' she asked.

Vallance wanted to say more but he needed to put aside his feelings of sympathy for a moment. 'No, not the car,' he said.

'What happened? What sort of accident was it?'

Accident? The only sort of accident that Vallance could imagine was the accident of being in the wrong place at the wrong time. 'Your husband was shot,' he said simply.

'Shot?' Mrs Cunliffe echoed, as though puzzled by the idea. 'How? By who?'

'We've yet to establish the facts,' he said, resorting to the sort of bland statement that hid the true nature of where they were.

Mrs Cunliffe stood up suddenly. 'But there's no hunting goes on around Elsham Stream,' she insisted. 'There's been a mistake, something's wrong.'

The tears were gone and in their place was a stubborn refusal to accept the truth. 'Mrs Cunliffe,' Vallance said, taking her hand and urging her to sit again, 'I'm afraid that there hasn't been a mistake. Your husband has been fatally wounded, he's dead.'

The tears came again and she slumped down in the sofa. Vallance stood up. There was no more he could say or do. 'We'll get your mum here as soon as possible,' he promised.

'He can't have been shot, he can't –'

Vallance motioned Quinn over. 'Stay with her for a while.'

Quinn nodded and sat beside Mrs Cunliffe. She put her arm around her and held her close. Vallance waited for a second and then left the room.

Vallance waited until Mrs Cunliffe's parents arrived, about an hour later, before he and Quinn left. There was no way they could get anything useful out of Mrs Cunliffe. Hell, she was probably going to need pills to get her to sleep.

In the mean time there were few developments worth noting. The possibility of suicide was discounted almost as soon as the body was delivered to the mortuary. The size and shape of the wound suggested that the blast had been fired from waist height, in an upward direction and from a distance of four or five metres. Quinn had been right in calling it a good clean kill.

The body still needed formal identification but Mrs Cunliffe's father had been volunteered for the job. The upper part of the victim's face had been smeared all over the car park but there was probably enough of his mouth and nose for identification.

Quinn was silent as she drove them back to Area. She still seemed shaken by Mrs Cunliffe's reaction. She'd shed tears which she had done her best to hide, though Vallance felt there was no shame in showing emotion in such circumstances.

'Do you fancy a quick drink?' he suggested as they neared the squat concrete and glass building that served as Area HQ.

She glanced at him and then turned back to the road. 'I'm supposed to be meeting someone,' she said.

Was she really meeting someone or was she playing safe? 'No strings attached,' he promised.

'It's not that,' she said, keeping her eyes on the road. 'I'm supposed to be going round to my mum's tonight.'

He canned the smile. She was still interested, by the sound of it, even if their relationship never moved beyond the casually sexual. Life was complicated enough for each of them and emotional involvement seemed the last thing they needed.

'What are you working on at the moment?' he asked when she had parked the car.

She shifted round to face him before answering. 'Credit card fraud,' she said, her face and voice suggesting that she found it less than interesting.

He nodded. Superintendent Riley had a habit of putting his best officers on the most boring cases. The idea of giving keen young officers some job satisfaction by putting them on interesting cases was anathema to him.

'It looks like this one's going to be a long hard slog,' he said. 'If this guy was connected to a local charity then there's a chance that some of the local worthies are going to lean on the Chief for a quick result.'

'Does that mean you want me on the case?' she asked, smiling at the prospect.

Vallance had worked with Quinn on one case previously and he'd been impressed with how sharp she was. Unlike some of the people on the investigating team, she had been instrumental in solving the Ryder case. 'Yes,' he said, also smiling, 'I think this'll be a good case for you. That's if Superintendent Riley is willing to let you go.'

She shrugged. 'I can only follow orders, sir,' she said softly, looking at him for a moment and then lowering her eyes.

Was she being deliberately coy? She knew how much it

turned him on when she acted that way. He looked at her and then turned away. How the hell could he think about sex after looking at a body sprawled in the mud? How could he think about sex after delivering such dreadful news to Jenny Cunliffe?

'I'll put in a request that you be assigned to the case,' he stated finally. His voice was emotionless. He couldn't play around no matter how much he wanted to, it just didn't feel right.

'Yes, sir,' Quinn said. There was a quizzical expression in her dark brown eyes, as though she had expected him to flirt with her.

There was nothing more to say. He needed a stiff drink more than anything else. Outside it had started to rain in thick, heavy drops that fell at a slant that was driven by a sharp cold wind. Shitty weather but it matched his mood.

'Do you want me to call my mum and cancel?' Quinn asked gently.

He looked at her, at her soft brown eyes full of sympathy. 'No, it's all right,' he said, 'you carry on.'

'I think you handled it really well,' she said, daring to put her hand on his shoulder.

'Thanks. It's just something that I can't get used to, that's all.'

'That's good, isn't it? It means that at least you're human, not some cold-blooded machine.'

He shrugged. 'Maybe it's better being a machine.'

'How are things with Mags?' she asked.

Discussing his private life with a junior officer was not something that Vallance did often, but there was something about Anne that made him trust her. 'She's moved out of the flat,' he said, speaking of his ex-wife. 'But she's still trying to make life hell for me.'

'She sounds like a real bitch.'

He smiled. 'That's probably why we got on so well in the first place,' he said. 'You'd better get going,' he added, glancing at his watch.

She peered out at the unwelcoming weather. 'I hope I do get the case,' she said.

'I'll see what I can do,' he promised.

She squeezed his arm and then opened the car door. The blast of cold air flooded in before she was out in the rain. She dashed across the forecourt into the back entrance of HQ.

Vallance shifted over into the driver's seat. It was early still but he had no inclination to get to his desk. It was too soon to make a preliminary report, even if that was what he was supposed to. It could wait. What he needed more than anything was a drink.

He backed the car out and then headed home. The Ryder case had been his first big job after his transfer from New Scotland Yard. It had been the sort of high profile case that should have secured his reputation and pushed him higher. Unfortunately it had merely served to highlight the gulf that separated him from his superiors at Area.

He could sense that the Cunliffe case was going to be pivotal in some sense. With no witnesses and no obvious motive there was going to be pressure on for a quick result. And local charities had a habit of being mixed up with local politics, of which he was totally ignorant. Central London still felt like home. It was where he spent most of his free time and where he saw his future. The suburbs were alien territory, as inexplicable and foreign as another country.

FIVE
Monday 9th December

For Vallance the morning had started badly. The hangover was manageable, just, but that he was suffering one so obviously did nothing to endear him to Superintendent Riley. The two of them were never going to get on, they hated each other on principle. That was fine for the most part, except that Riley had decided to hand pick the team investigating Cunliffe's murder.

It hadn't even been worth asking to have DC Anne Quinn on the team. For some strange reason Riley felt that it was better to shield his most junior detectives from working with Vallance. It didn't hurt to be thought of as a bad influence, in fact Vallance took it as a point of honour and would have been horrified if Riley thought any better of him, except that in this case it meant that the most able of the young CID officers was excluded from the case.

Knowing the way that Riley's mind worked, Vallance had not even mentioned Quinn as a potential team member. That would have to come later, or else Quinn herself would have to fix it up. The absence of Quinn from the team was the least of his worries. Much more serious was to be assigned Detective Inspector Roy Dobson as his assistant. Another Riley protégé, Dobson was an ambitious officer who was living testament to playing by the book. He was the perfect example of how to advance a career by crawling, showing no initiative and being good at playing with paperwork. Riley thought highly of Dobson, but not as highly as Dobson thought of himself.

It had been pointless trying to argue against Dobson but Vallance had done it anyway. Hell, how was he supposed to find Cunliffe's murderer when his right-hand man would be more concerned with looking good in front of his superior officers? It hadn't been much of an argument because Riley refused even to discuss it. As far as he was concerned he was the one picking the team and if it came down to it he would rather shift Vallance to some other case than drop Dobson.

And now, as Vallance sat back in the car on the way to interview Jenny Cunliffe, he wondered why it was that Riley had been so insistent. Ted Riley was tall, thin and had a face that was congenitally unable to smile. His eyes were forever frosted over with an icy sheen of hostility that seemed permanently directed at Vallance. What was it with the man? Vallance had tried to puzzle it out before but he'd never been able to work out what he had done wrong. Perhaps he just hated cops who looked more comfortable in leather jackets and faded jeans.

'How far now?' he asked, finally breaking the silence that had lasted most of the journey from Area.

DC Alex Chiltern was doing the driving. It was the second time he had worked with Vallance and he seemed pleased to be on the case. It was no surprise really, a good murder case never hurt anyone's career.

'Nearly there, guv,' Chiltern said, keeping his eyes on the clear road ahead.

Vallance was in no mood for conversation and it suited him that Chiltern was willing to drive in silence.

The yellow tape was still up at the entrance to the car park where the body had been found and as they approached it Chiltern started to slow down. A uniformed officer stepped forward and was about to wave them on when he recognised the unmarked car.

'Who's here?' Vallance asked, opening the car window a fraction.

'Scene of crime, sir.'

'Has the search through the woods happened yet?'

The young officer looked back towards the trees, where a dozen of his colleagues were waiting in the cold. 'It looks like they're just getting ready,' he reported.

'Thanks,' Vallance said, then turned to Chiltern. 'We'll come back after speaking to Jenny Cunliffe.'

As Chiltern accelerated away Vallance looked back at the group of uniformed men waiting in line. They looked freezing in the sharp white light of day. It was their job to track through the woods in search of evidence. There was always a chance that the murder weapon would turn up. The mounds of rotting leaves and the trunks of dead trees were good places to hide things quickly.

In the daylight Fenton Close looked no better than it had in the dull light of early evening. Most of the houses were without cars parked in the front, though with more light it was possible to see what people had done in an attempt to differentiate one house from the next. In most cases it was pointless. Fenton Close had been designed as one unit and there was nothing that could be done to break the monotony of sandy-coloured brickwork, casement windows framed in white, neat lawns and net curtains.

'That's it,' Vallance said, pointing to the Cunliffe's property at one end of the estate.

'The one with the Astra in the front?' Chiltern asked, turning the car left onto the estate road.

Vallance nodded, though he had no real idea whether the car was an Astra or not. The car belonged to Jenny Cunliffe's father, which meant that he and Jenny's mother had stayed over. Vallance hoped that Jenny would be in a fit state to talk. The investigation could not really start until they had a better idea of who the victim had been. It was up to him to build up a picture of the man in order to understand how he had come to end up dead with half his face blown away.

While Jenny was, Vallance hoped, going to provide most of the story, he knew that there was always more than one side of a man. The Michael Cunliffe that he would get from Jenny might be a completely different creature from the one that emerged in talking to his friends and colleagues.

'It's not a bad little place, is it, guv?' Chiltern said once they had stopped outside the house. He was looking around Fenton Close in general, and seemed genuinely impressed by what he saw.

Vallance smiled. 'Play your cards right,' he said, 'and one day you might end up here.'

'Bit pricey for me,' Chiltern said, 'but you never know.'

Vallance decided against saying more. Irony was wasted on people like Chiltern. 'Right, we might as well make a start,' he said.

The door was opened by Karen, Jenny Cunliffe's mother. She regarded Vallance with eyes that were edged with exhaustion. Nothing in her life had prepared her for the day she would have to comfort a widowed daughter.

'She's upstairs,' she said quietly, showing Vallance and Chiltern into the front room.

The fire was on and the room felt stifling. Jenny's father, Tom, looked up as the two policemen came in. He too looked exhausted, drained by the emotional shock that had exploded into their lives the previous evening. He had been reading the newspaper but he put it down immediately and offered to make some tea.

'Jenny's had an awful night,' Karen explained, speaking in hushed tones. 'We had to call the doctor out in the end. He gave her some sleeping pills.'

'Is she awake?' Vallance asked, standing in the middle of the room. The flames in the fire flickered gently and he could hear the hollow echo of the wind in the chimney.

'Yes, but she felt too weak to come downstairs,' Karen said. 'Is there any news, Mr Vallance?' she asked, her eyes looking into his as though she could divine an explanation for the tragedy.

'Nothing yet,' Vallance replied. 'We need to find out as much as possible about Michael to give this investigation a chance to succeed.'

'Please, sit down,' Karen said, gesturing to the sofa in front of the fire. 'Mike was a good man, Mr Vallance. I've never had any complaints, he always treated Tom and me like we were his own parents. And he loved our Jenny, no matter what happened he always loved her.'

Vallance looked at her. Was she hinting that something had happened between Jenny and Michael? He made a mental note to talk to Karen after he'd finished interviewing Jenny. She obviously didn't hate her son-in-law, but if Michael had a bad side then there was every chance that she would know about it.

'Do you think you could get Jenny to talk to us?' Vallance asked, unzipping his black leather jacket.

Karen nodded uneasily and then they heard her wearily climb the stairs.

'Poor cow,' Chiltern murmured.

Vallance's mouth was dry. He still felt dehydrated and the heat in the room was making it worse. Tom was in the kitchen making the tea, they could hear the kettle coming to the boil and the clink of cups being readied. Looking around the room everything was neat, ordered, regular. Making tea and sitting by the fire were the normal state of affairs. Bloody death and the presence of policemen were intrusions from a nightmare that should not be happening.

Tom came into the room bearing a silver tray stacked with pale blue mugs, a matching tea pot, a silver sugar bowl and an opened carton of milk. He walked slowly, careful not to let the tea leak from the pot, and set the tray down on a nest of tables by the sofa.

'Sorry about the milk,' he said, managing a weak smile, 'but I don't know where our Jen keeps the jug.'

'It's no problem, sir,' Chiltern said, his loud voice and emphatic manner contrasting with the sombre quiet and the lowered voices.

'Milk and sugar, Chief Inspector?'

Vallance nodded and waited for Tom to pour the tea before speaking. 'Did you identify the body?' he asked.

'I did,' came the reply. 'It's not the easiest job I've ever had to do.'

'What about Michael's parents?' Vallance wondered. 'They're not around then?'

Tom served Chiltern's tea before answering. 'His mother's

dead. I suppose that's no bad thing in the circumstances. She died two years ago, breast cancer. At least she's been spared the pain of having to grieve her son.'

'And his father?'

'No one knows. He and Hannah split up twenty years ago. Ran off with another woman from what I can work out. Michael never forgave him, and I don't suppose Hannah ever did either.'

'They didn't keep in touch?'

'No. Michael hated him with a vengeance, though he wouldn't talk about it very much.'

'What about brothers and sisters?' Chiltern asked.

'An only child,' Tom said, finally pouring himself a mug of tea. 'There are cousins and uncles and aunts but none that he was close with as far as I know.'

Any further discussion was terminated by the sound of footsteps on the stairs. Vallance took the chance to down most of the hot, sweet tea. It tasted awful but it was better than nothing.

Karen came down first, followed closely by her daughter. Jenny looked tired, her hair was a mess and her eyes bloodshot as though she'd been crying again. Dressed plainly in loose sweater and faded jeans she still managed to avoid looking unkempt. Vallance was once again struck by how attractive she was. Her husband, on the other hand, seemed to have been less of a catch. Bland, boring and older than her.

'I'll be all right on my own, Mum,' Jenny said as she entered the room.

It was a relief. Vallance had been afraid that the parents would insist on being present during the interview. They were concerned for her welfare. He was concerned with getting to the facts.

'Are you sure, dear?' Karen said, her voice filled with concern. She still held Jenny's arm though it looked to Vallance as though the mother was more in need of support than the daughter at that moment.

'It's all right, dear,' Tom said, taking his wife's arm. 'I'm sure that the Chief Inspector would rather talk to Jen in private.'

'Thank you,' Vallance said, making it clear that he wanted

the time and space to question Jenny on her own.

Jenny waited until her parents were safely in the kitchen and then closed the door. She looked around the room strangely, as if she had lost track of where she was, and then seemed to shake the confusion from her head.

'Do you want some tea before we start?' Chiltern suggested suddenly.

Vallance sighed inwardly. He needed to start and the delays were beginning to get on his nerves. The situation was fraught enough as it was.

Jenny shook her head again. 'No, I'm all right, thank you,' she said, and then walked across the room to an armchair to one side of the fire.

'I think I ought to apologise in advance,' Vallance began. 'There's no easy way of doing this and if at times I seem like an insensitive bastard it's because I have to be. I'm sorry.'

Chiltern looked at Vallance and then down at his notebook. He probably expected his boss to be a hard man. Had Vallance confirmed or destroyed that impression?

Jenny closed her eyes for a second. She looked exhausted, her face drained of emotion by the tears she had obviously shed during the long night and early morning. 'There's just one thing I want to know,' she said, her voice barely a whisper. 'Did he — was it — was it suicide?'

The answer was no, but Vallance stopped himself giving it. 'Why do you ask that? Do you think that he was suicidal or depressed?'

'He didn't look depressed when he left home yesterday morning. He looked OK, normal. I just never imagined that when he went it would be the last time —'

The sentence trailed to silence but Vallance couldn't let it end there. 'Why would you think he was capable of shooting himself? Have things been difficult between you?'

She stifled the sob that rose from her chest. With eyes firmly closed she nodded, unable to trust herself to speak. Her face was a picture of pain.

'I know this must be hard,' Vallance persisted, his voice soft but insistent, 'but we need to understand exactly what happened. Were things difficult between you?'

51

'Yes,' she replied finally. 'They've been difficult for the last six months – I just wish there was some way of turning the clock back –'

Unfinished business. The inevitable 'if only' and 'what if' questions that haunted every bereaved person, injecting pain and agony on top of the suffering of loss. Fruitless conjecture but Vallance knew that it couldn't be avoided. 'There's no point in hurting yourself,' he said, knowing that his words were futile. 'How were things difficult between you?'

The knock on the door was an unwelcome interruption. Chiltern opened the door a fraction, whispered hurriedly to Karen and then took the cup of tea she had brought for her daughter.

'Your mum's making sure you're being looked after,' he said, passing Jenny the mug of tea to her.

Jenny took a sip of tea and then put the cup down on the light grey carpet that matched the wallpaper and the curtains. 'Six months ago everything looked fine,' she said, speaking with more than a hint of regret. 'Mike was finance director at AlarmIC. Have you heard of it?' Both Vallance and Chiltern shook their heads. 'It made fire alarm systems, electronic ones. The company was doing really well and Mike was happy there. He'd been there for a long time and as the company got bigger he moved up with it. He worked really hard but he was a finance man, an accountant, he had no idea about the electronics, none. And then some stupid TV programme appeared and said that the alarms had design faults and that people had been killed because of them –'

Was there a possible motive lurking in the story? Vallance leaned forward. He'd never heard of AlarmIC but now he knew that it was the first lead in the case. 'Carry on,' he said, when Jenny lapsed into silence.

'Once the TV programme appeared that was it. Orders were cancelled and then the government started to get involved and then – The company was wound up, Chief Inspector, and all of a sudden Mike was without a job. We'd worked hard to get this place. Every penny was spent on doing it up and the mortgage was phenomenal. We'd been secure – You don't expect things to happen like that, not ever.

And because of the fuss he found that people didn't want to know. I mean he was a finance man, not an engineer. He didn't know one end of a soldering iron from the next.'

'I understand,' Vallance said, wanting to move her on. Protestations of her husband's innocence were fine but he needed to know more.

'After that he couldn't get a job for a while. It was hard on him, I mean he'd never been out of work before and — He found it hard to cope, that's all.'

It didn't gel. 'But he's working now,' Vallance pointed out. 'Why should he be depressed about what happened back then?'

She looked at him sharply, as though he touched a nerve that screamed with pain. 'Because he hated his new job,' she said bitterly. 'Good Neighbours is a pathetic little charity run by people who've got no idea of how good Mike is. They treat him like an office skivvy and he hates it.'

Lots of people hate their work. The majority of the population probably. If everyone who hated their job was a suicide case then the country would grind to a halt. 'Are you saying that because of this he was ready to shoot himself?' Vallance said, unable to keep the incredulity from his voice.

Jenny began to cry. She held her face in her hands and let the sobs burst from her lips.

Vallance looked at Chiltern who looked away. There was more to ask. Cunliffe hadn't shot himself, the suicide theory was just plain wrong. He bit his tongue and waited for a minute, glancing at his watch as the seconds dragged on.

'I have to know,' Jenny said, sniffing into a bunched-up piece of damp tissue, 'did he kill himself?'

'We're still waiting for a full pathologist's report,' he said. 'Did he have access to a gun, Mrs Cunliffe?'

'No,' she said flatly. 'Why would he need a gun?'

'Then why do you think he killed himself?'

She answered with tears streaming from her eyes. 'Because I had a fling with someone four months ago and he found out —'

Another potential motive. 'Is that why he was depressed?'

'He never really forgave me,' she admitted, unable to stop

the flow of tears. 'He said he did but he couldn't. My God, I wished I'd never done it. You can't know the number of times I've regretted it and now – I just wish I'd had a chance to tell him how much I love him.'

She kept mixing the present tense with the past. The shock of bereavement was overlaid with a heavy load of guilt. The poor cow, no wonder she felt bad.

'I'm sure he knew that you loved him,' Chiltern said quietly.

Vallance bit back his anger. Chiltern was there to take notes, not to offer sympathy or advice. Instead of calming the woman down his words brought on another flood of tears.

'I'm sorry, Mrs Cunliffe,' Vallance said, 'but all this information is needed for our enquiry. I need to know who you had the affair with and when.'

'But it wasn't an affair,' she wailed. 'It was just a fling. I was fed up. Mike was so depressed about AlarmIC and all he did was mope about at home, out of work. It was just a stupid fling, a bit of letting go. I wish to God I'd never done it, you can't know how much I hate myself for it –'

'I understand,' Vallance said, 'but I still need to know the details.'

'It was just some bloke I met in a pub –'

'Was he much younger than your husband?' he guessed. Her nodded answer was accompanied by another outburst of sobbing. No wonder her fling put a strain on their marriage. Michael Cunliffe was older than his wife and he had been out of work. What was more certain to destroy his self-confidence than his wife having sex with a younger man?

'What was this man's name?' Vallance asked.

'Trevor Watkins,' she whispered. 'I only met him a couple of times. I swear – Mike found out about it almost immediately.'

A couple of times? It hadn't been quite the one night stand that she had appeared to suggest at first. 'Do you have an address or a phone number for him?'

Suddenly Jenny's head seemed to clear. 'Why?' she demanded. 'You don't think that – No, that's stupid –'

'Please, Mrs Cunliffe,' Vallance told her, 'at this stage we need every bit of information we can get.'

'But that was over. I swear I haven't seen Trev since the time Mike found out.'

'Mrs Cunliffe,' Vallance said, 'we have to look at the possibility that your husband was murdered.'

She looked ashen, as though the possibility had not entered her head and now that it had, it had drained her of what little energy she had.

'That can't be,' she whispered.

'Tell me about AlarmIC,' Vallance said, sitting back in his seat.

'What have you got?' Vallance demanded when Chiltern came back to the car.

'Sausage and brown sauce or bacon and brown sauce, sir,' Chiltern said, opening the brown paper bag. The roadside cafe, in front of the car, was full of labourers from one of the new estates being built a little up the road.

'I'll have the sausage,' Vallance decided. His stomach was rumbling and the threat of greasy food did nothing to dampen his hunger.

Chiltern handed over the sausage sandwich. 'God, she was in a bad way,' he said, referring to Jenny Cunliffe.

'What else do you expect? If she's had it off with some younger bloke then she's going to feel even shittier with guilt.'

Chiltern bit into his sandwich, taking care not to drip thick brown sauce over his dark blue jacket. 'So what d'you reckon, guv? Is it this younger bloke in the frame or is it something to do with this dodgy alarm company?'

Vallance smiled. Chiltern had watched far too many TV cop shows for his own good. 'It's too early to tell. We need to find out how she's going to be doing financially now that hubby's out of the way.'

Chiltern looked shocked. 'You don't think –'

Vallance shrugged. 'Most murders are in the family,' he said. 'Never ignore the obvious.'

'Shit,' Chiltern said, glancing down at the brown stain dripping along the lapel of his jacket.

Vallance smiled. 'When you've cleaned yourself up then

you can drive us back to the scene. I want to see what else SOCO have come up with.'

The drive back from the cafe only took a few minutes. The tree-lined road carried a steady stream of traffic until the turn-off for the woods. The bright yellow police incident posters had gone up along the route. Not that Vallance expected much in the way of witness reports unless the murderer had been particularly stupid. The obvious thing to do was to use the woods for cover, perhaps to lie in wait and have a getaway vehicle parked up somewhere away from the scene.

DS Crawley was still at the scene. He had been directing the team of uniformed officers combing the woods but as Vallance and Chiltern arrived the search teams were on the way home.

'How'd they do?' Vallance asked, walking across the clinker surface of the car park to talk to Crawley.

'Lots of garbage but nothing that looks connected to the case,' Crawley reported. A thick black scarf was wound round his neck but his ears and his face were red with cold.

'What about forensics?'

'One of the lab sergeants has been waiting for you,' Crawley said.

Vallance knew a couple of the lab sergeants from previous cases. Detective sergeants from the Metropolitan Police Forensic Science Labs, the lab sergeants were the key officers on the forensics side of a case.

'Let's find him then,' Vallance said, hoping that there was something concrete to report.

The lab sergeant was still talking to members of the SOCO team but he straightened up as soon as he saw Vallance. A tall, gangly man, with a head of tight black curly hair, he walked over to Vallance immediately he finished.

'Well, Sergeant, what goodies have you got for me today?'

The sergeant grinned. 'Goodies is the right word, sir,' he said. 'We think we know how the murderer got here and out again.'

Vallance, Chiltern and DS Crawley followed the sergeant over to the entrance to the car park. The yellow police tape

56

fluttered in the breeze and a uniformed officer was still on duty. Only one side of the entrance was being used by the police themselves, the other side was off limits for the moment.

The lab sergeant squatted down to his haunches and pointed to the grid of tyre tracks in the thick mud. 'This is the victim's car,' he said, indicating a number of tracks that crossed the entrance and led in a slight curve towards the car which had yet to be moved. 'If you look here you'll see that the car's tracks have been overlaid with these.'

Vallance squatted down too. A second set of tracks cut through the tracks that Cunliffe's car had made. The second tracks were much thinner than the first, and there seemed to be two instead of four. 'What sort of motorbike?' Vallance asked.

'We've taken impressions of them and they'll be matched at the lab. It's definitely a motorbike though, it's not a mountain bike or anything like that.'

The lab sergeant stood up and led the procession towards the victim's car, pointing out the motorbike tracks along the way. In places the clinker surface was free of mud and leaves but it was not difficult to piece the short journey that the motorbike had taken.

'If you look here you can see where the bike was parked up,' he continued, 'and here you can see where our suspect got down.'

The footprints were indistinct in places but there was a good impression of the heel not far from the front of the bike. 'Boots or shoes?' Vallance asked, unable to decide for himself.

'It looks like he was pacing up and down a bit,' Crawley suggested.

'Boots, I'd say,' the lab sergeant replied, 'and I think you're right, he was pacing up and down. I'd say that he was pretty nervous while he was waiting for the victim to get back.'

'Get back from where?' Vallance asked, straightening up to look into the trees that lay beyond the car.

Crawley had the answer instantly. 'He went up a few hundred metres into the woods, sir. We've traced his route pretty clearly and there's no sign that he was followed or that he stopped for any amount of time in one place.'

'Then what happened?'

The lab sergeant took up the story again. 'The victim walked back to his car and stopped. He was still holding his keys and there was no sign of fresh mud in the car, so he didn't get back into it. The suspect walked along here,' he pointed out the tracks that were cordoned off with more yellow tape. 'He stopped here,' he pointed to the two foot-prints which were clearly impressed in the muddy layer of dead leaves.

'One shot to the head,' Vallance said, walking as far as the tape and looking towards where the victim had been found. The body had been removed but the signs of blood and gore were still on the ground.

The lab sergeant nodded. 'The suspect then turned back, walked to the motorbike and then drove out the way he'd come.'

'Any idea which direction?'

The lab sergeant nodded. 'Yes, sir, towards Epsley.'

'Is there any more?' Vallance asked.

'Not until we get the tyres matched and perhaps something from the boot prints.'

'Thank you, Sergeant,' Vallance said.

'If that's all, sir, I can head back —'

'Thanks, Sergeant, and if anything comes up I want to be informed instantly.'

When the lab sergeant had gone Vallance turned to DS Crawley. 'Any joy from DCI Simpson?'

Crawley looked disappointed. 'He's on leave, sir. I've asked a few other people but we didn't have much to go on.'

Vallance smiled. 'Find out where the hell Simpson is and I'll call him.'

'He's abroad, sir.'

'Let's hope he's somewhere nice and sunny when I ring him up.'

Crawley smiled too. 'Yes, sir. I'll get to it now.'

'Good. When we get back to Area,' he said, turning to Chiltern, 'I want you to find out more about this fire alarm company. Our lot must've been involved in an investigation somewhere along the line.'

'Yes, sir. Should I get a copy of this TV programme Mrs Cunliffe mentioned?'

It was a good idea, but there was probably a whole lot more that hadn't been covered on the programme. 'Yes, do that. And see what else there is — newspapers, magazines, whatever.'

'Yes, sir.'

'Right, let's get back.'

Once in the car Vallance radioed through to Area. He needed Jenny Cunliffe's lover, casual or not, checked out. Her relationship with Trevor Watkins sounded as though it had been a mistake born of frustration and anger on her part, but there was always a chance that there was more to it than that.

What if Watkins harboured deeper feelings for her? In that case he'd want to get her husband out of the way for good. Or what if the relationship had not ended? What if she and Watkins had cooked up the murder between them?

SIX
Monday 9th December

Good Neighbours. It was a stupid name for a charity. What did it mean? Nothing. It sounded more like the name of a soap opera than a charity. Dobson looked at his watch again. Ten after ten. Patrick Collins was late. Perhaps being a good neighbour didn't extend to the police.

The young secretary, her name was Jane, flashed Dobson another smile. At least she was friendly, though another cup of coffee would not have gone amiss.

'I'm sure that Patrick will be here soon, Inspector,' she said, speaking across the open plan office.

She didn't know about Michael Cunliffe yet. She had been a little surprised to find a Detective Inspector at the door but from her expression she showed no signs of being alarmed. He hadn't asked to see Cunliffe, though she herself had volunteered the information that it was most unlike him not to be at work.

Collins probably knew. That was why he was late, even though Jane had said that Patrick was often late into the office. Apart from Jane, the office was deserted, though there were plenty of desks around. Perhaps punctuality was not part of being a good neighbour.

Dobson wondered how DCI Vallance had fared with Mrs Cunliffe. Vallance was an oddball, there was no doubting that. Did he really think that the black leather jacket, the boots and the stubble suited a senior officer in the Met? Everyone was allowed a certain leeway but there had to be standards. And how would a recently bereaved widow respond to a man who looked like he was suffering permanently from a hangover?

'Morning Jane! Oh.'

The exclamation came from another young woman. Dressed in faded denims and an old sweatshirt, she had wandered casually into the office without a care in the world.

'This is Inspector Dobson,' Jane said. 'He's here to see Patrick.'

The girl looked warily at him. She had clear blue eyes and brown hair streaked with blonde highlights. 'Hello,' she said. 'Would you like a cup of coffee?'

She still regarded him with suspicion but at least she felt compelled to offer him a drink. 'Milk and one sugar please,' he said.

'Patrick's normally here by now,' the new girl said. 'Is everything all right?'

Dobson looked at her and then at Jane, who had being dying to ask the same question but had been unable to bring herself to do it. 'I need to speak to Mr Collins,' he said, deciding that it wasn't time to break any bad news. Besides, he wanted to see how Collins reacted to the news – assuming that Cunliffe's death was still news.

'Rosemary's usually here by now,' Jane added.

Who the hell was she? Another silly girl? 'Rosemary? This is something that only –'

'Mrs Collins,' the other girl said. 'She works here as well. It's not often that she's late. Where's Mike?'

Jane shrugged. 'He's late too. Is the traffic bad or something?'

When was Collins going to arrive? The idea of being trapped with the two girls and their inane chatter was enough to raise the blood pressure. 'Can you call Mr Collins at home?' he suggested. It might mean forewarning him that something was wrong, but news of Cunliffe's death was bound to be common knowledge by the end of the day.

Jane looked at her friend indecisively. 'Barbara?' she said.

Barbara shook her head. 'I'm sure they'll be here soon. Do you want me to call Rosemary?'

Dobson strained a smile. 'I need to speak to Mr Collins, not his wife. He runs this place, doesn't he?'

Jane and Barbara exchanged glances. 'Yes, sort of,' Barbara agreed.

Did that mean that the wife was the one who ran things? Patrick Collins was listed as the charity's director, surely he was the boss?

He was about to say more when he heard a car pulling up outside. He stood up and walked to the door to look outside. The car was a new Astra; the same type as Cunliffe's car.

'That's Rosemary,' Barbara said, also looking out of the window.

She would have to do, Dobson decided. If she did run things then she would be able to provide all the information that he required. He just hoped that she reacted calmly to the news. The last thing he wanted was to have to cope with a weeping woman. He didn't envy Vallance that task in the least.

He returned to his seat and a fresh cup of coffee. Barbara was sitting on the edge of Jane's desk and the two of them were whispering. They couldn't wait to find out what the hell was going on. They were clearly intrigued by his presence.

Rosemary was stony-faced when she came in. She looked at Dobson but there was no real surprise in her eyes. He introduced himself and she immediately ushered him into her office.

'It's about Michael, isn't it?' she said, taking her place behind her desk. She looked tired, not overly emotional but still obviously disturbed.

'How do you know?' he asked, setting his coffee down on her desk.

'I called him this morning,' she stopped and corrected herself. 'I called this morning and Jenny's mother broke the news. It's just so terrible, Inspector, I couldn't quite believe it.'

'What about your husband? How's he taken it?'

She sighed. 'Patrick's going to go over to see Jenny this morning. One of your colleagues is there at the moment but

62

Jenny's mum is going to call back later. The poor woman, she must be devastated.'

Vallance was still there. Dobson wondered how much useful information he'd get out of the grieving woman. His sardonic humour would do him no good in that sort of situation.

Dobson felt that the preliminaries were over. He needed to get to work. 'I'm here to find out as much as I can about Mr Cunliffe,' he said.

'Of course. How can I help?'

'When did you last see Mr Cunliffe?' he asked.

She answered without thinking. 'I saw him late on Friday afternoon. We finish work early, usually at around four o'clock. I saw him just as he left.'

'And he appeared in a good mood?'

She nodded. 'He looked fine. I mean I didn't really see him that much on Friday but just recently he's been fine.'

'He didn't see preoccupied or depressed?'

This time she was more circumspect. 'Not recently,' she said. Her eyes were clouded with doubt.

What did she know? Had Cunliffe been depressed in the past? 'When did he seem depressed?'

She sighed heavily. 'This is very difficult,' she admitted. 'Michael wasn't here very long. He came to us after the collapse of his last company. He'd been without work for a while but after interviewing him we realised that he had nothing to do with that awful business with the alarms.'

Bingo! Whatever she was talking about sounded significant. 'What awful business?' he asked cautiously.

She seemed surprised. 'I thought you knew,' she said. 'He worked for a company called AlarmIC. They made fire alarms which were riddled with design faults. Lethal things. But Michael wasn't a designer, he was an accounts man. We trusted him and offered him the job here.'

'How long ago was that?'

She looked blank. 'August or September,' she said vaguely.

'And he was still depressed about that?'

'Yes. And to be honest, Inspector, I think that he was having trouble adjusting to our way of working here.'

'What way of working?'

She managed the faintest trace of a smile. 'We're a charity,' she said, 'and we work according to our principles. We're not a business, and he never really got used to that.'

'And you think that made him depressed?'

She nodded. 'We'd talked about it, and I could see that he was unhappy with our way of working. He and Patrick never quite saw eye to eye on it.'

'They argued?'

Her eyes widened slightly. 'They discussed it,' she corrected.

Was she trying to back out of it? 'Heated discussions?' he suggested.

'We're Christians,' she explained, 'and that means a great deal to us.'

'Are you saying there was a lot of friction here?'

'No,' she explained, 'there were just a few occasional disagreements. Nothing more.'

He guessed that it was time to change the subject. 'If Michael did not appear overly depressed, did he appear preoccupied, distant in any way?'

'No,' she said categorically.

'Did he mention any kind of trouble? Did he have enemies?'

'Enemies? You're not seriously suggesting that someone murdered Michael, are you?'

She sounded appalled by the idea. What did she think? That he had killed himself? 'We have to entertain that possibility,' he said. 'Did he mention anything that you feel is significant?'

Again she sounded confident in her answer. 'No. I can't believe that someone would want to kill him. He was such a nice man, Inspector. He'd never hurt a fly, I can't imagine –'

Why was it that every murder victim was a saint? 'I'm sure that's true, Mrs Collins,' he said, 'but the fact remains that someone may have killed him.'

'I can't think of anything,' she said. 'He certainly never mentioned any enemies or anything that was worrying him.'

'How did he get on with the rest of his colleagues?' he

asked. There were two young women in the open-plan office. Had Michael been naughty with them?

'He was well liked.'

'Did he get on well with anyone in particular?'

'Not especially. He wasn't a great one for socialising. I mean he and Jenny came round to dinner a couple of times but that was all.'

She was sounding more and more defensive. There was nothing useful to be had. 'If there's anything you think of later then please call me,' he said. He handed her his card. 'Talk to me directly,' he added.

Vallance put the phone down and grinned. Andy Simpson had been none too happy at having his holiday in Lanzarote disturbed. He had recognised Vallance's voice immediately and his stream of invective would have made a sailor blush. Still, that was what mates were for. Once the swearing had stopped Vallance had given him the details. Simpson had listened carefully and then asked only one question: where had the victim been blasted?

'Simon Clark or Robbie Miller,' were Simpson's two suggestions, based on Vallance's answer.

The names were vaguely familiar. Miller at least had done time for armed robbery. Vallance could remember the case fairly well, even if he had not been in the team that had collared him.

'Is Miller still inside?' Vallance had asked.

Simpson's response had been swift but sharp. 'What is this? Twenty bloody questions? Do your own leg work.'

'Is that what you were in the middle of doing? What's her name?'

'Sod off, you bastard,' had been Simpson's parting shot. Which meant that he probably did have a woman stashed in his hotel room. Some men seemed never to tire of chasing nubile young WPCs, and Simpson was one of them.

Chiltern had done a computer check on Trevor Watkins. The man was clean apart from a string of petty motoring offences. It wasn't much to go on but at least half the offences involved motorcycles.

Vallance was about to order a check on Miller's and Clark's whereabouts when there was a quiet knock at his office door.

Quinn poked her head around the door. 'Can I come in, sir?' she said.

She obviously wanted to know why she wasn't on the case. 'OK,' he said, knowing that there was nothing positive he could say to her. If Superintendent Riley didn't want her on the case there was nothing anyone could do about it.

'I was wondering if you'd managed to get –'

He shook his head. 'Sorry, Anne, but Riley's giving me a hard time at the moment.'

She looked disappointed. 'But that's not fair. Why do I have –'

She was right. 'I can't help at the moment,' he admitted. 'But if you want to do some homework for me –'

'What is it?'

'Cunliffe worked for an electronics company called AlarmIC. Apparently there was something wrong with the alarms they manufactured and the company ended up dead after they were exposed on TV. Alex Chiltern's digging up a copy of the TV programme and whatever else he can.'

She smiled. 'Do you want me to check up on them too?'

He nodded. Quinn was good at getting information while Chiltern was the sort of detective constable who preferred to ride around in a fast car and kick in a few doors. 'He can get the TV programme, but I want someone to dig deeper. If these alarms were as dodgy as they say then I want to know if they were responsible for anyone dying.'

'You think that Cunliffe's murder might be a revenge killing?'

'It's possible,' he admitted. 'You can start by finding out who the other directors of the company were and what they're doing now. We wouldn't want anyone else to suffer an unfortunate accident with a sawn-off, would we?'

She looked pleased with the request, even though she knew she was taking a risk. Riley would hit the roof if he knew that she was doing work for Vallance. But then they both knew that it would be Vallance who'd carry the can.

'There is one other thing,' she said, her voice less certain.

He saw the look in her eyes. 'When?'

'Tomorrow night? My sister's away again.'

'You can pick me up after work,' he said, smiling.

The incident room was half empty when Dobson returned to it. Alex Chiltern was on the phone, DC Phil Matthews was doing paperwork and the rest of the team seemed to be doing nothing at all. If they had nothing to do then it was down to the commanding officer to make sure they were kept busy. Why hadn't Vallance set up a road block near the woods? Putting up posters was one thing, actually stopping people to question them was another.

Dobson stood by the door for another second then carefully opened it again then slammed it shut. He was gratified by the sudden change in atmosphere. The conversation clustered around one of the uniformed WPCs broke up instantly, and even Alex Chiltern straightened up as he spoke on the phone.

He strode into the room, glancing briefly at the pictures of the victim that had been plastered up on one of the white boards. The investigation was at its start, the incident room should have been a hive of activity not a bloody rest room. Few of the officers seemed keen to catch his eye, and those that moments earlier had been idle now seemed to have found work to get on with.

Sergeant Crawley was not around. He was probably the best man on the team. At least he'd keep things in order if Vallance wasn't around.

Dobson stopped by the cluster of desks closest to DCI Vallance's office. 'Where's Jim Crawley?' he demanded, directing the question to the room in general.

DC Matthews, only just out of uniform and assigned to CID, was the one who decided to answer. 'He's down at Traffic, sorting through the missing vehicles reports for the last few weeks.'

It was the sort of task that someone like Matthews should have been doing, not a seasoned sergeant like Crawley. Is that how Vallance expected to get results? 'What about DCI Vallance?' Dobson asked.

'In his office, sir,' Matthews replied, nodding towards the closed door to the office.

'Alone?'

'Yes, sir.'

'And what are you working on?' he asked coldly.

Matthews looked nervously towards his colleagues and then back at Dobson. 'I'm waiting for a call back from Mr Cunliffe's solicitor.'

Waiting? It sounded like Matthews was wasting time. 'And if he waits all day before he gets back to you?'

The room had gone quiet apart from the murmur of Chiltern on the phone. They were all listening, especially the newer members of the team. 'I'll call her again,' Matthews decided, nervously.

Dobson stared at the young detective. 'Do that,' he ordered coldly.

Matthews picked up the phone on his desk and started to jab the number with the tip of his finger. He wasn't about to make that mistake again. And neither, Dobson hoped, were the other members of the team. He turned and scanned the office but there were no takers, they were all engrossed in their work.

He knocked on Vallance's door and waited for a reply before going in. Vallance's desk was a mess. There were papers piled up and a small collection of coffee cups was occupying one corner of it. Vallance himself seemed as much of a mess as his desk. The man needed a shave and some decent clothes. No wonder the young DCs thought they could get away with doing nothing.

'How did it go at the charity?' Vallance asked, leaning back in his chair and fixing his dark brown eyes on Dobson.

Dobson met the eyes briefly. He and Vallance were not going to get on, even though they had never worked together on a case before. 'A waste of time, sir,' he replied finally.

Vallance looked surprised. 'Tell me about it,' he said.

Dobson grabbed the chair nearest the desk and sat down. 'The office's a tiny place behind a pub car park. I was there before the staff were, sir. They look like a right lazy lot. Not my cup of tea at all.'

Vallance smiled. His eyes shone with humour and for a second Dobson was sure that he was going to make some a joke. Instead he came back with a question: 'Did they know about Cunliffe's death?'

'Only the director and his wife seemed to know about it. I didn't get to meet him, he was waiting for you to finish with Mrs Cunliffe so that he could visit. I spoke with his wife, Rosemary Collins, and she seemed a bit shocked that was all.'

'And what did she tell you about Cunliffe?'

The answer was easy. 'Nothing.'

Again Vallance seemed surprised. 'Nothing?'

'Only that he wouldn't hurt a fly. The usual thing.'

'Did she talk about his previous job?'

Vallance knew about that. The wife must have talked about it. Dobson had hoped that it was a snippet worth keeping to himself until he understood the significance of it. 'She only said that he'd worked for an electronics company before,' he said. 'That's why he was having trouble fitting in with them at the charity. Seems he couldn't tell the difference between a charity and a commercial concern.'

The explanation seemed to suffice. 'Was there anything else?' Vallance asked.

'Nothing, sir.'

'I've spoken to a mate from New Scotland Yard. He reckons that the shooting sounds like the sort of job that Robert Miller or a bloke called Simon Clark would pull. I'm having them checked out, then I think we take one each.'

'Yes, sir.'

'You'll like Miller,' Vallance added, 'though I'd keep your bollocks away from his knee when you visit.'

Dobson nodded. He wasn't going to dignify Vallance's remark with the laugh he was so obviously looking for.

Chiltern arrived just as the information on Watkins was phoned through to Vallance. The details that Jenny Cunliffe had supplied had been out of date. Watkins had obviously recently changed address, and even the computer check that Chiltern had run earlier did not include his latest whereabouts. Now that his address had come through Vallance wanted to go out and talk to him immediately.

Chiltern was holding a fax that had just come through. 'It's that TV programme, sir,' he reported. 'I've been on to the production company and they're going to bike down a copy of the video. It should be here by about six or seven.'

It had taken Chiltern most of the morning and through to the middle of the afternoon to make the arrangements. Vallance knew that Quinn would have had it sorted it out much earlier, but there was no point in making a big thing of it. 'OK,' he said, 'let the others know. Make sure there's a video player about later, we might as well watch it when it arrives.'

'Yes, sir,' Chiltern said, turning to leave.

Vallance stopped him. 'I've just got an address for Trevor Watkins,' he said. 'You can drive.'

Chiltern grinned. He was good at driving.

The sky was already starting to darken when Vallance and Chiltern stepped out into the cold. Vallance turned up the collar of his leather jacket but it was no good. The thing was getting tatty and the lining was not up to keeping out the sharp gusts that seemed to slice through everything.

'It's getting a bit nippy, sir,' Chiltern said, noticing that Vallance was clenching his jaw as the cold hit him again.

'It's like bloody Siberia out here,' Vallance said. How come it was so cold out in the suburbs? Central London and civilisation were only half an hour away by car and yet sometimes he felt as though he'd been stationed in northern Iceland instead of the affluent suburbs to the south of London.

They walked to the car in silence. The high walls that surrounded the rear entrance of Area Headquarters were no good at keeping out the blasts of icy wind. Chiltern did the decent thing and slammed the heater on as soon as he switched the ignition on. The ice-cold draught made Vallance shiver but in seconds the air flowing from the vents was warm and nicely scented by the car fumes.

Vallance leaned back comfortably in his seat and closed his eyes. The car accelerated forward once it was on the road. Chiltern was always keen on getting out fast.

'Do you think this bloke's our man then, sir?'

Conversation? After talking with DI Dobson – the sort of miserable bastard that gave miserable bastards everywhere a bad name – even Chiltern was worth talking to. 'Probably not,' Vallance admitted. 'Jenny Cunliffe gave us his old address, which means she's either playing clever with us or else there's really nothing going on between them any more.'

Chiltern took a moment to consider the information. 'She's not a bad-looking woman,' he remarked. 'A lot younger than her husband was.'

Vallance couldn't fault his young subordinate's consummate skills of observation. It was easy to see why Chiltern had been moved out from the uniformed division. 'What do you think that means?' he asked, suppressing his own smile.

In contrast, Chiltern, his eyes fixed firmly on the road ahead, let his smile spread across his face. 'It means she's probably a bit of a goer. Must've caused him no end of grief.'

The conclusions were probably right, even if the phrasing wasn't the most delicate in the world. Vallance knew by experience that most murders were committed by immediate friends and family. Spouses killed each other with alarming regularity while spending most of their lives in fear of anonymous maniacs and random violence.

The question had to be asked. Could Jenny Cunliffe have murdered her husband?

'Just up here, sir,' Chiltern said.

The road ahead was treeless and lined on both sides by drab-looking terraced houses. Cars were parked on both sides of the road and along with the road humps they meant that Chiltern was driving at a snail's pace. The street lights were changing from pale pink to a dull orange glow as the sky turned from dark grey to a uniform cloudless black.

A cluster of sullen-looking school-kids were gathered around a doorway of one of the houses. They turned and looked at the car as it cruised by them. They'd spotted that it was an unmarked police car. Vallance could see the hostility clearly on their faces. Two of the kids were on bikes, the rest on foot, including one of the kids standing in the doorway of the house. They waited for the police car to move on before resuming their conversation.

'It must be that one there, sir,' Chiltern said, stopping the car in the middle of the narrow road. He pointed to one of the houses as functionally nondescript as any of the others in the street.

'There's a space further up,' Vallance said, pointing to a gap in the parked cars. He looked back and saw that the school-kids were still watching them.

'Don't worry about them, sir,' Chiltern said, 'they love us really.'

'I bet they do.'

They parked the car and walked back towards Watkins's house. Long strips of muddy grass bordered the kerb with paving between the grass and the front of the houses. Vallance skirted the grass carefully but kept his eyes on it as they walked towards the house.

'Notice anything?' he asked, stopping a few metres from the darkened front door.

Chiltern looked at the door. The frosted pane of glass showed nothing but the lack of light. 'No one's in,' he concluded.

Vallance shook his head. 'You're looking at the wrong place,' he said, pointing at the grass. Two thick tyre marks were etched deep into the mud, cutting through the unhealthy-looking verge. The marks looked fresh, as though only recently scored into the soft earth.

'He must be in the back,' Chiltern said. 'These houses have got gardens in the back,' he added.

The tyre marks became muddy tracks along the pavement and it was easy to follow them towards the gate that separated the lower storeys of the terraced houses. The gate was un-locked and there was light coming from the other end of the passageway.

'He's there,' Chiltern concluded.

'You know,' Vallance said quietly, 'you were wasted in uniform.'

Chiltern's expression was hidden by the shadows as he pushed open the gate and headed in. Vallance followed, glancing back at the kids who had walked down the street to get a better look.

The passageway was completely in darkness but it opened up to a small concrete courtyard that was bounded on left and right by small rectangular gardens and by brick-built sheds directly in front. The light was coming from one of the sheds, and with it the sound of the news coming from a radio.

Vallance stepped forward and peered into the shed that was lit by a single bare bulb. Tools and motorbike spares were pinned up on one wall, while the far end was occupied by a dismantled motorbike. But it was the motorbike up on a stand that took most of the attention, that and the figure hunched over it and fiddling with its innards.

'Trevor Watkins?' Vallance asked, knocking once on the shed door.

The figure straightened up, and it seemed to take all of five minutes for him to do so. It seemed that he was unable to stand straight and had to stoop in the confines of the shed. He looked at Vallance first, at the leather jacket, black jeans, boots and the unshaven face. Then he looked at Chiltern, younger, clean-shaven and wearing a blue suit and a tie under his thickly padded jacket.

'It depends who's asking,' Watkins finally replied as he wiped greasy hands on a rag that was even oilier.

Watkins spoke with the slow, deep tones of a big man lacking a few brain cells. He was as far removed from the staid appearance of Michael Cunliffe as was possible to imagine.

'You know who we are,' Vallance said, deciding that it was pointless trying any other approach.

'I'm clean,' Watkins said, a hint of protest in his voice.

'No you're not,' Vallance replied, 'you're filthy.'

Chiltern sniggered but Watkins looked confused. He was wary of the police and there was no way he was going to trust himself to laugh. 'This bike's legal,' he said, waving a dirty paw towards the motorbike he'd been working on.

'What about that one?' Chiltern asked, pointing at the carcase of a motorbike at the far end of the shed.

'That's clean too,' Watkins insisted.

Vallance smiled. 'I'm sure that the chassis numbers all check out,' he said brightly. 'How would you like it if we checked this little lot out for you?'

Watkins glared at Vallance but there was more confusion in his eyes than belligerence. 'I haven't done anything,' he insisted. 'I swear I haven't.'

'I'm sure you haven't,' Vallance agreed. 'Which is why you've got no problems helping us with a few questions. Have you?'

A slow smile appeared on the giant's face. He understood that a deal had just been offered. 'I'm always willing to help –'

'Chief Inspector Vallance,' Chiltern said, deciding that a formal introduction was in order. 'And I'm Detective Constable Chiltern.'

With that out of the way it was time to start with the questions. It wasn't a formal interview and if it looked like it was going to turn serious than Vallance was ready to issue a caution and take the obliging Mr Watkins back to HQ.

'What were you doing on Sunday?' Vallance asked.

'Sunday? I was working.'

'Where? Doing what?'

'Delivering. I do courier work,' Watkins explained then turned round so that they could read the garish advert for AAA Couriers on the back of his leather jacket. 'I was on a job,' he added.

'Details,' Chiltern urged.

'It'll be at the office if you want to check. I had to take a load of pictures up to Manchester Airport.'

'Times?'

Watkins shrugged. 'I left early, about half nine and I got there at about one. That's a bloody good time, three and half hours.'

'Very impressive,' Vallance agreed, though he had no idea how long the journey should have taken. Packages had to be signed for on receipt and on delivery. It wasn't an airtight alibi but for the moment it sounded real enough.

'It is!' Watkins insisted, hurt perhaps by an imagined slight on his driving skills.

It was time to switch topic. 'Tell me about Jenny Cunliffe,' Vallance decided.

Watkins smiled. 'What about her.'

'When did you last see her?'

He shrugged. 'Ages ago. Why d'you want to know?'

'Is that years ago, months ago or just last week?'

Watkins didn't have an instant answer so Chiltern urged him on after a few seconds. 'It must've been months ago,' he said finally.

'How many times did you see her?'

'Dozens,' Watkins said, grinning.

'That's not what she –' Chiltern started to say but Vallance stopped him instantly.

'How many times?' Vallance repeated, his voice more emphatic.

The stupid grin disappeared from Watkins's face. 'What's this about?' he asked.

'Just answer the question. How many times?'

'I saw her six or seven times when I did pick-ups from the electronics company where she works,' Watkins said. 'I saw her later in a supermarket and we met up for a drink after that.'

'And?'

For a second Watkins seemed quite embarrassed. 'And then I brought her round to my place a couple of times.'

Vallance decided not to relent. 'Here?' he demanded harshly.

'No, my last place. She's married,' Watkins added.

'Why did you stop seeing her?'

Again Watkins seemed embarrassed. 'I'm the one who stopped it,' he said. 'I found out she was married. I didn't know, honestly I didn't.'

Chiltern looked surprised, Vallance hoped that his own surprise didn't show as obviously. 'How did she react after you stopped seeing her?'

'She just laughed, said I was being pathetic,' he replied glumly.

A bashful biker. Vallance doubted that Watkins would have told the story quite so honestly in front of his mates. 'And you've not seen her since?'

'I saw her once more when I did a pick-up from

Components International. She didn't even bother to say hello. She's a right bitch if you ask me.'

'I'm not asking you,' Vallance snapped. 'What about her husband? Did you ever meet him?'

'The poor bastard? No.'

'What about any of the other drivers, were they seeing her?' Chiltern asked.

It was a good question. 'Or anyone else for that matter,' Vallance added.

'Not that I heard,' Watkins said. 'And I would've heard, believe me.'

It painted a different picture of the grieving widow but there was still a big difference between casual adultery and murder. 'I'm sure you'll have no problem making a formal statement of what you've just said,' Vallance instructed. 'And I'm sure you've got no objections if we take a set of footprints and tyre tracks from your bikes.'

Watkins looked back at his shed full of bits of motorbike. 'I got no problem with that,' he said, hesitantly, 'but, you know, I'm doing you a favour –'

Vallance nodded. 'We're just interested in the tyres for now. Don't worry, we don't even know what a chassis number is.'

'Thanks,' Watkins said, the relief clearly expressed in his voice and in the look on his face. 'What's this all about, anyway?'

Chiltern was about to answer but Vallance stopped him with a sharp look. 'Routine enquiries,' he said.

The answer seemed acceptable. 'No probs,' Watkins agreed. 'Anyway, I'm better off out of it. I mean now that she's hanging around with Jack Thomas I mean.'

The name rang bells. Jack Thomas. Jack Thomas. Chiltern picked up on it instantly. 'He runs a dodgy wine bar called Cagney's,' he said. 'A bit of a lad.'

'He was done last year,' Watkins added, 'for kicking ten tons of shit out of some poor bastard who he said cut him on the road.'

Vallance remembered the details. Thomas had a string of arrests but only the one conviction. His reputation for violence meant that anyone with sense preferred to drop charges, assuming the case got that far. And he was linked to Jenny Cunliffe? The case suddenly seemed ready to move forward.

SEVEN
Tuesday 10th December

The atmosphere in the media room was thick with smoke and banter, and the number of bodies present seemed disproportionate to the number that needed to view the film. Dobson stood in the doorway for a second, scanning the room while deciding who was going to stay and who was going to go. The blinds had yet to be pulled and the weak, grey light of a cold morning filtered through the big square windows.

DCI Vallance had yet to arrive, not that his presence would have made much of a difference to the informal atmosphere. Sergeant Crawley was there, sitting towards the back, away from the wide-screen television that they all faced. He was flicking through a pile of notes, his head bowed and his face, partly hidden from Dobson, was a picture of concentration. Crawley was the only man there who looked like his mind was on the investigation.

What the hell was DC Quinn doing here? She wasn't on the case. She had no business being in the video room. She looked relaxed, chatting amiably with DCs Matthews and Peters, standing at the end of the front row of seats.

Dobson strode across to her. Quinn was supposedly good at her job, but perhaps she was picking up the wrong sort of signals from Vallance. There was a fine line between informality and indiscipline. Vallance had blurred the two and it looked as though some of the junior ranks were headed the same way.

He stopped in front of her. Matthews and Peters shrank back visibly, becoming strangely silent as they stepped back. Quinn turned, a look of surprise in her dark brown eyes.

'What are you doing in here, Constable?' Dobson demanded, his voice booming through the room.

Quinn looked nervously towards her colleagues and then back at Dobson. 'I was just talking about the case, sir.'

'Which case would that be?'

She knew she was in the wrong. 'The Cunliffe murder, sir,' she replied quietly.

He glared at her. He was speaking to them all through her, and she knew it as much as the rest of the team. 'You're not working on this case, Constable,' he stated. 'And until the time that you are you concentrate on your own workload. Is that clear, Constable?'

'Yes, sir,' she whispered.

He turned towards the door. 'In that case get on with it,' he said.

Her face blazed red with anger or with embarrassment, it didn't matter which. 'Yes, sir,' she whispered, her voice on the edge of cracking.

She walked out in stunned silence, watched by everyone else in the room. Dobson knew that they all thought he was a bastard. It didn't matter. He couldn't stand sloppiness and if it meant courting unpopularity then it was a fair price to pay for imposing some standards.

He turned to Matthews and Peters, both of them looking nervously at their feet. 'Where's Chief Inspector Vallance?' he demanded. He was aware that as he spoke a couple more people discreetly slipped out.

'He's not here yet, sir,' Matthews responded.

'I can see that, Constable,' Dobson snapped. 'Do we know where he is?'

The door opened at that instant and Vallance wandered in, along with DC Chiltern. Vallance looked relatively cleaned up. He'd shaved and the black leather jacket was supplemented by a shabby white overcoat and an unruly black scarf. It was still hardly the correct attire for a senior officer but the overcoat at least was an attempt at respectability.

'All here?' Vallance asked, oblivious to the tense atmosphere in the room.

'Yes, sir,' Crawley replied.

Dobson walked over to where Vallance was going to sit. 'It finally arrived then,' he said. The film was a day late. The courier that had been promised for the previous evening had not arrived until close to midnight.

Vallance sat down and put his feet up on the back of the chair in front. 'It's not exactly a matinee showing,' he said, smiling, 'more like a case of breakfast TV. Anyway, we can catch up on things after this.'

Dobson sat down too. He was also wearing a heavy white overcoat, only his looked as though it knew what dry-cleaning was, and it was worn over a neat blue suit and a white shirt that had been ironed that morning. The contrast was telling. DCI Vallance looked as though he belonged on a police line-up as suspect number one.

DC Chiltern handed the Jiffy bag containing the tape to one of the uniformed PCs who ran the video room. He looked back and seemed disappointed to see that Dobson had taken his place beside Vallance. Dobson stared coldly at the young DC. That was another thing, Vallance had a tendency to pick young DCs to act as drivers for him. There was nothing wrong with having a junior do the driving, so long as it didn't imply any familiarity. Chiltern was already acting as though he and Vallance were partners. A DCI and a DC, it just didn't bear thinking about.

The blinds were pulled down and the lights extinguished apart from a spotlight near the video player. Thick tendrils of cigarette smoke curled around the room. The PC switched the equipment on and the TV screen came alive with jagged black and white waves of static. The last of the lights was switched off and the room was plunged totally in darkness.

'Have you got *Debbie Does Dallas?*'

The voice came from one of the PCs and elicited a round of ribald laughter. Dobson tensed instantly, but when he turned to Vallance all he could see, by the pale light from the screen, was the grin on his face.

'What about an ice cream?'

Again there was laughter and a number of murmured comments that Dobson could not make out. They were supposed to be seeing a film pertinent to the case and yet the younger constables were laughing and joking and threatening to turn the thing into a circus.

On screen the static had disappeared and the time codes superimposed on the picture had appeared. The video was a production copy, not something that had been copied from the television when it had been broadcast.

There were more comments and more laughter as the opening credits started to roll.

'Cut it out now,' Vallance said, his tone cool and calm.

It wasn't instant silence but it had the desired effect. Dobson seethed. Vallance had spoken conversationally where he should have reprimanded the silly buggers who were messing about. How the hell could discipline be imposed when it didn't flow naturally from the top?

Vallance leaned forward and tapped Chiltern, sitting on the row in front of him, on the shoulder. 'You didn't tell me that the programme's an episode of *Insight*,' he said quietly.

'Didn't I?' Chiltern whispered. 'I'm sorry, sir, I didn't think it was important.'

'I didn't say it was important,' Vallance corrected, but there was something in his voice which said otherwise.

Dobson recognised the programme instantly. He was glad that Vallance had made the same connection. 'Isn't this the series that carried that disgusting episode about police violence last year?' he said, leaning forward to join the huddle of Chiltern and Vallance.

'That's right, sir,' Chiltern agreed.

'Is it? I didn't see that one,' Vallance said, seemingly un-concerned by it.

'Yes, sir,' Dobson said. 'It was disgusting. A bigger collection of half-truths and distortions I've yet to see,' he spat angrily. 'It's the sort of television that makes you sick. I'm amazed that the buggers were allowed to broadcast it.'

The information seemed to have no visible effect on Vallance, though Chiltern was nodding agreement.'It's starting now,' Vallance said,'we'd better pay attention.'

Dobson sat back in his seat. He knew all about *Insight*. It was the sort of blatant left-wing propaganda that undermined everything it examined. The episode alleging police brutality was only one example, there were dozens of other hatchet jobs to its discredit. And now they were supposed to take it seriously as a source of objective information?

The room was in silence as the programme unfolded. The opening scene was enough to set the tone: a family house going up in flames, a mother and children asleep upstairs, the fire alarm that should have been squawking them awake and which was strangely silent as the smoke and the flames danced from room to room. The scene ended with a shot of the house from the outside, the flames exploding from windows and the blare of fire engines arriving too late to save the woman and her children. It cut to the presenter, a black man with an Oxbridge accent and the manner of a young priest, as he began to talk about the fatal consequences in the case of fire alarms that don't work.

The emotive language and the rhetoric of care and concern carried on throughout the programme. It was focused on the activities of a single company: AlarmIC. A supposedly impartial electronics expert described the design faults in the alarms that the company manufactured. Another expert, from the fire service, talked about the failings of the regulation authorities. One after another, expert after expert, talked damningly of AlarmIC and its potentially lethal products.

A key sequence of the programme featured a simulated test of the devices and showed how the alarm failed to go off even when the flames were directly under it. A number of directors from the company were also shown, harassed by the journalist, cowering from the cameras. A prepared statement was read out by a solicitor but it could do nothing to counter the bad impressions made by the rest of the programme.

The programme finished with a statement from the fire service, and it was read out calmly while the backdrop showed one of the alarms melting silently into flames. Then the credits rolled and the film was over.

Vallance walked to the head of the room as soon as the lights were on. He sat on the edge of the table next to the TV. 'That was who Michael Cunliffe had worked for in the past,' he said, folding his arms across his chest. 'We need to find out if there's a connection between the activities of this company and his death. There's no mention of anyone actually dying as a result of these alarms, but that might provide a motive for revenge. This isn't the only lead, it might not even be a major issue, but it's one that has to be eliminated.'

There were murmurs of assent from around the room. Dobson shook his head but kept quiet. The programme was as blatantly biased as the one he'd seen on police brutality. There was no evidence that the company's products had caused anyone to be injured let alone causing death. The evidence was so highly technical that he doubted whether anyone in the room had fully understood it. And the question of how the alarms had passed all the British Standards tests was never fully discussed. A hatchet job of the worst kind from start to finish.

Vallance spoke for a little longer but Dobson hardly listened. It was pointless. AlarmIC was a red herring and he knew it. Not that he cared. It was Vallance's case and if he wanted to waste resources then that was his prerogative. It was better to keep quiet and let Vallance carry the can later on.

He waited until they were back in the incident room before going in to see Vallance.

'I've located Robert Miller, sir,' he announced.

Vallance looked up from his seat. 'And?'

'And he's living up in the Midlands, sir. I've spoken to the Regional Crime Squad and they say that he's still an active criminal. Rumours say that he's switched from doing banks to dealing in drugs, but so far he's managed to avoid getting collared for anything.'

'Drugs? What about blowing away boring accountants?'

'One of the reasons that he's not been nicked is that people are scared of the man, sir. People know that he's got a reputation and that he's not afraid of using a gun when he has to.'

Vallance looked unconvinced. 'If he's involved with chemicals then I can't see why he'd be down this neck of the woods blasting at boring suburbanites like Cunliffe.'

Dobson knew that Miller still needed checking out. The local force had supplied lots of gossip but it was based on rumour and intelligence that he had no handle on. 'Do we forget about him and concentrate on Simon Clark?'

For a moment there was indecision in Vallance's eyes. 'No,' he said, 'have the local plod get an alibi for him. Make sure that it's checked properly.'

'What about Clark?'

Vallance grinned. 'I was saving that little visit for myself,' he said. 'But I think that this AlarmIC thing needs to be checked up properly. I saw Jenny Cunliffe's bit of rough yesterday and he's not our man.'

Dobson had been through the Watkins interview with DC Chiltern. 'How can you be so sure?' he asked.

'Because his feet are too big,' Vallance said. 'I took one look at the man's size 12 boots and knew that they didn't match the prints at the scene. I mean we still need to wait for forensics to put him in the clear but for now I say that Trevor Watkins out of it.'

'Simon Clark?'

'You talk to him,' Vallance said. 'At least he's reasonably local.'

Dobson nodded agreement. Clark sounded the most likely suspect and it was lunacy for Vallance to be so casual about it. 'And you, sir?' he asked, suddenly intrigued to discover what his commanding officer's next step was going to be.

'I'm going to follow up on this *Insight* programme,' he said.

For a second Dobson was speechless. He'd heard a lot about Vallance, not all of it bad, but the one thing that everyone agreed on was that he was sharp. A good detective despite the obvious flaws was the considered opinion. But if he was seriously interested in the AlarmIC story then received opinion needed to be revised.

Sarah Fairfax stared at the memo in front of her and tried to remain calm. She flicked through her notes and the presentation that she'd spent days putting together and then to the single sheet of paper that had come back from the commissioning meeting. One piece of paper. That was all. Just one. She looked up from her desk and out of the window at the concrete and glass skyline that sat under a grey misery of a sky. It felt appropriate.

She needed some coffee. Strong, black and blisteringly hot. She looked down at the memo once more and felt the anger rising again. They hadn't even the decency to come down from on high and tell her personally that the programme about Malik Alibhai was not going to be made. Instead she'd been sent a memo via e-mail. E-mail, the most impersonal form of communication ever devised. They didn't even need to put pen to paper any more.

And now the commissioning editors and the producer were keeping out of her way. They had no arguments that would stand up, and they knew it. Malik Alibhai's story was one that needed to be heard and yet no one had the guts or the decency to publicise it. Not even the famous *Insight* team.

Sarah closed her eyes and tried to remain calm. On the face of it she was working on the most radical programme currently on television, and yet she knew that most of it was hyped-up crap that presented a tough public image while being cautious in the extreme. After the furore surrounding the police brutality programme they were playing extra safe. They wanted nothing contentious though they were making the most of their campaigning reputation.

Malik Alibhai had only just come out of intensive care. The man had almost died as a result of his beating and yet his story had rated no more than a few sentences in the national newspapers and nothing on TV and radio. Alibhai was a trade unionist at odds with his union, at odds with his bosses and at odds with the police. Just about the only people who were on his side were his family and the strikers he represented.

He had been elected shop steward a week before the strike at Hinchley Bearings had begun. He had no experience of trade unions and none of politics, but when the crunch came he and his fellow workers refused to accept the new pay and conditions that were being imposed by the company. Pay and conditions which had been agreed with union officials who had no contact with people like Alibhai. Everyone expected the strike to collapse in days, especially as there was no official support for the dispute. Six weeks on and they had still been out on strike and the company was bussing in scab labour to keep things going.

On the seventh week Alibhai had been returning home from the picket line when he'd been attacked by three skinheads. He was so badly beaten up that his own wife couldn't recognise him. Loss of blood and a cracked skull had put him into intensive care. Initially it looked like a racial attack. An Asian man kicked half to death by a gang of racist skinheads. Big deal. It hardly merited a paragraph in the local papers. Except that his family maintained that the attackers were working for Hinchley Bearings. The police refused to investigate the company and the union took the chance to force the rest of the strikers back to work.

Sarah had been approached by Alibhai's family shortly afterwards and after meeting them once she had become convinced that what they were alleging was true. The company had been using a fly-by-night security company to guard the premises and to bus in the strike breakers. The security firm was run by a man with a dozen serious convictions for violence and most of the men he employed were also thugs. And a number were known racists who had used the strike as an opportunity to harass and intimidate the mainly immigrant work-force. Not that the police were willing to take any notice of it.

She had pieced the story together carefully, from Hinchley Bearings' history of bad employment practices, to the criminals running the security firm to the lack of police interest. Names, dates, places, everything was listed. It was a scandal and it needed to be aired. Malik Alibhai had been almost murdered, didn't that mean anything?

According to the memo in front of her it probably didn't. The programme had been rejected as being of local interest only. She wanted to scream with anger and frustration. Local interest only? And what had they decided to commission in its place? A programme about teenage hackers using the Internet to swap information with the Russian Mafia. It made her blood boil. No wonder the cowards upstairs in commissioning were unwilling to face her.

Coffee. She started to get up when the phone buzzed. For one second she hoped that it was Lucy or one of the other series editors but then she realised that they wouldn't be calling her so early after sending the memo. They'd wait for the air to clear first.

She was in no mood to talk to anybody. 'Sarah Fairfax,' she said, grabbing the phone angrily.

'Hi, Sarah, how are you?'

Detective Chief Inspector Vallance. She recognised the voice instantly. Vallance. She hadn't seen or heard from him since the court case surrounding the murders at the Ryder Forum. 'Who is this?' she demanded angrily.

There was a momentary pause at the other end. She hoped he felt suitably deflated. 'It's Anthony Vallance,' he said.

She was glad that he was unable to see her smile. 'Yes, Mr Vallance, what can I do for you?' she said.

Again there was a pause. He'd been expecting a more welcoming tone of voice. 'Well, er, I was calling to talk about one of your programmes.'

Now it was her turn to feel deflated. A business call. The last time they'd met he had invited her out to dinner. She had declined politely and was disappointed when he'd not called again. Not that she and Vallance were a possibility. He was different, interesting in his odd way, but that was all.

'It's the episode about a company called AlarmIC. They made dodgy fire alarms that didn't work,' he added.

She knew the episode he was referring to. It was one that she hadn't worked on and which she knew very little about. 'What about it?' she asked, deciding to stall for information rather than hand him over to Lucy.

He seemed to hesitate. 'I was wondering about information that hadn't been broadcast,' he said, sounding as though he were being uncharacteristically careful in his choice of words.

'And why would the police be interested in that?' she asked.

'Come on, Sarah,' he said, 'you know I can't go into that.'

He was calling her by her first name again. For a time she hadn't allowed him to get away with anything but Miss Fairfax. 'Mr Vallance,' she told him coolly, 'I can hardly discuss matters with you if I don't know what it pertains to.'

'In that case perhaps we can discuss this face to face?' he suggested. Was there a hopeful note in his voice.

'Of course,' she agreed. 'My office?'

'Your office,' he echoed, sounding none too enamoured of the idea.

'In that case I can come down to see you. I presume you're still attached to the same division?'

'Yes,' he murmured. 'When can you make it?'

She smiled. He'd probably been angling to meet for dinner. Did he really think she couldn't tell? She glanced at her watch. It was too late for a lunch-time meeting but she still had time to drive out to the suburbs that afternoon. 'Say five o'clock?'

'Today?'

'Of course.'

She could easily picture the smile spreading across his face. 'In that case,' she said, 'there's also a matter I'd like to discuss with you. It's about a man called Malik Alibhai.'

'Never heard of him,' he responded instantly.

'That,' she said, 'is precisely the problem.'

A name like Cagney's should have inspired visions of Chicago gangster opulence, the roaring twenties or Yankee Doodle Dandy. Instead the blacked-out shop front that nestled incongruously in a parade of suburban shops suggested a seedy dive with delusions of grandeur. Lodged between a turf accountant's on one side and the sub-post office on the other, the only remarkable thing about Cagney's was that the black glass, emblazoned with the logo, was free of the graffiti which marked all the other shop fronts.

'It's not exactly the West End, is it?' Vallance told DC Chiltern as they got out of the car.

'Try telling that to Jack Thomas,' Chiltern said, his breath misting as he spoke.

Vallance had looked at Thomas's police record, a long succession of violent assaults which was punctuated with arrests which failed to come to court. All except for the unprovoked attack on the motorist which had given Thomas his first taste of prison. Thomas was viewed as a hard man by people in the area, and the police certainly hated his guts, but was he really such a tough guy? A reputation like his was easy to garner, and once acquired it was easier to live up to it. Fear bred more fear which meant that thugs like Thomas could get away with things without even resorting to violence.

The shops were on the other side of a busy road and seemed to exist in the middle of nowhere. The surrounding streets were full of commuter-belt semis, and beyond them the uniform red brick of a post-war housing estate. It was a place without focus, a sprawl of featureless houses that survived thanks to a railway station with a direct link to London. It made Vallance depressed just visiting it.

He and Chiltern crossed the busy road and walked the length of the row of shops. A convenience store and newsagents; an off licence; a Chinese take-away with boarded up windows; a chemist's; the turf accountant; the seedy wine bar; the sub-post office and finally a bakery. It seemed the last place on earth that you'd open a wine bar, but then again the only competition was the pubs dotted around the area.

Vallance walked back from the bakery to the blacked-out windows of Cagney's. 'Does this place get busy then?' he asked Chiltern.

'Not sure, sir.'

It had been a surprise to discover that Jack Thomas also lived at Fenton Close. He and the Cunliffes were neighbours. Going by the addresses Vallance judged that they lived at opposite ends of the small estate. Neighbours. Good neighbours in fact. Did Michael Cunliffe know that his wife was seeing Thomas? And if he did what could he do about it? He could hardly dare confront a man with a reputation for violence like Thomas.

Vallance glanced at his watch. Sarah Fairfax was due to see

him in an hour or so. Lots of time to question Thomas.

The door to Cagney's opened when Vallance pushed it. The front of the place was in darkness, the tables and chairs hidden in alcoves partitioned off in red leatherette. The walls were decorated with silhouettes of gangsters carrying machine guns, with trench coats done up and hats pulled low. The bar was at the far end of the room, lit dimly by spotlights that focused a soft glow on portraits of Al Capone, Bugsy Seigel, Jimmy Cagney, Edward G. Robinson and Humphrey Bogart.

A door opened at the back of the bar and a man walked in. 'We're closed,' he said, looking at Vallance.

Vallance smiled and walked towards the bar. 'You've got real gangsters mixed up with pretend ones,' he said, pointing to the black and white portraits above the bar.

The man behind the bar was obviously Jack Thomas. He was tall, broad across the chest and well dressed. His fingers glittered with heavy gold rings which would cause serious damage to an opponent's face. He looked at Vallance coolly and then he smiled back. 'What does that tell you about me, then?' he asked.

Vallance shrugged. 'I can't be bothered to figure it out.'

'Well, in that case then,' Thomas responded, 'to what do I owe the pleasure of a visit from the old bill?'

Chiltern flashed his ID card but Vallance couldn't be bothered. 'We wanted to talk to you about one of your neighbours.'

Thomas looked up to the heavens, his face a picture of exasperation. 'Look,' he said pointedly, 'I can't help it if the bloody kids round here spray-paint everything but my place. If I knew who was doing it I'd get it stopped. I've told the bloke in the post office a dozen times and the stupid bastard won't believe me.'

'How would you get it stopped?' Chiltern asked, fixing Thomas with a look that was probably meant to scare him.

Thomas almost laughed. 'I'd get the little bastard, really get hold of him,' his face twisted into a vicious sneer, 'and then I'd threaten to tell his mum about it.'

Chiltern looked none too impressed but Thomas was

laughing anyway. Vallance wanted to laugh too but he guessed that Chiltern would feel that he was the butt of the joke. 'It's not that neighbour I'm talking about,' he said.

'Don't tell me that the other shopkeepers are having a go too.'

'I won't,' Vallance agreed. 'I want to talk to you about Jenny Cunliffe.'

The smile disappeared from Thomas's face. 'The poor cow,' he muttered.

'Why do you say that?'

Thomas walked to the other side of the bar and unscrewed the top from a bottle of brandy. 'I won't insult your professional ethics by offering you one,' he remarked, waving the bottle before pouring himself a generous measure. 'The poor cow's just lost that sap of a husband of hers, hasn't she?'

'You know them?' Vallance asked.

Thomas shook his head. 'They live near where I do. I mean I could point them out to you but that's as far as it goes.'

'You just said that he was a sap of a husband,' Vallance pointed out. 'Doesn't that imply you know more about them?'

Thomas downed a mouthful of brandy before answering. 'Nope. I could see he was a sap just by looking at him.'

'What about her?'

'She looks like a bit of all right,' he said, the smile returning to his face.

'But you've never met her?'

'Not even to say hello. But now that she's a free woman again —'

Chiltern seemed upset by the remark. 'She's just lost her husband,' he said disapprovingly.

'Never heard of a merry widow?' Thomas responded. 'A good-looking woman like her's not going to be short of love interest, is she?'

There was no point in beating about the bush. 'It's been alleged that you're her love interest,' Vallance said.

'Me?' Thomas demanded, incredulous. 'My missus would kill me,' he added. 'I swear that Isobel would go ballistic.'

'So you deny that you and Jenny Cunliffe were having an affair.'

'I do.'

'You know, Jack,' Vallance said, 'it's hard to figure you as the faithful type.'

'Never judge a book by its cover,' Thomas responded. 'Anyway, why'd you want to know about me and her? Her old man's topped himself, hasn't he?'

'Is that what you've heard?'

Thomas nodded. 'It's what all the neighbours are saying. They say he was a bit dodgy himself, don't they.'

'That must have been a shock to you,' Vallance said, 'finding out you live near a dodgy character like Michael Cunliffe.'

Thomas laughed once more, a big roar of a laugh that filled the room. 'What did you say your name is?' he asked.

'DCI Vallance.'

'A DCI? And you can't get yourself some decent threads?'

Vallance looked down at his coat, leather jacket and jeans which had once been jet black but which were now looking washed out. 'I suppose not,' he said. 'Just out of interest, Jack, what sort of clientele do you get here?'

'A very law-abiding one,' Thomas said.

Chiltern snorted but Vallance nodded agreeably. 'Enough of a clientele to finance an expensive house and a flash car?'

'I do all right,' Thomas insisted. 'You want to see the accounts?'

'No, not yet. I mean it'd be a shame if you and I fell out because of this Cunliffe thing.'

'What Cunliffe thing?' Thomas demanded, an edge of anger in his voice. 'I told you already, I don't know the woman.'

'Of course not,' Vallance said.

The old man sounded relieved. 'I thought you might be kids,' he explained, chuckling.

'You live next door?' Dobson guessed, indicating the house next to Clark's.

'That's right,' the old boy agreed. 'The name's Dennis McMahon. Do you mind if I ask what's going on. I saw that you collared young Simon. What's he done?'

The old man seemed friendly enough but Dobson wasn't about to risk anything. 'Mr Clark's just helping us with a few questions, Mr McMahon, that's all. Tell me, does he use his motorbike a lot?'

'His bike? Not since he got his car.'

'Has he used it at all in the last few days?'

The old man seemed unsure. 'I can't say, really. I hear him rev it up every now and then. You know, he's not silly that lad.'

Dobson felt surprised when Matthews decided to speak. 'I suppose he's got all the motorbike gear,' he said. 'Leather jacket, fancy helmet, boots, that sort of stuff.'

'That's right,' McMahon agreed readily enough. 'What's he done then? He's not in trouble is he?'

'Has he been in trouble before?' Dobson asked.

Again the old man seemed to hesitate before answering. 'He probably has, he's a bit of a rough diamond. But I've had worse neighbours, much worse. At least Simon looks out for people, you know what I mean? Not like some I could say.'

'Thank you for you help, Mr McMahon,' Dobson said. He'd heard enough. Simon Clark as the perfect citizen, kind to old folks and a good neighbour. Except when shooting people in cold blood.

The old man seemed reluctant to leave. Dobson turned his attention back to Clark's garden. He shone the light over the gate and peered over it. The grass would have been knee length had it not been flattened out by the wind and the rain. The back of the house was shrouded in darkness and the torch light hardly seemed to touch the back door and the kitchen windows.

'It's there, sir,' Matthews said, turning his light to the heavy plastic sheet that had been thrown over the motorbike.

Of course it was there. The whole point of being there was to look at the bike. 'Why do you think we're here?' Dobson snapped.

The cover had been thrown over the bike very loosely and it was possible to see bits of the underside, the lower half of each wheel and the stand. The bike was standing on a number of paving stones which had been arranged on top of the matted grass by the look of things. The tyres were caked in dried mud, some of which had fallen off in clumps onto the oil-stained paving stones.

Matthews was scanning the rest of the garden with his torch, the beam tracing back and forth in search of something other than grass and weeds. In places it was possible to discern a path of sorts where the grass had been walked on repeatedly.

Dobson wasn't interested in the rest of the garden, he knew precisely what he was looking for. He traced the path from the bike to the gate at which he and Matthews were standing. The pale white light picked out featureless mud and wilting grass that was still damp.

'At last,' he whispered, shining the torch down at the ground directly on the other side of the gate.

Matthews peered down for a moment, as though wondering what it was he was supposed to be looking at.

'The tyre print,' Dobson explained. 'Does it look familiar?'

Matthews stared at the impression of a tyre in the wet mud. Further up the tyre tracks were smudged or covered by the grass, but there, under the gate the impression was very clear.

'Do you think it matches the one at the murder scene?' Matthews asked, sounding unconvinced.

'Look at it carefully, Constable,' Dobson instructed. 'What do you think?'

'I can't – I'm not –'

'You do remember the tyre print we're interested in?'

'Yes, sir,' Matthews agreed reluctantly.

'And is it something like this?'

Matthews looked at it again and then he looked at Dobson. His eyes were all indecision but Dobson knew that the younger officer wanted to impress. 'Yes, sir,' he agreed finally, 'I think it might be a match.'

side of the table. It was the police side and armed with a tape recorder, clock and a notebook.

She suppressed her smile. He was impressed of course, though it had been easy to check back on the news from the previous few days and to pick up on the unexplained death. Once she'd got the victim's name the link to the AlarmIC story became clear. 'Basic research,' she said airily. She sat down and pulled out the transcript from the programme, the research notes and the other bits and pieces she'd gathered together.

'Ever thought of becoming a cop?' he asked, still smiling.

She looked at him coolly. 'No,' she answered. His eyes were so dark and intense, even when he was smiling, and his good humour seemed to light up his face.

He shrugged. 'Too smart for us,' he said. 'You're right, it is Michael Cunliffe's death that I'm looking at.'

'You suspect murder and you think it might be connected to the AlarmIC story,' she continued. The single paragraph that detailed Cunliffe's death had not speculated on murder, but it seemed unlikely that a man of Vallance's rank would be investigating the circumstances of a suicide.

'Right again,' he agreed. 'I want to know if you'd ever tracked down victims of these dodgy fire alarms. The programme implied that they were lethal but it didn't make clear whether anyone had actually died or been maimed as a result.'

'You think that Cunliffe's is a revenge killing?'

He shrugged. 'It's a line of investigation, that's all at the moment.'

The knock at the door interrupted the rest of Vallance's answer. 'I've got some coffee for Miss Fairfax, sir,' the PC explained, bringing in a big black mug of it.

Vallance smiled. 'Get me one too, there's a lad,' he said.

The PC nodded and disappeared quickly.

'It might be a revenge killing,' Vallance said, picking up where he'd left off. 'On the other hand there might be some other spin-off from the whole affair that we don't even suspect at the moment.'

The coffee tasted vile. She sipped it and put the mug down instantly. 'It was certainly an extremely messy affair,' she said.

'There were rumours that the regulations officials had been bribed into granting the safety certificates and the standards accreditations. And once the directors found out about the TV programme there was a great deal of activity with regards to the assets and the ownership of the company. When it collapsed the company was seriously in debt and the creditors were left carrying the can.'

Vallance was listening intently. 'How did you find out about it in the first place?' he asked suddenly.

She hadn't was the honest answer. The story wasn't one of hers and all she knew about it was what she had read in the few hours since Vallance's call. 'The initial lead came from someone working for the company,' she said.

'Can you tell me who?'

There was only one answer to give. 'No,' she stated firmly.

He nodded sagely. 'Journalistic ethics,' he said.

'Of course I'd never reveal a source,' she confirmed. 'But in this case we never did find out who'd written the letter to us.'

Vallance looked surprised. 'You mean you never bothered to find out who it was?'

If Sarah had been involved that would have been a priority. She hated the idea that the programme was part of someone else's agenda, but it hadn't been her story. 'No,' she said, 'though I'm aware that there could have been all kinds of reasons behind that initial contact.'

'You're not kidding,' Vallance said.

Was there a note of disapproval in his voice? She hated the idea that he'd think she'd been sloppy or unprofessional. 'The fact remains, Mr Vallance,' she said, 'that the technical information was true and that in exposing the company we were performing an important public service.'

'And getting good ratings,' he added.

'And what, exactly, is that supposed to mean?'

He sat back and raised his hands in mock surrender. 'I wasn't having a go at you,' he said, 'I was just remarking, that's all.'

He was right about the ratings. Ratings were the reason her programme about Malik Alibhai had been rejected. The earlier. The stairs were littered with discarded drink cans, household refuse and puddles of stale urine. He'd passed a couple of kids on the way. They'd recognised him as a police officer instantly and had tried to stare him out, as though he'd be intimidated by a pair of lads barely into their teens.

From the third floor he'd had a good view of Clark's house. The back garden was a jungle of weeds and uncut grass, though it was possible to make out a motorbike in one corner. The garden gate looked to be in working order so perhaps the long grass and the neglect were deliberate ploys. The front of the house looked similarly neglected. The windows were framed with peeling paint, the door was badly scuffed and a pane of glass that had been broken had been boarded up rather than replaced. Whatever the rewards of crime, Clark was hardly investing in his house.

The good view had been used to plan back-up. Although Clark had never resisted arrest there was always a first time. And if the gangland rumours were true he certainly knew how to use a gun. To date his arrests had all been for armed robbery, but that was a crime of desperation in the days of excellent security systems on the one hand and spectacular profits from big drug deals on the other. He had been out of prison for more than two years and in that time he'd been linked to a number of killings but the victims had always been other criminals. There were never any witnesses and the families of the victims were never interested in pursuing the cases.

Dobson had chosen to position police cars at either end of the road, unmarked vehicles manned by armed officers. He, sitting in a third car near to Clark's house, planned on taking no chances. He was willing to bide his time, wait for the right moment and then grab Clark as he came out of the house. He'd be cautioned instantly and then driven down to head-quarters for an interview. Vallance would probably have gone for a more softly softly approach, but Clark would only interpret that as weakness. A criminal like Clark understood power and violence more than anything else.

The street between the block of flats and the row of dilapidated houses was almost deserted. It seemed as though 'but it's not this division. Alibhai's on the other side of the Met. It's not local, there's nothing I can do.'

Sarah could hardly contain her indignation. 'Rubbish!' she cried. 'You're a Detective Chief Inspector, surely that counts for something.'

He shook his head. 'Believe me, it hardly counts for anything here, let alone in another division.'

She wanted to say more but there was something in the way he spoke that stopped her. She knew that he was an unorthodox policeman in many ways, and that in an environment that made a virtue of conformity this created problems, but was there more?

'Look,' he said, seizing on her hesitation, 'let me see if I can find out more on this Alibhai case, OK?'

Was he offering to share information with her? If it was true then he was taking a risk. His superiors would never forgive him. 'I never reveal a source,' she said quietly.

'I'm making no promises,' he said.

'I know. And if I make any progress with AlarmIC then of course I'll let you know.'

He looked at her quizzically. 'What does that mean?'

She allowed herself a smile at last. 'It means that I'm going to be working on this one too.'

Simon Clark was a nasty piece of work, a career criminal who'd been in and out of trouble since the age of twelve. If prisons were the universities of crime then Clark had graduated with honours. Dobson hoped that Clark was the one who'd killed Cunliffe. Collaring him would be a pleasure, especially as Clark was due a nice long sentence.

Clark lived in a run-down semi-detached house right on the edge of a council estate. It wasn't quite the inner city but it was not far from the main route into London, right on the edge of the Met's divisional boundary. Clark's house was overshadowed by a monolithic concrete monstrosity which had seen better days. The covered walkways were lined with pre-formed concrete slabs interspersed with reinforced frosted glass.

Dobson had walked up to the third floor of the block

'What are you doing these days?' Vallance began. 'You've been out of trouble for a couple of years now. Are you working?'

'Self-employed,' Clark said, sitting forward to cup his coffee in his hands. His fingers were thick, long, clean. No signs of calluses, no cuts, no thick layer of black grease.

'Doing what, exactly?'

Clark shrugged. 'This and that. The building trade mainly.'

'What, exactly, in the building trade?'

'Painting and decorating.'

There were no spots of paint on Clark's hands. 'Come on,' Vallance said, 'you wouldn't know one end of a paintbrush from another. A hard man like you doesn't do painting and decorating.'

'Yeah? What would I be doing?'

'You tell me,' Vallance suggested.

'I told you,' Clark insisted, 'I'm self-employed. This place looks like it needs a lick of paint,' he said, waving a hand at the room around him, 'you want me to put in a tender?'

Vallance laughed. 'Put in a tender? The only thing you're good at putting in is the boot,' he said, and then Clark was laughing too. 'Where were you on Sunday morning?'

It sounded as though a beat had been missed in the rhythm of Clark's laughter. He carried on for a moment too long and then stopped to answer. 'I was at home. Why?'

'Can anyone verify that?' Dobson asked, leaning forward to glare at Clark.

'Nope.'

'What time did you get up?' Dobson demanded.

'Can't remember.'

'Come on, man. Was it morning, afternoon, evening?'

Clark shrugged. 'Must have been early afternoon I suppose.'

There was no apparent note of concern in his voice but Vallance knew that Clark was covering up. 'You often sleep in, do you?' he asked.

'I'd been out the night before, to Cagney's,' Clark explained. 'I came back half pissed.'

Vallance smiled. So Clark was one of the law-abiding customers that Jack Thomas had been talking about. 'You're a mate of Jack's, are you?'

Clark grinned. 'Yeah, me and Jack get on all right.'

'Were you at his place all of Saturday night?'

Again there was a split second hesitation before Clark answered. 'I was there for most of the night. There's bound to be loads of witnesses if you don't believe me.'

'And you were half drunk when you left?'

'That's right,' Clark agreed.

'And you drove home?'

Clark grinned. 'Yeah. What're you going to do, breathalyse me half a week later?'

'Don't think you're so smart, lad!' Dobson snapped angrily.

'Look, I don't have to be here,' Clark responded. 'I can get up and go any time I like.'

Dobson was too uptight to handle people like Clark, Vallance realised. Dobson would have been happier dealing with stroppy teenagers who were intimidated by loud voices and an overbearing manner. 'You're also still under caution,' Vallance said calmly. 'So you were half drunk when you got home and you slept in until late on Sunday afternoon. Is that right?'

'Yep.'

'And there's no one who can corroborate your story?'

'That's right.'

'You didn't pick anyone up at Cagney's? There's no girl-friend or boyfriend around?'

'Boyfriend? Boyfriend?' Clark spluttered angrily. His face reddened and his hands clenched into tight fists that he pushed down hard on the table. 'What the shit do you mean by that?' he demanded, his face twisting with rage.

Vallance smiled sweetly. 'I don't know, do I? I mean it's not my business who you choose to sleep with, is it?'

'I ain't queer!' Clark insisted.

'Is there anyone who can corroborate that?'

'Don't sodding play clever with me!'

'Tell me about Jack Thomas,' Vallance suggested quietly.

'What about him?'

'He's not queer, is he?'

Clark laughed. 'Jack queer? Wait till I tell him that, he'll hit the bloody roof.'

few residents were willing to risk the cold or the dark. A group of teenagers had spotted the police in their cars earlier on and had decided to disappear. And the local beat officers had been told to keep out of the way as well. There was no point in taking chances.

Sergeant Crawley stirred suddenly. Dobson turned at the same instant. Someone was emerging from Clark's house. The light was too dim to see clearly but the figure had Clark's height and build. 'That's him,' Dobson snapped.

The car doors were open and officers running across the street before Clark had reached his car. Voices were raised and it seemed as though people were descending on him from all corners.

'I ain't done nothing!' he shouted, raising his hands above his head as the first of the police officers reached him.

Dobson rushed over, his heart pumping as the adrenalin rushed. Clark was looking surprised, his eyes darting from face to face as he tried to figure out what was happening.

'What the shit's going on?' he demanded when he turned to Dobson.

'We'd just like to talk to you, Mr Clark,' Dobson said, indicating to the other officers to step back.

'I haven't done anything,' Clark repeated, glaring at the ring of officers surrounding him.

'In that case you'll not object to helping us with our investigation.'

'What investigation? Am I being nicked?'

Unfortunately there was no warrant for Clark's arrest. There was no direct evidence to point to his involvement with the crime, yet. 'No, Mr Clark, you're not under arrest,' Dobson confirmed.

Clark grinned. 'Then I'm free to go,' he said. 'I know my rights.'

'I'm sure that you do, Mr Clark,' Dobson said, doing his best not to display his anger. Clark knew his rights, more than most law-abiding citizens did, and he'd use them to his advantage too. 'I'm asking you to voluntarily help us with a serious enquiry, Mr Clark. I'd say that it would be in your interest to do so.'

'And if I don't?' Clark demanded defiantly.

DS Crawley stopped forward. 'You know what'll happen, Clark. Do you come back with us now or do we have to find something to nick you for?'

Clark smiled. 'Bugger it,' he said, 'what's this about?'

Dobson nodded sharply and Clark was led away by Crawley to one of the cars which had pulled up close. Crawley was a good cop and he knew exactly how to handle scum like Clark.

Dobson waited until Clark was in the car before he turned and headed back to his own vehicle. He was already looking forward to the confrontation back at HQ. Before that, however, there was one more thing that needed to be done.

DC Matthews was already waiting by the car. At least the lad could follow orders.

'I've got the torch, sir,' he said, standing stiffly to attention.

'Follow me then,' Dobson ordered. It was gratifying to see the way Matthews was shaping up once a little bit of discipline had been applied. The younger officers were always the easiest to handle. It was the old hands who got sloppy and disrespectful.

Together they walked round to the side of Clark's house, which was now completely in darkness. Clark had been alone all afternoon. If he had a girlfriend she was notable by her absence. There was a narrow alley that ran by the side of his house. The powerful beams from the torches cut through the darkness to reveal a muddy path. Black dustbin bags were piled into one corner, and beside them stood a couple of plastic bins which were overflowing with rubbish.

'Along there,' Dobson said, flashing the light towards the end of the alleyway. Clark's garden was on the other side of a high wooden fence. The garden gate was definitely in working order, the hinges were oiled and the bolt was padlocked shut.

Dobson turned at the sudden noise behind him.

'Who's there?' a voice demanded.

Matthews turned the torch towards the voice and almost blinded the elderly man who'd crept up behind them.

'We're police officers,' Dobson explained, making Matthews remove the light from the man's eyes.

NINE
Wednesday 11th December

It was still dark. And it was cold. Vallance yawned, reached out across the bed and was disappointed to find nothing but empty space. He opened his eyes to the dim light and sat up. He could just about make out the dial on the small clock by the side of the bed. Almost seven. The door to the bedroom was closed but he could see that there was light somewhere else in the cramped flat. Was Anne making coffee? He hoped so, he didn't fancy getting up in the cold to make it himself, especially not as it was her sister's flat and he had no idea where anything was.

He sat up properly and propped a pillow up on the bed. He yawned again and stretched hard to wake himself up. Coffee and then a shower. And then more coffee before he got Anne to drive them in to work. She'd want him to do the decent thing and get out near HQ so that they wouldn't be seen driving in together. She had a boyfriend to think about.

He heard her approaching, the muffled sound of bare feet on carpet accompanied by the clink of cups on a tray. She came in quietly, inching the door open with a consideration that made him smile.

'I'm awake,' he said. She was wearing nothing but the black camisole he'd stripped from her late the previous evening. In the dull light her body looked pale, warm and sexy.

'Good,' she said, smiling, 'it saves me having to shove you awake.'

She walked round the bed and put the tray down on the cabinet on her side. The coffee smelt good and so did the buttered toast beside it. She climbed back into bed, fluffed up her pillows and then reached across to pass him his coffee.

'Thanks,' he said, taking it gratefully. Her arm brushed his and her skin was silky smooth.

She cupped both hands around her own mug and smiled. 'I like doing this,' she said.

'Making me coffee?'

She laughed. 'No, getting cosy early in the morning, especially if it's really wet and miserable outside.'

Wet and miserable. 'A day like that just makes me want to turn over and get back to sleep,' he said.

She pulled a face. 'Even with me beside you?'

He liked it when she was coy. And she was good at it. When she wanted to she could be so girly and sexy. It turned them both on.

'Well?' she demanded.

'Well what?'

'Would you really just turn over and go back to sleep?'

There was something in her tone that stopped him being flippant again. He just hoped that she wasn't about to go all serious on him. 'You know I wouldn't,' was all that he could think of saying.

'Mark does, sometimes,' she said, looking away from him.

Why was she talking about her boyfriend all of a sudden? It was a deal that they never talked about relationships. He tried to think of something to say but it was too early to think straight.

There was a long silence before she spoke again. 'I saw that Sarah Fairfax was back again,' she said suddenly.

Quinn had been involved in the Ryder case too, though he wasn't sure how much she and Sarah Fairfax had had to do with each other. 'Yes,' he said, 'she works on the programme that covered that AlarmIC business.'

'Oh, yes,' Anne said, looking at him with raised eyebrows.

'It's true,' he said, 'that's the only reason she was in yesterday.'

'Good man,' Dobson said, grinning. 'I think that counts as reasonable suspicion. If Clark decides he doesn't want to let us look around, or he doesn't play ball in the interview, then we'll have no problems getting a warrant.'

The penny dropped and Matthews smiled. 'Yes, sir,' he agreed, 'I think that's definitely reasonable suspicion.'

'Right then,' Dobson decided, 'we need to get one of the uniformed boys to keep an eye here until we get back to it. Now,' he added, relishing the thought, 'to get stuck in to Clark.'

There was no doubting Sarah's determination. If she said that she was going to look into Cunliffe's death then that was it. It made Vallance wary, of course, especially as she'd almost got herself killed when she had got mixed up in the Ryder case. He was aware also that she still thought that she could teach the police how to catch criminals. Her arrogance was one of the things he'd noticed about her first. After he'd noticed how good she looked, of course.

'You have to agree, Mr Vallance,' she said as he opened the door of the interview room, 'that if it hadn't been for our programme you'd have no leads in this story at all.'

He didn't have to admit anything. 'Firstly,' he countered, 'this isn't a story, it's a murder investigation. Secondly we were already looking into his background –'

She didn't bat an eyelid. 'The police would never have discovered the truth about AlarmIC,' she stated with total conviction.

It wasn't so much what she was saying that annoyed Vallance, it was the total certainty with which she approached everything. Doubt played no part in her thinking, shades of grey did not exist.

She was waiting for him to respond. Her eyes, strikingly blue, looked into his and he could see the sparkle of excitement there. She liked to argue with him, she obviously got a buzz out of it. 'On the left,' he said, gesturing with his arm. She looked disappointed and he smiled.

Her heels crashed down hard on the corridor floor as she walked with long, measured strides. She gave every indication of being in control of the situation. Vallance followed closely, wondering whether to risk another invitation to dinner. She'd turned him down after the Ryder case and it rankled still. Why bother asking again? Because he knew that she was interested. He could feel it, even though they couldn't be in the same room for five minutes without getting into an argument.

Sarah stopped at the end of the corridor, near the stairs that led up from the rear car park. She turned to Vallance just as DI Dobson and DC Matthews appeared. Dobson looked at Sarah with unconcealed distaste. She saw it of course and she stared back haughtily.

'We've got Clark, sir,' Matthews reported, unable to hide the excitement in his voice.

Dobson looked momentarily pained. He obviously hadn't wanted the news broadcast yet. 'Our suspect's in room one,' he said. 'We're just going in to talk to him now, sir.'

'I'll join you in a minute,' Vallance decided. 'Don't start without me.'

Dobson's face dropped. Matthews looked ill at ease too, as though he realised that he'd ruined Dobson's chance to get first crack at Clark. It probably meant that Dobson was going to come down hard on the young DC. 'Yes, sir,' was all that Dobson could manage to say, and even that was issued through gritted teeth.

Sarah stood her ground until Dobson and Matthews were out of earshot. 'You have someone under arrest already?' she asked.

Vallance shrugged. 'We've got someone in for questioning.'

'Clark,' she repeated. 'Is he linked to AlarmIC?'

Vallance walked ahead, aware that the corridor was not a good place to talk. She trailed after him, matching stride for stride even though she was inches shorter than he was. They breezed through the front of the building and out past the reception desk.

'I'm parked over there,' she said, pointing to her car.

The temperature had been falling steadily throughout the day and Vallance had no intention of spending time out in the cold. 'Look, Sarah,' he said, 'I don't think it's a good idea for you to get involved in this case. It's a criminal investigation, that's our job, not yours.'

Her blue eyes widened. 'You've no right to say that,' she snapped. 'I'm well aware of the difference between what you do and what I do, Chief Inspector. And I don't need you to tell me what I can and can't do. We started this investigation, remember? The media, not the police. And now I intend finishing it.'

What was wrong with the woman? He wanted to grab her by the arms and give her a shake. 'For Christ's sake! It's dangerous! Cunliffe was shot in the head at close range. I saw his brains smeared over his car –'

'Very dramatic I'm sure,' she responded, 'but that's got nothing to do with it.'

He stepped back and shook his head sadly. 'Why are you so stubborn? Just for once why don't you listen?'

'Because doing what I'm told is not what I'm about,' she stated defiantly. 'Doing what we're told is what people in power are always wanting us to do. What about people like Malik Alibhai? Who'll look after them if we're all so busy doing what we're told?'

It was bloody pointless talking any more. He turned on his heel and walked back into the building. She'd made up her mind and wouldn't listen to reason. Sarah Fairfax was always right, never wrong. Never. God she knew how to wind him up.

Dobson was waiting for him inside. He looked pissed off, even more than Vallance did. 'What is it?' Vallance snapped.

Dobson looked a bit shocked. 'Nothing, sir,' he said, 'I was just keen to start with Clark, sir.'

'He's not said anything yet?'

'No, sir. I sent him up here with Sergeant Crawley. So far he doesn't even know what he's here for.'

That was good, it was just the way that Vallance liked it. 'Good,' he said, starting to calm down.

'He's got a big motorbike in his garden, sir. And there's a good print just inside the back gate –'

'Get a warrant,' Vallance said. There was no need even to think about the decision.

'Yes, sir. I'll get Matthews on to it.'

'Let's go in then.'

Matthews was waiting by the interview room. He was looking glum, as though he knew he'd screwed up and wasn't looking forward to the consequences. It had been stupid to blurt out a suspect's name in front of a civilian, Dobson was right to be angry.

'Next time you blab like that,' Vallance warned him, 'you'll be back in uniform so fast –'

Dobson cut in quickly. 'I've warned him already, sir,' he said.

Why the hell was Dobson suddenly so protective? Vallance couldn't figure it out, it seemed so out of character. 'Get a search warrant sorted out,' Vallance ordered.

'Yes, sir,' Matthews mumbled.

'He was hoping to sit in on the interview,' Dobson explained as Matthews walked off down the corridor.

'Until he learns to keep quiet he's no good with people like Clark,' Vallance said. 'We'd better get started.'

Simon Clark was sitting comfortably in the interview room, feet up on the chair beside him, a cigarette in his hand and a cup of coffee on the table. The air was already smoky and as Vallance and Dobson walked in he puckered up his lips and released another smoke ring to float up above him in an ever widening and diffuse circle.

'The big boys,' Clark said, grinning.

'I'm Chief Inspector Vallance and this is Inspector Dobson,' Vallance said, taking the seat directly opposite Clark.

'Do you think I ought to call my solicitor in?' Clark asked, stubbing out his cigarette.

'You have that right,' Vallance said. 'You're not under arrest, Simon, you know you're free to go if you don't want to help us.'

Clark grinned even more. 'And then what? You'll just nick me for something stupid so that you can keep me here. There's no point, I ain't done anything.'

Dobson reached over and started the tape. He spoke clearly the names of the officers present, the name of the suspect, the date and time and the rest of the information that was required.

Crawley come up with the connection to Jenny Cunliffe? 'I need you on this case,' he declared vehemently. 'And it's got nothing to do with how I feel about you,' he added.

'And how do you feel about me?' she asked softly.

He looked at her and smiled. Her nipples were points against the silky black satin of her camisole. He put his coffee cup down and reached for her, curling his arm around her shoulder.

She looked up at him as he drew her closer, her eyes sparkling in the faint light. He kissed her softly on the mouth, simply touching his lips to hers and letting his breath mingle with hers. She responded by snuggling up closer and rubbing her cheek against his arm. There was something about her manner that was different, something nervous and unspoken. It wasn't just that she was turned on, the way she had been the previous evening, there was something deeper and more exciting going on.

He took her hand and placed it flat against his chest, letting her fingers rest in the tangle of dark hair. She looked up at him questioningly.

'You know what I want,' he told her, a hard edge to his voice.

Her eyes widened. 'Yes, sir,' she whispered, her breath warm against his skin.

Sir. When the mood took her it was what she liked to call him in bed. The way she said it — soft, quivering and slightly frightened — turned him on too. She had to be told what to do, that was part of what she wanted. Part of what he wanted too.

He stroked her breasts for a moment, rubbing the silky camisole against her nipples until they were fully erect under his fingers. 'Is your pussy wet?' he whispered.

For a second he thought that she wasn't going to answer but then she nodded. In the dim light it was impossible to be sure, but he was certain that her eyes would have been full of shame and guilt and excitement.

'Show me,' he said, kissing her once more on the mouth.

She turned over slightly and slid her hand down under the covers. She was naked apart from the camisole. It was a

'The only reason?'

She was right of course, but there was no way he could admit anything. 'Why else would she be here?' he asked.

'Because she fancies you,' Anne said, looking directly into his eyes for his reaction.

'That's rubbish,' he said, looking away.

'You know it isn't,' she responded. 'She fancies you and you know it. Don't you think I haven't noticed the way she looks at you?'

He tried not to smile. Did Sarah really fancy him? It was so hard to tell sometimes. 'You're seeing things,' he said, without conviction.

'And you fancy her too, don't you?'

Was she jealous? It sounded crazy. 'I don't,' he insisted. 'You're not about to go all serious on me, are you?'

She looked into her coffee while she answered. 'No, you know I'm not.'

Now they were both half-lying. It was time to change the subject. 'I've had no luck getting you switched to the case,' he admitted. They'd agreed the previous evening not to talk about the case but now it seemed the most expedient thing to do.

'I know,' she sighed, 'you're not flavour of the month. Anyway, I've done some digging around and there's something you need to check out. Jenny Cunliffe works for a guy called Graham Scott.'

The name rang bells immediately. 'The bloke who owned AlarmIC?'

She nodded. 'One and the same,' she confirmed.

Vallance knew that Mrs Cunliffe worked for an electronics company, it was where Trevor Watkins had picked her up. He hadn't made the connection with AlarmIC. Perhaps the dead company wasn't so dead after all. 'Have you got anything on him?' he asked.

'Nothing yet. He seems to have slipped through all the investigations after the collapse of the company. He's completely legit as far as we're concerned.'

Why hadn't anyone else come up with the information about Scott? Why hadn't Chiltern or Matthews or even DS

'I can just see his face,' Vallance said, smiling. 'But anyway, he's still having it off with Jenny Cunliffe, isn't he?'

Clark was still laughing. 'Wait till I tell him you called him queer. Try telling that to Jenny Cunliffe's old man. And the others.'

Dobson tensed but Vallance touched his arm to keep him quiet. 'You know that Jenny's married?' he asked, trying to keep the conversation going.

'Yeah, so what? If her old man can't satisfy her why shouldn't Jack take her in hand?' Clark demanded, a lecherous grin spreading over his face. 'And it's not just her, I know Jack's got a couple of others on the go too.'

Vallance laughed. 'It's a surprise he's still got time to run Cagney's.'

'Jack's the lad,' Clark said, and it sounded as though he were repeating a catchphrase that he still found funny.

Pulling Clark in had already proved to be useful. Was there anything more to get out of him? 'And what about you, Simon? You don't have a bit on the side to satisfy your unnatural cravings?'

It took a moment for Clark to get the message. 'You're a funny bloke,' he said. 'You're wasted, mate. What the shit are you doing in the old bill?'

'Answer the question,' Dobson said, obviously irritated by the banter that excluded him.

'What question? Do I have a married bit on the side?'

Vallance hadn't specified married or single but Clark had provided the answer. 'Who is she?'

'Can't say,' Clark responded instantly.

It was time to get heavy. 'We're investigating a murder, Simon,' he said. 'We've heard that this one's right up your street. If you were with someone on Sunday morning then tell us now and save us all a lot of hassle.'

'I was on my own,' Clark insisted.

'You're sticking to that even though telling us her name might put you in the clear?'

Clark leaned back in his seat and crossed his arms. 'That's right,' he said.

'In that case we're going to have to arrest you on suspicion,'

Vallance said. 'We'll turn your place over from top to bottom. What's the point?'

'I was on my own.'

'Who are you scared of?' Vallance asked, suddenly realising why Clark was so unwilling to name a name.

'I ain't scared of anyone,' Clark responded angrily. 'I told you, I was on my own.'

'Is it Jack Thomas? Are you screwing his wife?'

Clark shook his head. 'I ain't saying another word. You either arrest me now or let me go.'

Vallance shrugged. 'In that case I'll hand over to Inspector Dobson,' he said. 'He'll arrest you and make sure that the search warrant is sorted out. Are you sure you want to do this?'

Clark looked defiant. 'I ain't saying a word,' he insisted.

'You're an idiot,' Vallance said sadly.

He knew the truth already. Simon Clark had been with Isobel Thomas on Saturday night and the following morning. In which case where had Jack Thomas been?

She inched forward too but where he had only the kerb to worry about she was facing the oncoming traffic.

The other car moved forward suddenly and she realised that he'd won. His car was six inches in front of hers and the road narrowed into a single lane. She took a deep breath and gritted her teeth. The bastard was looking so pleased with himself. The thought that he'd be ahead and looking at her in the rear-view mirror for the next few miles made her go cold. She glanced ahead, saw the gap in the oncoming traffic and took her chance. The tyres squealed with pain but she accelerated out into the other lane, swerved round the car in front and then cut in. She was ahead and there was no way that the driver behind her could get back in front.

The other driver was less than happy, and he made a big show of mouthing obscenities at her when she glanced in the mirror. She smiled in response and that made him shout even more. When the lights changed she accelerated away from him in the hope that he'd rage even more. Did he really think that because she was a woman she'd give him right of way? There was something immensely gratifying in putting male drivers in their place.

The address of Good Neighbours wasn't very clear. It sounded as though the charity were based in a pub, which couldn't be right. She turned off the main road and down a side street that was lined on each side by big Edwardian detached houses. It was so obviously a prosperous sort of area that it was hard to imagine why a local charity like Good Neighbours existed. The big houses, expensive cars and wide open spaces were the epitome of London's commuter belt. It was a part of the world that Sarah knew well. She had been born and brought up somewhere very similar.

The Coach and Horses boasted a big old-fashioned pub sign that looked no more than two years old. Sarah parked on the road in front of the pub and switched the engine off. She carefully folded the map and put it away in the glove compartment and then retrieved her pad and the tape recorder from her bag. She'd replaced the batteries the previous evening and had inserted a new cassette in it, pre-ferring to take no chances that the thing would not work.

He could hold back no longer. He thrust hard and tensed, crying out blissfully as he spurted thick waves of come into her pussy. She pressed herself against him and then shuddered as she climaxed too with a long low moan of pure pleasure.

The sharp breeze seemed to have cleared the thick layers of cloud that had turned the morning a dark and depressing grey. It felt as if the sun had come out for the first time in days, and, sitting in the warmth of her car, Sarah found it hard to believe that it was so late in the year. The traffic had been light too, though the long drive from central London out into the suburban fringe was never particularly easy. It was not nearly as bad, however, as the commuter drive in the other direction. Watching the slow-moving traffic as it inched into London was extremely dispiriting and she was grateful that she no longer had to do it.

She glanced at the open map on the passenger seat beside her and then, as the traffic lights changed to green, she accelerated sharply, getting away before the other cars had even started. A quick glance in the rear-view mirror at the cars behind her brought a smile to her face. There was something about being first, about being out front while everyone else was still registering that the lights had changed, which was profoundly satisfying.

It had been no problem getting her bosses to agree to her looking at the Cunliffe case. They owed her one after Malik Alibhai. They were almost pathetically grateful for the chance to redeem themselves in her eyes, though they all knew that she wasn't one to forget things in a hurry. If she was willing to work on the Cunliffe case for a while it was because she needed time to work out what to do next with the Alibhai story.

The traffic started to snarl up just as she neared the next set of lights. The dual carriageway ended and turned into a single lane that was packed solid. She edged the car forward slowly, trying to cut in on the car to her left in an effort to get in front. The other driver glared at her but she pretended not to notice him. He edged the car nearer to hers until they were almost bumper to bumper. He wasn't about to give way.

hard to imagine too men more dissimilar. Duncan, who still imagined that Sarah was going to marry him, was solid, dependable and good-looking. He was also dreary, dull and humourless.

The door opened suddenly and she looked up. It was only a uniformed PC. 'Yes?' she snapped, angry because her heart was racing and she could sense that her disappointment was visible.

'DCI Vallance will see you now,' the PC reported politely.

She stood up, grabbed her leather case and glared at the cop. He made way for her, letting her glide past on high heels that crashed on the stone floor. Her long black coat fell open, revealing a short tartan skirt that contrasted with black Lycra stockings that matched the heels.

The PC seemed unsure as to whether he should be leading or following but Sarah went ahead anyway. She headed down a corridor lined with offices passing other officers, some in uniform and some in civvies. Her escort followed meekly, pointing the way when she stopped at the end of the corridor.

'The Chief Inspector will be along in a minute,' the PC said, showing her into one of the interview rooms.

'Is there any chance of some coffee, please?' she asked, carefully setting her case down on the table.

'I'll see what I can do,' the PC promised.

She waited for him to disappear before she relaxed again. Her heart was still beating too fast and she didn't like it. DCI Vallance was just another cop, that's all. Another person to deal with in her job, that was all. She glanced down at her skirt, brushing it carefully so that the pleats looked perfect against her shiny black stockings.

'Yes?' she called when there was a knock at the door. Coffee, she hoped.

DCI Vallance walked in, smiling, and offered his hand. 'Hello, Sarah,' he said. She smiled and shook his hand quickly, hardly daring to meet his dark brown eyes.

She turned away from him and opened her case. 'You're interested in Michael Cunliffe's death, aren't you?'

He looked more than a little surprised. 'How did you work that one out?' he asked, walking around to sit at the other

EIGHT
Tuesday 10th December

Sarah was shown into a neatly antiseptic waiting room almost as soon as she arrived at the police divisional headquarters building. In one sense it was a relief to be given the time to recover from the drive down from central London. The rush-hour traffic heading out to the suburbs had been heavy and unforgiving and more than once she had been provoked into outrage by bad drivers, all male, who thought that because she was female she was fair game to cut up, overtake or block in.

Was Vallance going to be late again? Punctuality was not one of his strong points. Neither was grooming come to that. Nor being organised. She had her list of key words which described him perfectly: unkempt, infuriating, facetious. He was also intelligent and attractive, though it was hard for her to figure out what attracted her to him. Not that she ever dared admit to the attraction.

The waiting room was kitted out with low-slung arm-chairs, a table laden with uninteresting reading materials and an empty fish tank. The walls were decorated with the kind of public information posters which seemed to have been drafted with the functionally illiterate in mind. She looked at her watch once more. It was getting close to six o'clock. There was a long drive home to think about, and then an inter-minable evening in with Duncan. Duncan and Vallance. It was pity because he liked to tease her panties down slowly between her thighs. He felt her shudder slightly against him as she stroked her fingers between her pussy lips.

His cock was hard and as she moved he pressed it against her, delighting in the feel of her warm body next to his. She withdrew her fingers and gingerly brought them out from under the covers. The light was beginning to improve but not enough for him to see clearly. He took her hand roughly and brought her fingers to his lips. He dabbed his tongue at her fingertips, felt the moisture of her sex there and then licked it away.

'Again,' he ordered, 'show me how wet you are.'

'Yes, sir,' she whispered. He waited for a second and then licked away the pussy taste from her fingers.

'Now you,' he instructed, 'I want you to taste yourself.'

She obeyed instantly. She stroked her pussy until her fingers were nice and wet and then she licked the moisture with the tip of her tongue.

He touched her lips and she licked his fingers too. 'Do you want me to touch your pussy so you can lick it up?' he asked.

'I don't know —' she replied coyly.

He turned onto his side and then pushed her down so that she was flat on her back. Her knees were up and her thighs already parted in preparation. He kissed her roughly on the mouth and she tried to draw him towards her by wrapping her arms around him.

'Put your hands down,' he told her gruffly. 'I'll tell you when you can touch me.'

She whimpered meekly but obeyed. Was that what she wanted? She liked to be told off as well as being told what to do, but he wasn't always sure how far to go. In lots of ways it still felt like she was calling the shots.

He slid his hand down between her thighs and let his fingers gently touch her between her pussy lips. She closed her eyes as he began to stroke her, rubbing his fingers up and down in the slick wet groove of her sex. He curled his middle finger and pushed it deeper into her wetness so that she sighed and moved closer.

'Why are you wet?' he demanded, beginning to play

117

with her clitoris with his pussy-soaked fingers.

'Because you make me wet —' she responded, her voice a sigh of pleasure.

'Is it?' he hissed, moving his hand faster and faster.

She sighed and moved with him, opening her thighs, shifting her body as the pleasure seemed to burst through her.

'Why are you wet?' he demanded, his voice louder and more insistent.

'Because — because I want you —'

He forced his mouth over hers and she squirmed for breath as he kissed her violently. His hand was smeared with her juices as he played with her pussy bud, edging her closer and closer to orgasm.

'You want my cock,' he said, pushing himself against her.

'Yes — I want your cock inside me —' she cried urgently.

He moved quickly between her thighs and she curled her arms around him tightly. She lifted her bottom off the bed, moving herself so that his hardness pressed between the wetness of her pussy lips. He reached under her and held her in place, pressing the very tip of his cock at the opening of her sex. It felt like heaven and he closed his eyes to the pleasure.

'Please — please —' she moaned, thrusting herself upwards, trying to open herself fully to his hardness.

'Is this what you want?'

She sighed loudly as his stiff cock pressed into the tight warmth of her body. He could feel her tensing up as he entered her fully. She was clinging to him, quivering on the verge of orgasm as he moved and positioned her as he desired. He eased out slowly and then penetrated again, just as slowly so that she moaned softly and dug her nails into his back.

'Is this what you want?' he demanded again.

'Yes — yes — please, please.'

He began to fuck her properly, moving in and out with a rhythm that she matched each time. It felt so good that he wanted it to last for ever. She moaned with pleasure again and again, moving her hips with ever greater urgency as the sensation overtook everything else.

Vallance seemed pleased. 'Thanks, Sarah. I appreciate you coming out like this.'

Did he really think that the interview was over? 'We haven't finished yet,' she told him.

They were interrupted once more by the uniformed constable bearing a mug full of coffee. The stuff was undrinkable but she waited for Vallance to discover it for himself. He swallowed a mouthful of it and winced. 'Horrible stuff,' he said, setting his cup next to hers.

'Firstly,' she began, leaning forward for emphasis, 'it seems to me that the AlarmIC story we covered isn't finished yet. Michael Cunliffe's death is another chapter in a scandal that has yet to be completely uncovered.'

'That's only supposition,' he cautioned.

'Granted, but for the moment there are enough unanswered questions surrounding AlarmIC to merit further investigation. Secondly,' she paused, 'there's the case of Malik Alibhai.'

Vallance looked perplexed. 'I did some research too,' he said. 'And all I could find out was that the guy had been jumped by a gang of skinheads. It's bad and all that, but why the interest?'

She tensed up as the anger surged inside her. She had hoped for more from Vallance. Despite appearances he had more integrity than most of the policemen she'd ever met, and he was not the heartless macho bastard that most of them pretended to be. Disappointment mingled with anger and for a second she couldn't trust herself to speak.

'Have I screwed up?' he said, the look on her face finally registering with him.

'Malik was not just another victim of racist violence,' she said through gritted teeth, 'though that would be bad enough. He was deliberately attacked because he was leading a strike at the factory where he worked.'

'There was nothing on that on the police computer,' Vallance responded.

'Then that just shows you how much concern your people have for what's happened to him.'

Vallance shook his head. 'I'm sorry, Sarah,' he said quietly,

TV company couldn't see that anyone would be interested in the story of a man half killed for daring to go on strike. 'I'm not interested in ratings,' she declared, 'I'm interested in the truth, Mr Vallance.'

'I know,' he agreed, 'I wasn't saying any different. Now, about Cunliffe, is there anything you can tell me about him?'

'Only that he was the company's money man. He wasn't technical and there was nothing to suggest that he knew that the company was producing alarms that could have been death traps. But once the investigation was under way he would have been the man handling the transactions that meant assets disappearing and invoices unpaid.'

'That's why he couldn't get a job afterwards,' Vallance said, as though realisation had only just dawned.

'That's right,' she agreed. In amongst the paperwork were several reports from the liquidators which pointed the finger of suspicion directly at Cunliffe. She fished one out and slid it across the table to Vallance.

He flicked through it quickly. 'But there were no charges ever brought,' he said.

'That's right. He was a good accountant. No laws were broken and so no legal proceedings could ever be instituted. On the other hand no reputable company would touch him with a barge-pole. He'd broken no laws but what he did was entirely unethical.'

Vallance smiled. 'It's ironic then that his next port of call was a charity.'

Now it was her turn to be surprised. 'A charity?'

'That's right. He was working for a local charity called Good Neighbours.'

'A charity,' she repeated. 'That's the last place I would have expected him to go.'

Vallance seemed to think that the interview was coming to a close. 'It looks like there's a whole new angle to investigate,' he said. 'If he was moving money and assets around then there's a chance that some of the creditors might have taken action to get their cash back.'

'Or else someone wanted to make sure that the full details of what he did never got out.'

From her seat in the car she could see that the pub itself had only recently been refurbished. The brewery had decided on the rustic look and had probably installed oak beams, fireplaces and other artefacts from the days when the surrounding area had been farmland and not occupied by executive estates and tree-lined avenues. How did that fit with Good Neighbours?

She replaced the pad and tape recorder in her bag and got out of the car. The bright sunlight brought no warmth with it. It felt like December even if the sky looked like it belonged to April. She walked across to the pub and saw that she'd been right about the decor. The interior was worked in brass and oak, though the effect was spoilt by the tendrils of tinsel and the other brightly coloured Christmas decorations.

It was too early for the pub to be open but she tried the door nevertheless. It was locked so she walked round to the back and into the concrete car park. There was a pub garden on one side and at the very back a small two-storey building that looked like a converted outhouse that had once belonged to the pub. Now it served as the office for Good Neighbours.

Sarah checked herself quickly, smoothing down her skirt and straightening her long overcoat. When she looked up again she saw a woman emerging from the office building. She looked completely preoccupied and hurried from the office to one of two identical cars parked in bays next to the office. She threw her bag into the car and then got in quickly, starting it almost as soon as she had the door closed.

Was that Rosemary Collins? Sarah started to walk towards the car but it moved off quickly, sweeping past her before she had a chance to call out to the driver. Damn it! It had to have been Rosemary Collins and Sarah had wanted to talk to her first.

There hadn't been time to book an appointment with anyone at the charity but she had assumed that she'd have time to talk to the people who ran things. She'd only had time to do a brief background check but she knew that Good Neighbours was the brainchild of Patrick and Rosemary Collins, and that Rosemary was head of fund-raising. That was why Sarah wanted to talk to her first.

As she walked past the other car parked in a bay she saw the 'Jesus Saves' sticker in the back window. If the first car had been Rosemary's then it meant that her husband was in, which was some consolation. And knowing that he was religious, assuming the car did belong to him, was useful.

The door opened onto an open-plan office that looked cosy enough to work in, though to Sarah it looked like it could do with a tidy up. There were half a dozen desks arranged in two rows of three with an aisle clear between them. The walls were almost bare apart from a few token Christmas decorations and a number of posters for charity events plastered here and there. At the back of the large room there was a single partition wall that looked as though it were still new and which divided the rest of the office into three rooms.

There was a quiet murmur of voices in the room. Three of the four people present were on the phone. Sarah flashed a smile at the only person not on the phone and then walked towards her.

'Can I help you?' the young woman asked, returning Sarah's smile.

'Yes, I was hoping to speak to Patrick Collins,' she said, looking towards the far end of the room.

The young woman looked doubtful. 'Do you have an appointment?' she asked.

'No,' Sarah admitted. 'I was hoping to talk to Rosemary but I've just missed her, haven't I?'

The girl nodded. 'Something urgent just came up,' she said. 'It's always the same at this time of year. Christmas is one of our busiest periods.'

'Of course, in that case can I have a word with Mr Collins?'

The girl still looked reluctant. 'Perhaps I can help you? Is it about a donation to our Christmas Fund?'

Why the reluctance to let her meet Patrick Collins? 'No, I think I need to speak to Mr Collins directly,' Sarah said insistently while trying to remain polite at the same time.

'Who shall I say is calling?'

'My name's Sarah Fairfax.'

The young woman stood up. 'And can I tell him what it's in connection with?'

Sarah was tempted to say no, but she knew that would get her nowhere. 'It's to do with your work here.'

The answer was obviously less than satisfying but the young woman said no more. That was the trouble with working in a small place, Sarah thought, everyone wants to know what's going on. The woman walked off to get Patrick Collins and Sarah sat on the edge of her desk. The desk next door was occupied by another young woman who smiled at Sarah while carrying on her telephone conversation. Sarah eavesdropped for a few seconds but she grew bored listening to the woman trying to wangle a donation to the Christmas Fund.

'No luck,' the woman sighed, putting the phone down.

Cold calling. The very idea of it made Sarah's heart sink. Even if it was for a good cause there was no way that she had the patience or the inclination to ring people at random and plead with them to buy something or to make a donation. 'It sounds like hard work,' she said, smiling sympathetically.

The woman made a face. 'It is hard but we're having a good Christmas so far. It already feels like we've collected more than we did last year, not that it's buying us more –'

She stopped mid-sentence and Sarah turned to see Patrick Collins come rushing out of his office. A tall, ruddy-faced man, he towered over the young woman who had gone to fetch him.

'Can I help you?' he said, and it sounded almost like a demand.

Sarah stood up straight, suddenly aware of the man's height and his stiff almost hostile manner. 'I'm Sarah Fairfax,' she said, offering her hand. 'I was hoping to talk to you about what you and your team are doing here.'

He looked at her coldly. 'You're a journalist?' he guessed.

Was it that obvious? 'Yes, that's right,' she said, still smiling.

'Are you here to talk about Good Neighbours or about Michael Cunliffe?'

The smile wavered but held. 'Both,' she admitted. 'I'd like to talk –'

He didn't let her finish. 'We can talk in my office,' he snapped.

It wasn't the friendliest welcome in the world and for a moment she had been certain that he'd throw her out. He didn't come across as the most charitable person in the world. Charitable. It was a good word and she made a mental note to use it well.

His office was a cramped little room at the far end of the building. Apart from the desk and a couple of chairs there was little else in there apart from a book shelf that was half empty. The Bible was there of course, and a couple of other Christian books and then a few stacked-up reports and folders. One wall was decorated with a number of framed photographs of Collins and his wife attending what looked like conferences in different parts of the world – Africa, Russia, South East Asia. The view from his window looked down on the car park and beyond that the back of the pub. All in all it was hardly the most impressive office Sarah had ever seen. How much did the charity spend on running costs?

'Who do you work for?' Collins asked, slumping down heavily in his seat. His eyes were cold and angry and fixed rigidly on Sarah.

She sat down in the seat opposite him, aware that he hadn't asked her to sit down yet. 'I work for a TV programme called *Insight*,' she said.

His face showed no flicker of recognition. 'I don't watch television,' he announced. 'I find it a very destructive medium. There's no room for the spirit. There's no room for faith in television.'

So, he was that kind of Christian. 'We covered the AlarmIC story,' she said. 'I assume you've heard about that.'

He nodded. 'Is that why you're interested in us?'

'Partly.'

'Quite frankly, Miss Fairfax, I see no reason why we should be involved in any of this. Michael Cunliffe had no part to play in what happened with the alarms at his old company. He was a money man, not an electronics expert. And to be honest I'm not even sure that he would have remained with us here for much longer.'

'And why's that?'

Collins moved forward to rest his arms on his desk. 'Because we're here as a charity not as a business. It's a truth he could never come to terms with. We exist to help people, not to make profit or loss or any of that business.'

She smiled. 'That's very commendable, Mr Collins,' she said. 'That's also partly why I'm here. I'd like to know more about what you're doing.'

He looked distrustful again. 'You'll pardon me for my reluctance to deal with the media,' he said. 'I can think of nothing more corrosive, more permissive or more destructive than the media. I'm not one to preach but —'

She cut in quick, before he had a chance to launch into his sermon. 'What about what we do? Do you really think that we exposed AlarmIC because we're only interested in destroying things?'

'No,' he agreed with a slight smile, 'you're interested in advertising revenue. And of course you have your own agenda. The media wields inordinate amounts of power, Miss Fairfax, and very little of it is used for the common good.'

'I'm not here to argue about that,' she snapped. 'I'm here to talk about why Michael Cunliffe was murdered.'

Collins's smile broadened. 'I see that my points are hitting too close to home. Do you believe in God, Miss Fairfax?'

'That's my business,' she said coldly.

'Then I'd ask you to examine your conscience and ask yourself whether what you are doing is good or bad.'

She gritted her teeth to stop the scream of anger escaping. 'I've got nothing on my conscience to worry about,' she managed to say, in a voice so calm she hardly recognised herself. 'Now, if —'

Collins wasn't about to give up. 'There are dark forces at work in the world,' he said softly, as though imparting some terrible secret.

Not only was the man born again, he was hot on the book of Revelations. No doubt he watched the sky for portents and was eagerly awaiting the end of the world. Sarah knew there was no point in trying to argue with him, he had the total conviction and the sure-fire knowledge that he was one of the chosen and everyone else was going to fry.

'Can we talk about Michael Cunliffe,' she said, pointedly ignoring his last remark.

'But just now you were asking about the work of Good Neighbours. Or was that merely an attempt to put me at ease?'

Sarah wanted to wipe the smug grin from his face. He was getting to her, no matter how hard she was trying to remain calm. 'The two are connected, aren't they? You yourself said that he never quite fitted in with working at a charity. So, tell me what it is you do here.'

It took a moment for him to reply and for a second she was certain he was going to refuse her again. 'As you can see,' he said, 'we're based in what is said to be one of the most well-off parts of the country. However in the midst of plenty there are still pockets of need. You people,' he added, 'prefer to report on the horrors of famine in some far-off part of the world which you can blame on the machinations of politicians and bankers, but what about the hungry and the lonely around us?'

'Look, I'm not –' she started to say and then stopped. He'd done it again and he was enjoying it.

'Can I continue? There are people in this area who are lonely, poor and in need of help. There's a gap which only we can fill. Social services are useless, they too have their own agenda and looking after the old and the infirm is low on their list of priorities. There's a space for Christian charity and the virtues of good neighbourliness. For example during the Christmas period we're putting together over a hundred and fifty food parcels, we've collected hundreds of pairs of shoes and boots, extra blankets and clothes –'

He was warming to his theme, his voice was increasingly animated and the traces of paranoia were absent. However Sarah had heard nothing to cause her the same feeling. 'I'm sorry,' she said, deciding to stop him there and then, 'but I know of primary schools who do a better job than that. Surely you don't need a staff of half a dozen people, three executives with company cars and an office this size to collect up a couple of hundred food parcels over Christmas.'

It was a message that Collins obviously hadn't been

expecting. The smile drained from his face and his eyes seemed to ignite with anger. 'That's so typical! All you people do is carp at other people's good work! I should have known better than to talk to someone like you –'

She looked at him with raised eyebrows. 'Please,' she said calmly, 'carry on and vent your spleen, Mr Collins, but you're not doing yourself any favours. If this is how you react to a few simple questions then I wonder how you'd cope with some real criticism?'

'What the hell is that supposed to mean?' he demanded, his voice a low growl of anger.

Sarah glanced at the door nervously. Collins was a big man and the rage that had been below the surface was starting to show. 'It means you ought to calm down, Mr Collins, that's all.'

He stared at her coldly before answering. 'Did you threaten me?'

She shook her head. 'No, I was just making a point, that's all.'

'I don't like you, Miss Fairfax,' he stated finally. 'I don't think we should continue this interview. I'm sorry it even started.'

She wasn't sorry that it was over. She stood up and walked quickly to the door. 'For a Christian preaching the values of charity,' she said, opening the door, 'you're not exactly a paragon of virtue, are you?'

'I think you ought to leave,' he stated coldly. 'Now.'

She shrugged and slammed the door as hard as she could. There was silence in the open-plan part of the office and all eyes were fixed on her. She stared at them coolly, trying to ignore the shakiness that she felt. Did they feel sympathy for her or were they all of the same mind as Collins? No wonder Cunliffe had never quite fitted in at Good Neighbours.

She walked through the office in silence, looking neither left nor right but listening intently in case Collins decided to come after her. The man was dangerous, she had no doubt about it.

TEN
Wednesday 11th December

Doris was just coming in with the tea and biscuits when Superintendent Riley arrived. Vallance was sitting on the edge of Doris's desk, quietly scanning the paperwork while she had been brewing up and retrieving some of Riley's secret supply of chocolate biscuits.

'Morning, Mr Riley,' Doris called, 'it's just brewed, do you want a cup?'

Riley ignored her completely and walked directly to where Vallance was sitting. 'What the hell do you think you're doing?' he demanded.

There were a million ways to answer but most of them would have sent Riley's blood pressure dangerously high. It was tempting but Vallance needed his help. 'I was waiting to see you, sir,' was the most politic reply he could think of.

'In my office now,' Riley snapped.

Vallance winked at Doris who smiled back. She was used to working with Riley and his foul moods did nothing to dent her own permanent good humour. Riley took his coat off and hung it carefully on the rack beside the door before marching briskly into his office.

There were no social niceties with Riley. 'Where are you with the Cunliffe case?' he said, sitting stiffly behind his desk.

Vallance would have liked to sit down but in Riley's domain you could only do that when you had permission and there was no way that Vallance would ask for it. 'We've made an arrest, sir,' he reported. 'His name's –'

'Simon Clark,' Riley said, finishing the sentence. 'Is he the guilty man?'

Clark had been arrested late the previous evening, well after the time that Riley had left for home. He'd only just arrived at work. So how come he was so clued up about the case? 'No, sir, I don't think so,' Vallance replied.

'Why not?'

Vallance was caught off guard. His chat with Riley wasn't going as planned. He hated having to explain himself to his superiors. Most often there was nothing to go on but gut feeling and instinct. Riley was a man who distrusted everything but office memos. The only gut feelings he ever had were sorted out with indigestion tablets.

'Why not?' Riley demanded impatiently. 'He's got no alibi, he's got a criminal record and your friend at Scotland Yard thinks he's the most likely candidate.'

Someone had been feeding Riley with information. It had to be Dobson, that was why he'd been appointed to the case in the first place. 'I think he does have an alibi,' Vallance said, 'I think he's just too frightened to tell us.'

The look on Riley's face was pure scorn. 'Don't be so ridiculous, man. Clark's a convicted robber, he's probably a murderer too, why should he be afraid to offer an alibi?'

Vallance could barely bring himself to speak. The pompous bastard in front of him had no idea what he was talking about. The last time he'd investigated a case the death penalty was still on the statute books. How the fuck could a desk-bound bureaucrat like Riley tell him how to run a case?

'I'm waiting,' Riley said.

'Because he's scared of someone far more dangerous,' Vallance said, his eyes half closed so that he wouldn't have to look at Riley.

'Jack Thomas?' Riley said, showing once more that he was completely up to date on the case.

'Yes, sir. I also think that Jack Thomas is still having an affair with Mrs Cunliffe. That gives him the prime motive for murder.'

'Thomas is a petty villain with a big reputation, that's all,' Riley stated. 'He hasn't got the history that Clark has.'

'Maybe that's because he's smart enough not to get caught.'

Riley stood up suddenly. 'Jack Thomas has been operating around here for years, are you suggesting that we've let him get away with things?'

The answer was yes but it came out as silence.

'If Thomas was the criminal you think he is then we would have had him by now,' Riley insisted. 'Unless you think that the rest of us are incompetent idiots without your policing skills, Vallance.'

'I'm not saying that,' Vallance lied. 'We're keeping hold of Clark for now, sir. I just wanted some extra manpower, that's all.'

'Why?'

'I want to confirm or deny that Jack Thomas is still sleeping with Jenny Cunliffe, sir. I was hoping to institute a house to house at Fenton Close.'

'Why can't you do that with the people that you've got?'

'Because they're looking at the AlarmIC connection and following up on Simon Clark, sir.'

'You can have one of the uniformed lads,' Riley suggested.

It was make or break time. 'I think this would make a good job for Anne Quinn, sir.'

Riley sat down again. 'Why Quinn?'

'Because she's good, sir. And we really need a feminine touch here, sir. I mean who's likely to know all the gossip on Fenton Close? You know that we always get better results when we –'

'Cut the crap, Vallance, what's the real reason?'

It was crap of course, but Vallance had hoped that his appeal to Riley's sexism would do the trick. 'She's a good officer, sir, that's all.'

'Request denied,' Riley said, in a tone that indicated the conversation was over.

Vallance stood his ground. 'Why? What reason is there to deny me an extra officer on this investigation?'

Riley smiled. 'Because that's the way it is,' he declared. 'You've got some good officers on your team already. If you can't make effective use of human resources then that's your problem, Vallance, not mine. Ever heard of chain of command? Ever heard of discipline?'

'It's not a question of resources —'

'The decision has been made, Vallance. Now, get out of here.'

Vallance resisted the urge to vault Riley's desk and throttle him there and then. His fists were clenched deep in his pockets and he was trembling with rage. He turned and walked out, unable to even look at Riley's skeletal face.

Dobson. He was the one feeding info to Riley, there was no one else with the inside knowledge and the motive. The bastard was angling for promotion and he'd decided that using his tongue to lick Riley's arse was better than using his brains to solve crimes. If that was the way the game was played then Vallance wanted no part of it. Hell, he was a copper and his job was to catch the man who'd murdered Michael Cunliffe not to secure himself a comfortable desk, chair and pension for the future.

Sarah listed her key words to describe Patrick Collins: obnoxious, dogmatic, paranoid and uncharitable. The latter word seemed so mild compared to the others, but somehow it was the one that mattered the most. She wrote the words in order on her pad and then stared at it blankly for a while. Finally she added the word 'confrontational' to the list. Collins had been looking for an argument from the moment he had set eyes on her.

What next? She felt inclined to dig deeper into the activities of Good Neighbours. However that was undoubtedly due to her dislike of Collins, and the fact that she had felt so shaken by his anger. Did Good Neighbours have any bearing on Cunliffe's murder? Tangentially perhaps. She could see a strange symmetry in the dead man's life. First he had worked at a company producing life-saving devices that were lethal, then he worked for a charity that was run by the most uncharitable man she'd ever met.

She glanced at her watch. It was still early and the long drive back to the office didn't appeal to her very much. So, what next? The obvious thing to do would be to interview Jenny Cunliffe but she felt wary of approaching the woman so soon after her husband's death. The only other thing was to follow up on the AlarmIC connection.

The notes were in her bag, neatly filed away after her talk with Tony Vallance. She smiled to herself at the memory of the previous evening. He had seemed genuinely surprised that she was going to look into the Cunliffe case. It was funny how he always underestimated her. For a man who was so obviously good at reading people his faculties seemed to fail when it came to her. How could he imagine that she'd not want to become involved in the case?

Tony Vallance. Tony. She never allowed herself to call him that. He was always Chief Inspector, sometimes DCI Vallance and most often Mr Vallance. Why was she thinking about him? There were more important things to do than sit in the car and ponder on Vallance's name. She retrieved her notes and started to read, doing her best to get Vallance out of her head.

She turned to the page of her notes on Graham Scott. The faded photograph clipped to the top of the page showed a rather plump, middle-aged man hiding behind thick round glasses that magnified his shifty-looking eyes. It wasn't the most flattering of portraits but Sarah knew that it had probably been snapped on Scott's doorstep first thing in the morning. No wonder he looked shocked. His address was local, she noted, but the file was old and it was more than possible that the information was out of date. There was a list of contact numbers for him. Some she recognised as mobile phone numbers which had probably been replaced, some were the numbers for AlarmIC, which left a single private number.

She punched the number into her mobile and waited. The number was still active and after half a dozen rings the call was picked up by an answer-phone. She listened to the dull, nasal tone of the message which confirmed that she was through to Graham and Jocelyn Scott. She reached for her pen just as the message got to the good bit and she noted down the number Graham Scott had obligingly provided for Components International.

The AlarmIC debacle had obviously done nothing to dent Scott's enthusiasm for the electronics business. She was guessing that the company was his, or that he was running it with someone else as the front man or woman. There was always a chance that he worked at Components International as a hired hand but that didn't fit with the ambitious personality that had emerged during the course of the earlier TV investigation.

The next call was to directory enquiries. It only took a minute to confirm that Graham Scott was still listed at his old address and then to get the full address of Components International. She was beginning to feel the familiar excitement of an investigation going well. What next? She was on a roll and she didn't want to break the flow. Now that she had a handle on Scott she needed to catch up on what his current commercial activities were.

Who would know about the electronics industry? There was no one back at the office who'd even know where to start. She had friends in the computer business but she wasn't sure that Scott was into that kind of technology. Who else? She flipped open her personal organiser and turned to her list of information sources. She ran a glossy red fingernail down the list of names and then stopped at George Reid. He was an acquaintance more than a friend, but he worked at one of the big corporate information suppliers in the City and was a useful source of commercial information.

She dialled the number immediately and then spent a frustrating five minutes navigating her way through the voice-mail system until she was finally through to him.

'George? How are you? It's Sarah,' she said.

He paused before answering. 'Sarah? Sarah Fairfax?'

'Yes, that's right. I know you're probably in the middle of something –'

'Do you know,' he interrupted, 'the only time you ever call is when you need help.'

He wasn't going to whine, was he? 'That's not true, George,' she lied. 'It's just that you never seem to have the time for a proper chat.'

'So this is purely a social call?'

133

She raised her eyes to heaven. He was going to be difficult. 'Not exactly. Listen, how's –' she hesitated while she searched her memory for the name of his mousey little girlfriend.

'We've split up,' he announced, saving her the trouble of putting a name to her.

'I'm sorry to hear that.'

'She left me last month,' he sighed. 'It's been a really bad time for me –'

'Why don't you give Duncan a call?' she suggested desperately. She had met George through Duncan and she could think of no better way of extricating herself from what looked to be an interminable and wretched conversation about George's personal woes.

The answer came back by rote. 'How is he?' George asked, and Sarah could not detect a trace of real interest in his voice. It was no surprise. Duncan was her partner and he elicited the same response in her.

'He's fine. Give him a call, maybe the two of you could arrange a boys' night out, or something.'

'Sure, that's not a bad idea,' George said, sounding a bit more enthusiastic.

'Listen, George, while we're on the phone, could you –'

'What is it you want to know?' he responded.

'Ever heard of a company called Components International? They're based at the Surrey end of the suburbs. The chief's a guy called Graham Scott, who used to run AlarmIC. Ever heard of him?'

'I've heard all about AlarmIC,' George confirmed. 'Listen, Sarah, give me fifteen minutes and then call back.'

'Thanks, George. I'll get Duncan to give you a call,' she promised.

'In fifteen minutes,' he repeated and then put the phone down.

Good, that was out of the way. Fifteen minutes was time enough to drive out to Components International to get some idea of the scale of operations there. She reached in the glove compartment for the street atlas immediately. The idea of waiting in the car so close to where Collins worked was distinctly unappealing. She knew that if he saw her waiting there he'd assume that she was there for him. His paranoid suspicions would be confirmed and then God only knew what his reactions would be.

As she worked out her route she realised that she was actually very close to Scott's home address. AlarmIC had been a fairly large company but when it collapsed there was nothing there for the creditors to fight over. How much of it had been sunk into Scott's house and car? Come to that, she thought, how much of it had ended up in Michael Cunliffe's pocket?

The day was still cold but bright, with wisps of white cloud high in the clear blue sky. If it were not for the festive displays in the shops it would have been hard to imagine that it was so close to Christmas. She suddenly thought of Jenny Cunliffe. Her Christmas was going to be anything but jolly. Sarah hoped that she had family and friends around her to cushion the blow, though even that wouldn't be enough to soften the raw pain of bereavement. It was a depressing thought and Sarah almost shook herself to clear it from her mind.

Luckily Graham Scott's house wasn't hard to find. A large Edwardian detached house with a sloping roof, bay windows and a big front garden which had been partly paved, it sat well back from the road. It looked expensive, the whole street did, but Sarah had no idea whether in the grand scheme of things the house was worth more or less than a fortune. The sheer scale of the property, and the quiet road on which it was sited, suggested an asking price that was measured in the hundreds of thousands. It wasn't quite the millionaires mansion that she had hoped for, but it was expensive nevertheless.

She waited for a while, debating whether to ring George back but then decided that she ought to make her way to Components International. It was edging closer to lunchtime and she wondered about stopping off somewhere for a bite to eat. Should she call Vallance? She'd refused him dinner, but he'd never asked her to meet for lunch. Should she ask him? No, it was a bad idea, she decided. Vallance might think that an invitation to lunch meant she was interested in something other than work.

Components International sported an altogether less salubrious address. It wasn't much of a drive from Scott's home but it crossed one of the main arterial routes into London, which meant it might as well have been on the moon. The houses in the area were smaller, dingier and crowded together on narrow roads that looked as mean and as neglected as anything London had to offer. The social apartheid that existed in the suburbs was nowhere better displayed than in the different status attached to addresses on each side of a main road. On one side there was affluence and success and on the other failure and neglect.

The industrial estate looked like a run-down relic from another age. It owed nothing to the fashion for hi-tech units, steel and glass and the quiet concentration of new technology. Instead the units were built with pre-formed concrete slabs with arched roofs of corrugated iron and the only steel around was used to shutter doors and windows. Spray paint added lurid colour to an otherwise bleak landscape.

Sarah slowed the car to a crawl and drove onto the estate, peering intently at the empty units in the hope that she'd see life somewhere. There were cars clustered at the end of the estate and she headed towards them. She had seen the glossy brochures put out by AlarmIC and so she knew how much of a contrast the premises of Components International provided. Graham Scott had definitely taken a step down in the world.

The sudden roar of an engine startled her. She gripped the wheel instinctively as the transit van sped passed her. It had to belong to a courier company, only one of their drivers would take so much pleasure in overtaking a car that was crawling along at barely ten miles an hour. It screeched to a halt in front of one of the big units at the end of the estate and as she drew closer the driver jumped out and jogged up a flight of rickety steps on the outside of the building.

She parked her car next to his van and peered out to get a better view. The front of the building was dominated by a loading bay that was firmly closed, the laminated steel door, alive with swirls of graffiti, locked into place. Two square windows, both protected by thick black bars, were positioned above the loading bay. On the second floor of the unit a sad-looking sign that said COMPONENTS INTERNATIONAL sat above the windows and just under the curved roof. The only way in appeared to be the rickety steel steps at the side, and even they were covered with spray paint.

A minute later she heard movement and saw that shutters on the loading bay were being pulled up. The van driver sprinted down the stairs and jumped back into van. He backed out of his space, turned in a tight circle and then slammed the vehicle into reverse again to position it directly in front of the loading bay. Once the shutters were completely up Sarah caught her first glimpse of Graham Scott. Compared to the man pictured in her file he was slimmer, older and the glasses had been replaced by contact lenses.

She watched him bustle about, barking instructions to a couple of his employees as they started to load packages into the van. The driver was standing to one side watching the other men work. He looked up and saw that they were being watched. He started to smile and then Sarah turned away. When she looked up the man was gone and she sighed with relief. It wouldn't have been good to draw too much attention to herself, not yet at least.

It was way past the time she had to call George back. She cursed herself for being sloppy and then hit the redial key on her phone. Again there was an interminable route through the voice system as she keyed her way through different options until finally she was speaking to him once more.

'Why are you interested in a two-bit operation like this one?' was his first question.

'Because of the AlarmIC connection,' she admitted.

'I've looked them up too,' George told her. 'They were a pretty big operation, way way ahead of Components International. I mean we're talking about a turnover that was measured in the millions compared to the few hundred thou' that the new company manages.'

'What do they do?'

'Import high-power components from the Far East. It's a good sector to be in but you need the turnover to make real cash on it. The margins just aren't big enough. If they switch to computer components, especially memory, then they'd easily double their profits. It's a much more crowded market though.'

It was probably good information for a stockbroker but not of much use to Sarah. 'George, what kind of profit are we talking about?'

'Peanuts. The last lot of accounts that were posted show that Graham Scott earned less than my secretary did last year. He's got himself a company car, but to be honest it's nothing to write home about. The bottom line, Sarah, is that this company is going nowhere, fast.'

Sarah had one last question. 'Tell me, apart from importing and distributing these power things, does the company do anything else?'

The question seemed to throw George completely. 'Give me a for example,' he suggested.

She tried to think back to what AlarmIC had been doing before its collapse. 'Manufacturing, exporting stuff, design –'

There was a pause and then George came back with his answer. 'No way according to my information,' he stated categorically.

'Thanks, George, I'm grateful.'

'Listen, Sarah, about me and Duncan going out –'

'Yes?'

'How about you and I going out instead?'

'Sorry, you know that's not on –'

She heard his resigned sigh. 'It was worth a try,' he said.

'Bye, George, and thanks again.'

She put her phone away and sat back in her car to re-consider her next move. She needed to find out more. For example, was Scott's house paid off? There was no way that he could afford a substantial mortgage on his pittance of a salary. And was it true that Components International did nothing more than import electronic components? The industrial unit was pretty big, surely a small turnover didn't need such a big space?

The slamming of the van's doors was followed by the screeching of the steel shutters as the loading bay was closed up again. The van driver winked at Sarah as he climbed back into his cab. She looked at him disdainfully as he drove off, preferring not to acknowledge his gesture with anything remotely like a smile. It was only after the van had disappeared from view that the name emblazoned on its side registered.

The AIR EXPRESS HEATHROW logo was a blur of blue and white on the side of the dark red van. It hadn't clicked at first but now she realised that the van had been loaded rather than unloaded. If Components International was an importer why was it sending stuff out to Heathrow Airport? Belated recognition of the fact was tempered by the knowledge that there were endless legitimate explanations for what she had seen. Perhaps the courier company did other runs apart from Heathrow? Even if Heathrow was the destination, perhaps components were being flown up to Scotland or elsewhere in the UK.

The industrial estate was quiet once more. From the outside there were no signs of life coming from the Components International unit. Sarah knew what her next step had to be. She got out of the car and walked towards the rickety steps leading up to the entrance. It was too early to let Graham Scott know what was going on, but it wasn't too early to find out more about what his company was up to.

She hesitated at the bottom of the steps until she heard the sound of a motorbike coming towards her, a big black bike being ridden by someone in black leathers and a big black crash helmet. Cunliffe had been murdered by someone on a bike. Another courier, she saw, as the biker drove directly towards her. She stood and watched, transfixed by the speed and the power of the sleek bike as it roared to a stop only inches away from her. When it stopped she swallowed hard. Her hand had been clenched tight around the hand rail at the foot of the stairs and her throat was dry.

The biker pulled off his helmet and grinned at her. 'Didn't scare you, did I, love?' he asked innocently.

'No, not at all,' she said, feeling stupid for the sudden fright that had overtaken her. Just because Cunliffe had been murdered by a biker, it didn't mean that –

'Going up?' the biker asked, pulling out a bundle of papers from under his battered leather jacket.

'No, after you,' she said, making way for him.

'It's all right,' he assured her, 'I don't make a habit of running innocent women over.'

'Sorry?'

'It's just the guilty ones I go for,' he said, and then laughed loudly at his own joke. She watched him blankly and then he shrugged and started up the stairs.

She followed him a second later, aware that with her short skirt the biker would have had an ample view of her legs if he'd followed her. Her heels clanged on the metal steps but it was nothing compared to the echoing cacophony the biker's heavy boots had created. The stairs led to a single door that opened to a tiny reception room with a couple of dirty chairs and a counter on the other side.

'I'm picking up an order,' the biker was explaining to a middle-aged man at the counter.

The man at the counter looked over the biker's shoulder at Sarah as she walked into the room. 'I'll be with you in a sec, love,' the man called to her.

The floor of the room was grimy with dirt, and a bin in the corner was over full with drink cans, chocolate wrappers and the discarded contents of an ashtray. A pit, and it smelt like one too. Sarah decided not to risk her skirt on the chairs, and she was careful where she stood too, she didn't like the idea of having to scrape stuff off her heels either.

'Picking up an order?' the biker asked, coming over to stand next to Sarah while his own order was being packaged up.

Did she look like a courier? Looking into the man's eyes it was hard to see that there was any spark of imagination there at all. 'No, not really,' she said.

He nodded knowingly. 'Mine should be ready in a few minutes,' he added.

'What are you picking up?' she asked, deciding to make the best use of her time.

'Components for a company out in Kent,' he said. 'It's a good little run. See, if I do the M25 I'm laughing.'

Sarah copied his knowing nod. 'Do you often collect from here?'

'Now and again.'

'Do you ever take things to Heathrow? You know, things for export?'

He shook his head. 'No, can't say I have. Mostly it's small orders like this one.'

'But they do have orders like that, don't they? Export orders?'

Again the man shook his head. 'Don't know, love. Ask Charlie on the counter, he'll know.'

Sarah turned to look at the counter but the man hadn't returned with the order yet. Which meant she was stuck with making conversation with the biker for a while longer. 'He won't be long,' he assured her.

She turned from the counter to look at the posters stuck on the wall. For the most part they were catalogue pictures of different types of electronic components. Uniformly boring. Her eyes blurred rather than attempt to take in the details.

'Fancy a para jump?' the biker asked suddenly.

Sarah turned to him. 'What?'

'A parachute jump,' he explained. 'It's for charity. Look,' he added, picking up a leaflet on the counter.

Sarah took the photocopied sheet and scanned it quickly. The Good Neighbours name was printed in bold black letters across the bottom of the flyer. They were organising a sponsored parachute jump and the leaflet listed all the details as well as featuring a sponsorship form on the reverse side.

'Fancy it then?' the biker asked, grinning once more.

'I don't think so,' she said politely.

He laughed. 'I wouldn't mind having a go but I screwed up my leg last time,' he said, slapping his hand across his thigh to prove it.

'You've jumped before?'

'No, not that. I had a go in the sponsored motocross they put on a couple of months back.'

'You mean this lot,' she tapped the Good Neighbours name on the flyer, 'organised it?'

'That's right. Good Neighbours they're called.'

Suddenly Sarah was smiling. 'How many of you were there?'

'About fifteen. I went over the bars,' he explained, motioning with his arms, 'came down on the bastard in front. Put me out of work for a month.'

'How awful for you,' she cooed sympathetically.

'It weren't too bad. They were good to me, gave me enough cash to pay the rent and that.'

'Who was good to you?'

'Good Neighbours. I mean we collected a fair amount of dosh on that day.'

'Was Patrick Collins there too?' she asked.

'Collins? Big bloke, bit of a religious nutter?'

'That's him.'

'He was all right. He even had a go on one of the bikes. Said he used to have one when he was a lad. Said that once you know how to ride a bike you don't forget.'

Patrick Collins as a young biker? It made a warped sort of sense if aggression was anything to go by. 'And could he handle a bike?'

Another laugh preceded the reply. 'He was a bit rusty to start but he picked it up real quick. Well, how about it?'

Charlie arrived back at the counter. 'How about what?' Sarah asked.

The biker grinned. 'The parachute jump?'

She smiled. 'It's not for me,' she said, 'but I'd like to push Patrick Collins out of a plane.'

The biker was still laughing as Sarah headed for her car.

ELEVEN
Wednesday 11th December

Vallance was still seething two hours after his confrontation with the Superintendent. Waves of anger flowed through him along with a desire to beat the hell out of Riley's man on the case. Luckily Dobson was still checking up on Simon Clark. The search warrant had come through and Dobson had decided to be in on the search himself. As if Clark would have the murder weapon stashed away at home somewhere. Dobson was even more deluded than Riley if he seriously thought that a man like Clark was a cool and calculating killer.

In the mean time Vallance had gone through all the files on Jack Thomas. There was precious little real information and most of the rumour appeared to be sourced from people too afraid of the man to put detail to their accusations. The Jack Thomas that emerged from the files was a successful and ruthless career criminal. His known associates included hard men from some of the East London gangs, streetwise criminals from South London and most of the big local villains. His seedy little club was nowhere near busy enough to fund a fairly lavish lifestyle.

As far as Vallance was concerned, Simon Clark was no longer suspect number one. That honour had been usurped by Jack Thomas. He had no doubt that Thomas was having an affair with Jenny Cunliffe. It was the key to the case. Either

Thomas had decided to do Jenny a favour and get rid of her husband, or else between them they had cooked up the murder in the hope of some financial reward. Cunliffe was an accountant by inclination as well as by trade. He was the sort of man to hoard every penny, to see everything in terms of investment and return. Which probably meant that he was well covered by insurance. If nothing else Jenny Cunliffe would have the house to herself and from what people had said that was worth a small fortune.

The next step was to talk to Jack Thomas once more. Vallance had decided to spare the grieving widow for the moment. He hoped to get some idea of whether Thomas had acted alone or not before he saw her again.

DC Chiltern was driving once more. He seemed more than happy to be sitting at the wheel ferrying Vallance around. Perhaps it gave him a nice warm glow inside to be seen as the guv's driver. He drove in silence after his attempts at conversation had been greeted with stony silence.

'Here we are, sir,' Chiltern announced, pulling in to a parking space opposite Cagney's.

'He's not here,' Vallance guessed. The blacked-up windows of the wine bar gave nothing away but he felt certain that Thomas was not the sort of man to appear at work before lunch-time.

Chiltern hesitated before offering to go and look.

'Good idea,' Vallance agreed, settling back in his seat. He felt too pissed off to do anything but wait. Why the hell couldn't he have Quinn on the case? The question kept coming back to him. The answer was simple: because it was what he wanted.

Chiltern walked over to Cagney's and banged loudly on the door. He waited for a reply that obviously didn't come because he tried again, and again. He bent down almost double to look through the letterbox and when he straightened up he gestured to Vallance that there was no one there. It was no surprise but Chiltern seemed reluctant to return to the car.

'He's not there,' he said, climbing back into the driver's seat of the car after banging on the door of the wine bar again.

'You catch on quick,' Vallance murmured. 'Let's try him at home,' he suggested.

Chiltern ignored the sarcasm. 'We could drop in on Jenny Cunliffe as well,' he said.

It was too early for that. 'Not yet,' he cautioned.

'Do you think they're in on this together, sir?'

Vallance was in no mood for explanations. 'Just drive,' he said.

Chiltern accepted the reprimand in silence. He backed out onto the road and then accelerated away sharply. At least he had some way of venting his anger, Vallance decided. Driving like a maniac was as good a way as any of letting go of aggression. Was it significant that Thomas's only conviction was for a road rage attack on an innocent motorist?

'Slow down,' he said, deciding that Chiltern's driving was way too fast.

'Sorry, sir, I thought we were in a hurry,' Chiltern replied.

'We are but that doesn't mean you take risks. Understood?'

'Yes, sir,' Chiltern said.

The allure of driving the guv around was probably wearing off fast for Chiltern, Vallance decided. Hell, what difference did it make? One more person on his back wouldn't make any difference.

Fenton Close was much nearer to Cagney's than he'd realised. They were turning onto the estate before Vallance had clocked where they were. It wasn't quite walking distance but it had taken only a few minutes. He twisted round in his seat to look at the Cunliffes' home. There was nothing about it to say that it was a house in mourning – assuming that Jenny was really grieving and not secretly celebrating.

'Looks like he's in, sir,' Chiltern said, indicating with a sharp nod of the head the sleek black Mercedes parked outside the Thomas home.

The car gleamed in the bright sunshine as Chiltern steered the unmarked police car into the space next to it. Of course Thomas's car featured a personalised number plate, just in case anyone had any doubts that it was driven by a flash bastard. Not that many people would have the temerity to get in

145

Thomas's way. His beating of the other driver had made the national headlines.

Chiltern seemed keen to get a closer look at the car. 'Expensive set of wheels,' was his considered opinion.

'You fancy it, do you?'

Chiltern pursed his lips before deciding that he did. 'I wouldn't mind,' he admitted. 'Not sure I'd have it in black, though,' he added.

Vallance glanced across the length of the estate but there was no sign of life at any of the windows in Jenny Cunliffe's house. He guessed that from the front room she'd have a clear view to them. 'Come on,' he said, 'we don't want to hang around out here all day.'

Jack Thomas answered the door a second after Chiltern rang the door. He was dressed casually in blue jeans, a V-neck cashmere jumper and a pair of moccasins. His sleeves were rolled up and the gold watch that glittered around his wrist caught the eye.

'Well, well, well,' Thomas exclaimed, 'Mr Vallance, to what do I owe the pleasure?'

Vallance smiled. 'I was hoping you'd invite us in for a coffee and a chat, Jack.'

Thomas stood back for from the door. 'Of course, always happy to help.'

Vallance and Chiltern stepped into the hallway and Thomas closed the door. The place was warm, the heating must have been turned up high. A creature of comfort, Vallance decided. Jack wasn't the sort of man to shiver in the cold in order to keep heating bills down to a minimum.

'The missus is out,' Jack explained, pointing towards the kitchen, 'so you'll have to make do with my coffee.'

The kitchen overlooked the garden and with the light streaming in through the glass door and windows it seemed to be as big as Vallance's entire flat. The room was done out from top to bottom in pine, from the large round table and matching chairs to the units on the walls and even the spice rack on the wall by the hob.

'What's this about, then?' Thomas asked, filling the kettle with water.

There was no point in an indirect approach, Vallance decided. 'It's about Jenny Cunliffe,' he said.

Thomas plugged the kettle in and turned to face the two police officers still standing in the middle of the room. 'Please,' Jack said, 'sit down. Jenny? What about her?'

Vallance sat down at the chair nearest the door. Chiltern took the seat next to him. 'I don't think you've been entirely honest with us,' he said.

'Haven't I?'

'You told me that you didn't really know Jenny,' Vallance reminded him.

Thomas grinned. 'Well, I suppose I do know her,' he admitted. 'Has some bastard been blabbing?'

'How well do you know her?'

The grin grew broader. 'Well,' Jack said, 'I know her well enough to have screwed her.'

There was more than a note of swagger in his voice. 'Are you still sleeping with her?' Vallance asked.

'Listen,' Thomas said, lowering his voice, 'this is strictly between us, right?'

'Us and the rest of Surrey by the sound of it,' Vallance responded.

Thomas laughed loudly. 'I know I've got a bit of a reputation,' he said, 'but come on, what can I do about that?'

The kettle was growing colder again. 'Coffee?' Vallance reminded him.

'Sure,' Thomas said, reaching up for a cafetiere on a high shelf behind him. 'Rumours are rumours, I can't help that. What I don't want is for my missus to go ballistic when she finds out it's true.'

'She doesn't know?' Vallance asked, not bothering to mask his surprise.

'Course she don't,' Thomas responded as he began to make the coffee. 'She knows the rumours but that's all they are, see? I mean if she believed everything that people said about me −'

'What do people say about you?'

Thomas grinned once more. 'Mr Vallance,' he said, 'you know as well as I do that people like to gab. Look at all them rumours about you.'

147

Vallance became aware that Chiltern was staring. 'What rumours?'

'Come on, Mr Vallance,' Thomas said, 'there's no need for any of that. I mean you know what people are saying. From what I hear you ain't exactly Mr Popular are you?'

No wonder Thomas had survived for years without any real trouble from the police. If he had contacts in the force with an ear to the ground so that even inconsequential office trivia was picked up –

'How do you like it?' Jack asked, already pouring the hot water into the cafetiere.

'You don't know? Frankly, Jack,' Vallance said, 'I'm disappointed.'

'Black as hell,' Thomas guessed. 'What about the boy?'

Chiltern bristled. 'I have it black as well.'

'Course you do,' Thomas said. 'So, what about me and Jenny?'

'You told us that you didn't really know her. Now you're admitting that you've slept with her.'

'That's right.'

'Are you still having an affair with her?'

Thomas poured the coffee slowly then passed the first cup to Vallance before answering. 'I never said I was having an affair with her, did I?'

'Are you saying that your relationship was purely sexual?'

Thomas passed the second cup to Chiltern and then poured his own. 'That sounds a bit coy, Mr Vallance. But yes, that's all there was to it. I had sex with her.'

'How often?'

Thomas laughed. 'Three times a night usually,' he replied.

Vallance ignored the remark. 'And are you still seeing her?'

'No, not since her old man died.'

'Why is that?'

Thomas shrugged. 'She's decided that she loved the sap after all. Now she's gone all guilty, like. I mean it was all right before, but now she's not interested.'

'Do you believe her?'

'Don't care to tell you the truth, Mr Vallance. I mean it's not as if there's any shortage of women, is there?'

148

'You mean like your missus?'

'Isobel's a darling, I love her deeply, Mr Vallance. But, you know, I've got a healthy appetite. I mean there was more to it than just Jen.'

'So I've heard,' Vallance admitted.

'You ever done it with two women at once, Mr Vallance? Have you?'

'We're not here to talk about me,' Vallance said. Thomas had stopped being amusing and was now getting more and more annoying.

'It's great,' Jack continued. 'I mean it. There's nothing like having two women going down on you. I love it. Two women taking it in turns to suck your cock –'

Vallance had had enough. 'I don't give a shit what you get up to in bed, Jack,' he snapped. 'It's Jenny Cunliffe I'm interested in.'

Thomas laughed again. 'That's who I was talking about. She loved sharing my cock with another woman. She loved it...She'd do anything in bed, anything. Sod it, Vallance, she even liked sucking my cock after I'd come inside another woman's cunt.'

'Enough!' Vallance cried.

Thomas drank deeply from his coffee but his eyes were full of malicious amusement. He'd won, he'd managed to rile Vallance without even having to try too hard.

'Where were you on Sunday morning?'

'You mean when the sap was gunned down?'

'Yes.'

'I was at home all day.'

'With Mrs Thomas?'

He shook his head. 'No, she was out. At her sister's.'

Did he know that Isobel was having an affair with Simon Clark? There was no way that Vallance could find out without jeopardising Clark's life. 'Can anyone else corroborate the fact that you were here?'

'I was with company,' he admitted.

'Female?'

'That's right,' he said, smiling.

'How many?'

Thomas laughed. 'Just the one this time.'

'Name and address.'

'Can't remember.'

Vallance stood up. 'Don't make me get serious, Jack,' he warned.

'Straight up, Mr Vallance,' Jack insisted. 'I picked her up at the wine bar. I ain't got a clue where she lives and all I've got is a first name. You're a geezer, you know how it goes.'

'Tell me,' Vallance asked, 'did you ever meet Michael Cunliffe?'

Thomas shook his head. 'Nope. He wasn't my type of bloke. I'll tell you what else,' he added. 'Just because I was screwing his missus it doesn't mean I shot him.'

'I'm not convinced,' Vallance said. 'Prove it, Jack. Where's your alibi?'

'She was married,' Thomas said.

'You like married women, don't you,' Chiltern said quietly.

Thomas glared at the younger DC. 'Listen, sonny,' Jack warned him, 'you let the adults do the talking. All right?'

Vallance indicated to Chiltern to keep quiet for the moment. 'Who was she? Come on, Jack, you're not scared of some little accountant finding out you've been giving it to his wife, are you?'

The mere suggestion that Thomas was afraid of someone brought an instant reaction. 'That ain't what I'm worried about,' he said. 'Her old man's not fit to wipe the shit from my shoes, Vallance.'

'So give me her name.'

'And screw things up with her? This woman's the dirtiest cow I've ever met. There ain't anything she won't do in bed. I though Jenny Cunliffe was a hot bitch, but she's like a nun in a convent compared to –'

He wasn't about to slip up with the name. 'In that case I'm going to have to dig deeper,' Vallance warned.

Thomas shrugged. 'I ain't worried, Mr Vallance. See, I had nothing to do with that poor sap getting it. Nothing. I'm clean, always have been and always will be.'

'Yes,' Vallance agreed, 'you're a model citizen, Jack.'

★

Clark was sitting on the edge of his unmade bed. The duvet was bunched up behind him, a mountain of soft white where it had been unceremoniously dumped by one of the uniformed PCs. Clark's anger had dissipated and in its place there was nothing but calm resignation, its tempo measured in the slow, sure way that he drew hard on a cigarette. It was easy to pin him down as an ex-con, it showed in every fibre of his being.

'You finished, Inspector?' he asked, looking up to see Dobson standing in the doorway.

Dobson glared at his prisoner. There was precious little to show for the time and effort in carrying out the search of Clark's house. 'Not yet,' he replied, deciding it was better to play for time than to admit the paucity of results.

Clark nodded and sucked back hard on his cigarette once more. He looked unconcerned by the mess in his room, most of which had been there before the start of the search.

Dobson looked at him for a moment longer and then headed downstairs. There was no sign of the gun. No sign that Clark had ever stored a weapon in his house. But of course Clark was too clever for that. The gun was stashed away somewhere safe, probably at the home of an accomplice or perhaps hidden in a lock-up garage somewhere.

He stopped in the kitchen and peered out into the garden. Two uniformed officers had donned rubber gloves, protective face masks and plastic aprons as they pored through the disgusting contents of the rubbish bins. As Dobson watched he saw one of the PCs carefully unravel a thick bundle of toilet paper only to reveal a used condom that hung limply from the end of the tweezers that were used to pick it out.

It was no use, Dobson decided, turning away from the sick sight of Clark's filthy debris, the search was going to get them nowhere. It didn't prove that Clark was an innocent man. It served only to confirm that he was far cleverer than had first been suspected.

He turned at the sound of footsteps on the stairs. 'Yes?' he barked, staring at the uniformed officer who had come looking for him.

'Clark wants to use the toilet, sir,' the constable reported nervously.

The toilet had been the first place that was searched. The cistern had almost been taken apart but there was nothing lodged in it that shouldn't have been there. 'Tell him to wait,' he said. Clark had been for a piss once already and Dobson saw no reason to let him go again so soon afterwards.

'Yes, sir.'

The PC turned to go and Dobson followed him up the stairs. The sight of Clark's room offended him once more. The place was a pit overflowing with empty drink cans, dirty dishes and cups that were live with fungus and bacteria.

'I need to piss,' Clark complained.

'What you're doing,' Dobson responded, 'is taking the piss, Clark. If you think that we've finished then you're wrong, sonny. We can take the floorboards up, we can rip the tiles from the roof, we can dig the garden up –'

'Can you? Then do me a favour, Inspector, dig it up proper and plant me some veg,' Clark said, smiling. He dropped the cigarette on the threadbare carpet and then ground it under his heel.

He thought he was funny. Did he think that he was dealing with Vallance? Did he really think that a smart remark would get nothing but a laugh and a joke in return?

'If you don't keep quiet,' Dobson warned, 'I'll call in that slag Isobel Thomas for an interview. How do you think Jack's going to react to that? Perhaps I ought to wheel him in too?'

Clark's face showed no emotion. The threat was enough to silence him. 'Good,' Dobson said. 'Now, Clark, I want the full story on the Cunliffe murder.'

'But I don't know anything about it –'

'I'm getting bored with that same old refrain,' Dobson said. 'Tell me something new.'

Clark sighed wearily. 'Look, Inspector, I'll tell you the truth. I don't know anything about it. All right, I admit it, me and Isobel have got something going. She can tell you, I was here with her on Sunday morning.'

Damn it! It wasn't the story that Dobson wanted to hear. But then again what kind of alibi was Isobel Thomas? Married to a gangster, there was no way they could let Clark off the hook on her testimony alone.

In the mean time there was only one sensible course of action. 'In that case we can get back to the station and you can make out a new statement,' he said.

Clark had only one thing on his mind. 'This ain't going to get back to Jack, is it?' he asked in a nervous whisper.

Was Jack Thomas lying? Vallance sought for an answer but the truth was he didn't know. The man was vain, arrogant, supremely self-confident and in no doubt that he had nothing to fear from the police. Part of Vallance wanted to believe that Thomas's self-confidence was down to the fact that he had got away with things for so long. On the other hand there was the strong possibility that he had been telling the truth.

'I think he's lying, sir,' Chiltern said, venturing to voice an opinion as he drove back to Area.

Vallance decided not to agree or disagree. 'Why?' he asked, hoping perhaps that the young detective constable had picked up on something that he himself had missed.

'Because I can't see a man like him willing to put up with too much snooping around.'

It was a good point. 'But what if he's so used to getting away with things that he's not bothered? Let's face it, it's not as if he's had a tough time from us, is it?'

'Still can't see him inviting us to dig deeper,' Chiltern insisted. 'I mean no bit of skirt's worth that much trouble, is she?'

Vallance declined to answer. Thomas had been goading him and the anger it had aroused had been twinged with not a little jealousy.

Chiltern obviously felt that silence did not automatically mean the end of conversation. 'It's him, isn't it, sir? He's the one who shot Cunliffe in the head.'

'Tell that to Inspector Dobson,' Vallance suggested. 'I'm sure that he'd be willing to entertain the theory.'

Chiltern grinned. 'Inspector Dobson's not the sort of man who takes kindly to theories from the likes of me, sir.'

The subject was too close to home for discussion. 'When

we get back I'll get Sergeant Crawley to organise a house to house at Fenton Close. Do you want to be in on that?'

It took a while for Chiltern to answer. 'What's the alternative, sir?'

'I need to start talking to people that Jack's crossed in the past. I can't believe that the man's such a big villain that there isn't one person willing to talk about him.'

'You'll need a driver, sir,' Chiltern pointed out.

Vallance nodded. 'You've got the job.'

Sarah Fairfax was parked at the rear entrance to HQ, her car positioned so that she could see who was going in and out. She was bored, sitting right up against the steering wheel, her hands locked together in a gesture of impatience which Vallance recognised at once. She was waiting for him.

'I'll get out here,' Vallance told Chiltern as the car stopped in front of the electronic barrier.

'Here, sir?'

'Get Sergeant Crawley for me, I'll only be a minute,' Vallance said, getting out of the car.

Chiltern looked across to where Sarah was sitting. It seemed to take a moment before he put it all together and then he grinned. 'I'll see you in a minute, sir.'

Vallance waited for Chiltern to disappear before he walked over to Sarah's car. The passenger side window wound down with electronic smoothness and she leant across the passenger seat to talk to him.

'I've got something important to tell you,' she reported.

'You've cracked the case,' he said. 'You've sussed out who the killer is and you've performed a citizen's arrest.'

She glared at him with angry blue eyes. 'If that's your attitude then you can forget about it,' she said.

He inhaled sharply. The woman had a fuse too short for her own good. 'It's called humour,' he reminded her. 'You're supposed to laugh.'

'I'll laugh when you say something funny,' she replied sourly. 'Now, do we have to freeze out here?'

'You can freeze in there if you like,' he said, gesturing towards HQ.

She looked vaguely disappointed but then nodded her

agreement. 'I just hope the coffee's better this time,' she said.

They walked round to the front of the building, saying little of substance. She was bursting to deliver news but there was no way she was going to be pressured. It seemed to Vallance that if they talked in the street she would think that it demeaned her work in some way. She was weird like that.

He sorted things out with the desk sergeant and then she was allowed through. The obvious place to talk would have been in his office but there were too many things going on and he didn't trust Sarah not to pick up on it. He knew that she'd be scouring the walls looking for information and that no piece of paper on his desk would go unread.

'We'll take one of the interview rooms,' he told her, escorting her down the corridor to the row of secure rooms.

Three of the four rooms were being used. He noted that Simon Clark was back. It probably meant that the search of his home had produced a blank. It was no surprise, except perhaps to Dobson and Riley.

'In here,' he said, opening the door to the last room just as the door to the next room opened.

'You're here, sir,' Dobson said, looking a little discomfited to be meeting Vallance so unexpectedly.

Vallance was aware that Sarah was watching and listening. 'Sarah, if you'll just wait inside,' he suggested.

She smiled at Dobson sweetly. 'Is that Simon Clark you've got in there?' she asked.

'Wait inside!' Vallance snapped angrily. What the hell did she think she was doing?

She looked at Vallance strangely and then went into the room. He waited until the door was firmly closed before turning to face Dobson.

'What's going on, sir?' Dobson demanded. 'You know who she is, why the hell is she allowed to wander the building?'

'Who is she?' Vallance demanded, his voice raised higher than Dobson's.

'She works on that bloody left-wing TV programme, you know that. She's not on our side, she hates everything we do.

I can't for the life of me see why we even let people like that into the building.'

'That's my decision, Dobson. Understood? You're the one who makes a bloody song and dance about lines of command and the need for discipline. Why the hell don't you live by what you preach?'

Dobson's face was ice cold. 'This isn't the place,' he whispered hoarsely. 'This is going to be all over the building –'

'I don't give a shit,' Vallance snapped.

Dobson looked pained. 'Look, sir, I don't know what's going on but I hardly think that the corridor's the right place for two senior officers to have a slanging match.'

'Where the fuck do you suggest is a better place?'

Dobson glared at Vallance but said nothing. The aggression was there but it was locked behind a demeanour that might have been carved from stone.

Vallance inhaled deeply. 'What's the story with Clark?' he asked, his voice back to normal volume. He was aware that people from further up the corridor were peering at them. It would have been the perfect time to waste a career and get a life by belting Dobson in the mouth.

'He's admitted that he was with Isobel Thomas on the morning of the murder. He's just doing a statement now.'

'That's it?'

'Yes, sir,' Dobson admitted quietly.

'In that case you can pull her in for questioning now,' Vallance said. 'Her old man's just told me that she was at her sister's on that Sunday.'

Dobson looked pained by the news. 'Yes, sir.'

'And before you ask,' Vallance added, 'she's not at home. Get back in to Clark and find out where she is.'

'Yes, sir. What about Jack Thomas?'

'I'm dealing with him,' Vallance said decisively. It felt good to be putting Dobson in his place. The man talked about the need for command but he hated to be on the receiving end of it. Especially when the orders came from a scruffy bastard who didn't give a toss.

Dobson went back in to Clark immediately. Vallance felt sorry for Clark. Now that Dobson was all riled up he was going to be a real bastard. All the anger and frustration would come pouring out on the first hapless soul who came into the line of fire.

'What was all that about?' Sarah asked when Vallance entered the interview room. She was already sitting on the other side of the table, as though she were preparing to interview him.

'An exercise in communication skills,' he said, taking a seat. 'You know how hot we are when it comes to human resources these days.'

There was not a glimmer of a smile on her face. Her blue eyes regarded him with a detachment that was painful to see. Just for once why couldn't she smile and put him out of his misery?

'Was it about me?' she asked.

He had been staring. He looked away quickly, aware that she had caught him looking. 'No,' he said, 'it's nothing to do with you.'

'I heard every word,' she insisted. 'I know it was about me. He hates the idea of having a journalist around.'

She was up to her old tricks again. 'The room is sound-proofed,' he said. 'You couldn't have heard any of it.'

'I could if I didn't let the door close properly,' she pointed out. 'I'm sorry if my presence unsettles some of your colleagues, Mr Vallance, but I'm here for a reason.'

She was there to see him, according to Anne Quinn, but Vallance wasn't so sure. 'You're just a handy blunt instrument to batter me with,' he said bitterly. 'Now, what's so important that you're willing to risk police canteen coffee to tell me.'

'Have you spoken to a man called Patrick Collins?'

He was one of the people who ran the charity that had employed Michael Cunliffe. Vallance hadn't spoken to anyone there, and as far as he could remember Dobson had only spoken to Rosemary Collins. 'No, not yet,' he replied cautiously.

'The man is extremely dangerous in my opinion,' she said. 'I've never seen a man so close to violence after only a few questions – That's not funny,' she said.

Vallance was smiling. He could easily picture someone

157

driven to violence by Sarah's disdainful attitude and arrogant questioning. 'I'm sorry,' he said. 'But it's hard to figure anyone getting angry with you.'

She clenched her jaw and pursed her lips. 'If you're not interested –'

He was sure she'd have no compunction about getting up to leave. 'I'm sorry,' he said. 'Tell me about Patrick Collins.'

'He's paranoid, aggressive, dogmatic and thoroughly obnoxious. He's some kind of religious fanatic as well. Not once did he show any feeling for Michael Cunliffe and he all but admitted that in time Cunliffe would have been given the push.'

'So?'

'The charity he runs is also not very charitable from what I've been able to find out,' she said, flipping open her note-book. 'According to my calculations only a small percentage of the money raised actually ends up with the people it's meant to. Good Neighbours manages to support three very good executive salaries, three company cars, a relatively high figure for director's expenses and also enough money to send Collins and his wife on business trips abroad.'

'Evidence?'

She looked unfazed by the question. 'My own eyes. Collins, his wife and Michael Cunliffe all had identical company cars. I've seen where they live and I've seen the pictures of Collins abroad at various conferences. The money they're raising isn't being spent on the shabby little office they inhabit, and it's not going on the pathetic little parcels they're putting together for Christmas. So, where is it going, Mr Vallance? It's being swallowed up by Patrick Collins and his wife, I'm certain of it. I've absolutely no doubt that a quick call to the Charity Commission will prove that I am right.'

It all sounded interesting but what was the point? 'So?' he repeated.

'So, Collins is very touchy about it. He almost exploded when I started to talk about it. Now, what if Cunliffe did the same? What if he started asking awkward questions too?'

Vallance smiled. 'I get it. Cunliffe asks awkward questions so Collins gets out a shotgun and blows his head off.'

Anyone else would have rephrased the accusation but not her. 'Yes,' she stated boldly, 'that's it. I know that Collins can ride a motorbike. He organised some kind of rally where he was showing off on a motorbike. Add that to his blind rage and his persecution complex and you've got a case.'

Unfortunately it was not a case that made any sense. 'I'm sorry, Sarah,' he responded, 'but I think we've got a stronger lead than that.'

'What?'

She didn't sound impressed, as usual. 'I'll put one of my men on to it,' he promised.

'Quite frankly, Mr Vallance,' she started to say but was interrupted by a sharp knock at the door.

Chiltern was in the room before Vallance had a chance to respond. 'Can I talk, sir?'

Sarah looked at Vallance as though she dared him to say no. 'That depends,' he said.

Chiltern decided to take a gamble. 'Something's happened at Fenton Close, sir.'

Vallance stood up instantly. 'Like what?' he demanded.

'It's Jack Thomas, sir,' Chiltern said. 'He's dead.'

'Shit!' Vallance cried angrily.

Sarah looked at the officers calmly. 'Does that mean you've just lost your strong lead, Mr Vallance?'

TWELVE
Wednesday 11th December

In the race to Fenton Close DC Chiltern proved his value as
a driver. He drove like a maniac to get Vallance at the scene
minutes before Dobson turned up. It wasn't quite chaos, but
there were too many people around and the officers at the
scene seemed not to know what was going on. Thomas's
neighbours were milling about, chattering excitedly as more
and more emergency vehicles arrived.

Even before the car had pulled to a stop beside an ambulance with flashing blue light, Vallance realised that the
house was full of people. How in the hell was evidence
supposed to be preserved if the crime scene was trampled on
by all and sundry?

Vallance jumped out of the car and raced towards the
house. He pushed passed a uniformed PC who looked as
though he were enjoying the spectacle as much as the neighbours who'd wandered over to gawp. The front door of
the house was open and one of the ambulance people was
standing in the doorway smoking a cigarette.

'Police only,' he said, looking up at Vallance rushing towards
him.

There was no time to flash ID. 'I am the police,' Vallance
snapped. 'Now get out of the bloody way.'

The man stepped aside promptly and Vallance stepped into
the house. Everything looked in place, nothing had changed

since his visit earlier that morning. There were voices coming from the kitchen but he checked that the front room was empty first.

'Get a cordon around the front of the house,' he barked at Chiltern who had made it into the hallway.

Chiltern nodded curtly. 'I'll get the uniforms on to it,' he replied. Ordering his colleagues in uniform was still a new experience and he seemed pleased by the opportunity to do it.

Vallance stopped in the doorway of the kitchen. The body that had once been Jack Thomas was sprawled across the kitchen table and had dripped a pool of blood on the polished floor. Its arms were flung back over the sides of the table. Two policemen, the second ambulance man and an unidentified woman were arranged around the table, chatting quietly.

One of the PCs turned and saw Vallance. He straightened up instantly. 'He's dead, sir,' he reported stiffly.

'I didn't think he was having a nap,' Vallance responded.

'Looks like two gunshots,' the ambulance man said, moving closer to the body. 'One took a chunk out of his shoulder and neck and the other took most of his head off.'

Vallance looked beyond the table at the spray of blood that had run down the white painted wall. 'And who are you?' he asked, turning his attention from the corpse to the middle-aged woman standing between the two police officers.

'Emily Grant,' she said. 'I live over the road.'

'Mrs Grant called us in,' the first officer added.

'Has anything been touched?' Vallance asked, voicing his chief concern.

The para-medic got in first with his reply. 'He was alive when I got here,' he said. 'I tried to keep him going but it was hopeless.'

'Did he say anything?'

'No, sir, he was too far gone,' the first policeman said.

There were voices in the hallway. Dobson had arrived. 'We're in here,' Vallance called. 'You might as well join the party.'

161

Dobson came in and walked straight to the table to stare at the dead man. 'A shot to the head,' he said. 'Do we have any witnesses?'

'I think that's your cue,' Vallance told Mrs Grant. She looked at him nervously and then nodded.

'Right, everybody out until the scene of crime people get here,' Vallance decided. 'One of you two take a statement from him,' he added, pointing to the para-medic. 'And if you'll just step outside, Mrs Grant, you can tell us all about it over tea and biscuits.'

'Tea and biscuits?' she said.

Vallance smiled. 'You do have some biscuits at home, don't you?'

They all trooped out of the house. The scene outside had been transformed. The fluorescent yellow cordon around the house kept everyone at bay and most of the neighbours had melted away. There were still flashing blue lights everywhere but it looked less like a road accident than it had a few minutes earlier.

DS Crawley was talking to a group of officers, most of them in uniform apart from DCs Chiltern and Matthews. When he spotted Vallance and Dobson he broke off and jogged over to them. 'You've just got time to put the kettle on,' Vallance said, dismissing Mrs Grant with what he hoped was a charming and friendly smile.

'I'm just organising a house to house,' Crawley explained. 'I've also put out a request to traffic division to keep an eye out for our phantom motorcyclist.'

'Good man,' Dobson said, getting in first to commend the detective sergeant.

'Keep some of your people back to do a quick search round the back of the house,' Vallance added. 'Oh, and your house to house doesn't include Jenny Cunliffe, I want to talk to her myself.'

'Yes, sir,' Crawley said.

Vallance was just about to head off with Dobson to Mrs Grant's house when he spotted Sarah Fairfax's car turning on to the Close. Damn it! Why the hell didn't she keep her head down? How long was it before Dobson started to complain about her to Riley and from then upwards to Chief Super Larkhall and beyond?

'Keep Sarah Fairfax away from the scene,' he told Crawley, pointing out her car as it headed up towards them. 'Treat her the same as any other member of the public,' he added. 'Just because she's a journalist it doesn't mean she's got a right to know any more than Joe Public.'

Crawley looked at Sarah and then back at Vallance. 'Yes, sir,' he said and for a split second Vallance was certain that there had been a smile on Crawley's face.

'Mrs Grant, sir,' Dobson said.

Vallance and Dobson walked across the front lawn of Mrs Grant's house in silence. Vallance was aware that Sarah was watching him, he could sense that her eyes were on him. Those eyes. It was better not to look at her.

Mrs Grant was at the door waiting for the two police officers. She seemed excited by what was happening. She hadn't even blanched in the presence of a body with most of its head splattered across a kitchen wall.

'Chocolate Bourbons all right?' she asked. 'If I'd known I would have got something in special.'

'You could have baked a cake,' Vallance suggested. He went in first and was shown into the front room where the tea was already waiting. A coffee table had been pulled into the centre of the room and a silver tray set down on it. Silver tea pot and best china were on display and Mrs Grant looked fit to burst with pride.

Vallance sat on the edge of a big three-seater sofa under a large and poorly executed print of an Alpine landscape.

'How do you take it, officer?' she asked, lifting the tea pot.

'Milk and sugar for me please,' he said.

Dobson sat on the other end of the sofa. 'No sugar for me,' he said sombrely.

She poured the tea and passed a cup to each officer in turn before offering the biscuits which she had arranged neatly on a tea plate. Vallance took a couple before Dobson politely declined. No sugar and no biscuits, Vallance noted. Dobson was scared of losing his figure. Yes, he looked like the sort of copper who'd turn into a fat bastard with the passing of time.

163

'Now, Mrs Grant,' Vallance began, 'tell us what happened.'

Mrs Grant took her tea and sat down on the two-seater sofa at right angles to the one the policemen occupied. She was sitting closest to Dobson but her attention was focused on Vallance. 'Well, officer,' she said, 'I was just in the middle of phoning my sister when I heard the gunshots —'

'At what time was that?' Dobson asked sharply.

'Only thirty minutes ago, I think. I can find out if you like, I mean we've got itemised billing on the phone and it's all there. Well, as I said, I was just talking to Audrey when I heard the gunshots. Of course I knew what it was straight away. My husband's got a gun, you see. I know lots of people can't tell but as soon as I heard it I said to Audrey that someone's been killed.'

'Is that when you called the police?' Dobson asked. He seemed not to want to hear the full story told in Mrs Grant's homely way.

'No of course not,' she replied, she glanced irritably at Dobson and then looked to Vallance again. 'Well, I thought I could be wrong. So I told Audrey to hold on and I rushed over to the window.' She pointed to the big square window which looked across to Jack's house. 'That's when I saw the man on the motorcycle. Well, I saw the back of him. He was roaring off and then I knew I was right. So I rushed back and told Audrey that I'd call back. Well, really it's her turn to call me now but never mind.'

Dobson was dying to hurry her up but Vallance decided to let her carry on. It was worth the wait to see Dobson squirming impatiently.

'Anyway, I rushed out of the house and went over to Jack's. I banged on the door but there was no reply so I went around to the back. I know Isobel's away and his car's still in the drive so I knew he had to be there. Well, him and some fancy woman probably but that's another story. You know, he's always bringing women back with him —'

'And you saw the body in the kitchen,' Dobson suggested.

'Well, yes. He was right over the table and there was blood everywhere. Now most people would have panicked but I used to be a nurse. It was a long time ago, of course, but I suppose you never really lose it. I don't like the sight of blood, but, well, I'm not easily afraid. Well, I tried the door and it was open so I went in. I couldn't find a pulse and with those gaping wounds I knew that he was a goner. I know what you're thinking,' she said, looking at Dobson and then back at Vallance. 'I could have tried to save him but I honestly couldn't find a pulse. I know the ambulance man did but then that's what he's paid for. Well, once I saw the body I called the police first and then the ambulance. I could have come home but I thought it would be better if I waited there.'

She stopped abruptly and both policemen seemed taken by surprise. 'This motorcyclist,' Vallance said, 'can you give us any description?'

'Tall, muscular and dressed head to foot in black,' she said. 'Well, I know it's not much but it's better than nothing.'

'Did you hear him arriving?'

'No. I was on the phone to Audrey and that woman talks and talks. I sometimes think that it'd take a bomb dropping to shut her up for a minute.'

'Did you get a look at what type of bike he was riding?' Dobson asked. He looked as though he wished he had a bomb handy to stop Mrs Grant mid-stream.

'No, I only got a back view as he drove off.'

Vallance shot in with a question before she decided to expand on her answer. 'And when you went in through the kitchen door did you see any signs of forced entry?'

'Oh, no, the door was unlocked. This is a safe place to live, I'm sure most of the back doors are open. Well, mine isn't but then you can't be too careful. Last year one of the people at the other end of the Close had someone walk off with all —'

Dobson didn't want to hear about the local crime wave. He leant forward anxiously. 'You said that Jack was always bringing women home,' he said, 'did that include Mrs —'

Hell! It was too early to drag Jenny Cunliffe into the story. 'Yes,' Vallance said, raising his voice slightly, 'tell us about Jack Thomas and his women.'

Mrs Grant looked as though she'd just been granted her

165

dearest wish. A born gossip she had free rein to gab to a captive audience who was really interested in what she had to say. 'Well,' she began, leaning forward conspiratorially, 'it's no big secret. He's a ladies' man, oh yes, he's got a real eye for the women. Not that it's hard to understand. You know, he wasn't a bad-looking sort of man. A bit flashy at times, but, well, he had that something if you know what I mean. He liked them young usually, sometimes they only looked half his age. Young and leggy is what he liked.'

'Does anyone stick out in your mind,' Dobson asked, still obviously angling for the main catch.

'Well,' she continued eagerly, 'a few weeks back there was this young black girl,' she said, sounding scandalised by it. 'All legs and boobs, she can't have been out of her teens. He did like them young, half his age some of them. This young black girl she had a skirt on so short you could almost see her backside. She came back with him and didn't go home until the next day —'

'What about his wife?' Vallance asked.

'She was away again. I'll be honest, officer, me and his wife never saw eye to eye. She was all high and mighty with us, I can tell you that. Anyway, she's been away a lot recently, not that she was that bothered by his goings-on.'

'Apart from the black girl,' Dobson persisted, 'does anyone else come to mind?'

Mrs Grant shook her head sadly. 'There's been so many,' she said. 'Honestly, sometimes it seems like there's been a different woman every week. He runs a club, you know that, don't you? A horrid little place called Cagney's. Not that we've been there, it's not our sort of place at all. Too full of young 'uns getting drunk and showing off. That's where he used to meet his fancy women,' she added for good measure.

It was time to give the subject a rest, Vallance decided. 'Did he ever ride a motorcycle himself?'

'Oh, no,' she replied immediately. 'Cars, always cars. You've seen the Mercedes but before that he had a BMW and before that another Mercedes. He likes big, fast cars. Well, that's how he got into trouble when he had that spot of bother on the road.'

'But no motorbikes.'

There was no doubt in her voice. 'No. Never a motorbike, just big flashy cars.'

Dobson looked at Vallance. The question he wanted to ask was obvious. For some reason Vallance was loathe to broach the subject. Surely if Jack's affair with Jenny was such a big deal than Mrs Grant would have mentioned it? There was no way she was being discreet. Discretion was not part of her nature.

'Just recently,' Vallance said, 'have you noticed if he had a new girlfriend?'

Dobson closed his eyes and sat back. He didn't know about Jack's new woman, all he wanted to know about was Jenny Cunliffe.

'A new woman?' she repeated, obviously intrigued by the prospect. 'I can't say that I have. Well, I would have noticed. I know what his women were like: young, leggy, big boobs and a bit brassy. He did like them young,' she repeated, just in case the information hadn't sunk in.

'When you say young you mean early twenties,' Vallance said.

'Or younger,' she replied, again over-doing the shock horror of it all.

Jenny Cunliffe was in her early thirties and although she was attractive it was difficult to imagine that she could be mistaken for someone in her late teens. Jack hadn't put an age on his latest, married woman but Vallance had imagined that she was also around Jenny's age. 'What about this weekend?' he asked. 'Did you notice if he had a woman round?'

'Well, I know that his wife was away, but I can't say that I noticed any of his girlfriends round. Come to think of it, I would have expected him to bring home some young thing but he didn't. In fact I can only remember his sister coming round at the weekend.'

'His sister?'

Mrs Grant nodded. 'Oh, yes, I've seen her a few times now. She's older than he is by the look of things. That poor woman.'

There were no feelings of sympathy for the wife, Vallance noted. 'How do you know it's his sister?'

'Well, I saw them together once and he introduced us. Just briefly mind, I'm not one to get too familiar.'

'You said that she was here at the weekend. Can you be more specific?'

Mrs Grant wasn't the type to think to herself, everyone had to be party to her thought processes. 'Well, I think it was probably Saturday. You see Mr Grant and I went out on Sunday morning. We went to Audrey's for Sunday lunch. Once a month we go over to hers and once a month she and John come over to ours. We were back on Sunday afternoon so I'm sure that Jack's sister must have been round on the Saturday.'

'So you can't say for sure if Jack had company on Sunday morning?' Vallance asked. After all that it looked as though Jack's alibi for the morning of the murder was still unconfirmed.

'Well, it depends on what you mean by sure,' Mrs Grant replied. 'I can't remember another car parked outside his house on Sunday morning, and though I was in bed when he came home on the Saturday night – Well, I say Saturday night but it was really early Sunday morning. He closes late on the Saturday and sometimes he doesn't get in until two or three. The noise he makes sometimes, especially when he's got a girl with him –'

The real answer was that she wasn't sure but there was no chance of her admitting that. 'Apart from his sister you're sure there were no other visitors?' Vallance said.

'Well, I'm not one to snoop,' Mrs Grant said, 'but I can't remember anyone else coming round. His house is right opposite,' she explained, as though Vallance hadn't noticed. 'I can see right across to his front door.'

But only if you make an effort and run to the window each time you hear a noise, Vallance thought. But then again he knew that no effort was too great for Mrs Grant. 'You're in the Neighbourhood Watch scheme, aren't you?' he guessed.

She grinned proudly. 'We like to do our best, officer. This is a good place to live and if we don't look after each other, well, what sort of neighbours would we be?'

Vallance stood up. 'Thank you, Mrs Grant,' he said, signalling to Dobson that it was time to go. 'You'll be asked to make a formal statement later to one of my uniformed colleagues,' he added. 'Oh, and I'll be recommending your tea and biscuits.'

She smiled proudly. 'Thank you. I do like to help out.'

'Why didn't you ask about Jenny Cunliffe?' was Dobson's first question as soon as he and Vallance were back out in the Close. The sky had started to darken and with it the temperature was falling. The tape around Jack's house fluttered in the stiff breeze. The ambulance had departed and so too had most of the police cars.

'Because she didn't mention it,' Vallance said. 'If the affair between Jack and Jenny was so obvious then Mrs Grant would have talked about it. You saw her, there wasn't anything that she was keeping back. God, at one point we were going to get chapter and verse on the local crime rate.'

Dobson still seemed unhappy. 'Perhaps she didn't mention it because she saw it as an entirely innocent relationship, sir.'

Vallance laughed. 'Mrs Grant doesn't believe in innocent relationships. She didn't mention it because it was kept secret. For Christ's sake, Jenny Cunliffe wasn't going to do anything public in case her husband found out.'

'Will we be talking to her now?'

'No,' Vallance replied, '*we* won't be talking to her, *I* will. You can get back to Simon Clark and find out where the newly widowed Isobel Thomas is. You can have the honour of delivering the bad news. Oh, and get her or his sister to identify the body.'

Understandably Dobson looked less than happy with the prospect. 'Yes, sir,' he mumbled.

'I've already done it once,' Vallance pointed out. 'Telling one woman her husband is dead is more than enough in one investigation.'

'Do I release Clark now?'

'Unless you can think of anything else we can usefully do with him. How does it feel to be his alibi for this one?'

Dobson didn't appreciate the humour but then again

169

Dobson didn't appreciate any humour. 'I'll see you later, sir,' he said.

There wasn't much point in getting a look at the crime scene again. The place was probably crawling with forensics people. He turned towards the Cunliffe house and saw that Sarah Fairfax was still in her car. Obviously she was still waiting for him. Why the hell hadn't she gone home? Dobson had noticed her too but hadn't said anything, which was a relief, though Vallance was sure that her presence was bound to be reported back up the line.

For the moment there were other more pressing things to think about. A policeman had been posted outside Jenny's home. Had she been out to investigate all the fuss? And how would she react to the news that her lover had been murdered?

Vallance walked slowly towards her house. Jenny Cunliffe was the key to the case. She was the only link between the two men who otherwise had nothing in common. Had she done it? The idea was crazy. Would she be so stupid as to murder her husband and then her lover? And anyway, Mrs Grant had seen the motorcyclist roaring off into the distance. However, ludicrous as it sounded the possibility had to be addressed and discounted.

Sarah Fairfax got out of her car as he approached. He exhaled slowly, resigned to the fact that she was going to collar him before he made it to the Cunliffes' house. 'Yes, Sarah?' he said, detouring towards her car.

'Jack Thomas was your favoured suspect, wasn't he, Chief Inspector?' she stated calmly.

'So?'

She smiled. 'Petulance doesn't become you, Mr Vallance. Now that he's comprehensively proved his innocence –'

'What makes you think that's happened?' he demanded. 'What's to say that he didn't murder Michael Cunliffe?'

'You mean there are two black-clad motorcyclists who make a habit of blowing people's heads off?'

'Cheap sarcasm's my line,' he said, allowing himself a smile. She was right of course, everything pointed to one murderer.

'Will you now be interviewing Patrick Collins?' she asked.

'After what I've found out surely he must be high on the list of suspects?'

Vallance shrugged. 'What's the link between Collins and Jack Thomas?' he asked.

She had no answer. Vallance wasn't sure but he guessed that she didn't know that Jenny Cunliffe had been having an affair with Jack Thomas. For the moment he wasn't going to tell her. It would only give her more excuse to meddle in the case.

'If I can find a link between them then will you listen?' she responded finally.

'The police are always grateful for information from members of the public,' he said, smiling.

She looked at him coldly. 'Yes,' she said, 'cheap sarcasm is definitely your line.'

He waited for her to slam her car door and then stepped back as she accelerated away. Sometimes it was just so easy to trigger her off. He smiled to himself. So easy.

'Has Mrs Cunliffe been out to see what's going on?' Vallance asked the unformed officer stationed just outside her front door.

'No, sir,' he responded sharply, 'there's been no sign of her.'

Vallance steeled himself and then rang the doorbell. He waited a moment and then heard the patter of footsteps on the stairs. The door opened an inch and Jenny Cunliffe peered out nervously.

'It's Detective Chief Inspector Vallance,' he said, showing her his ID.

The door opened fully and she made way for him to enter. She looked haggard. Her hair was limp, unkempt and her eyes lifeless. She hadn't done herself any favours in the way she had dressed either. Her jeans were badly creased and her top looked unwashed.

'What's happened to Jack?' she asked, walking into the front room after Vallance. She sounded tired and emotionless and there was no hint of urgency in her voice.

'He's dead.'

She sat down heavily on the armchair near the door. Her eyes were closed but other than that there was no obvious sign of emotion. 'I knew it was something bad,' she said quietly.

'What was your relationship with him?' Vallance asked. It felt bad to be pushing but he felt that there was no other option.

'It was over between us,' she said, keeping her eyes closed. She leant right back in her seat, her arms resting on each side of the armchair.

Vallance sat down too. 'Since when?' he asked.

'It was over before Michael died,' she said.

'That's not what Jack told me,' Vallance said sharply. 'He claimed that it's only since the death of your husband that things have stopped.'

Tears began to stream from her closed eyes. 'That's not true,' she said. 'There was never anything but sex between me and Jack. I loved Michael. I loved him even though I was a bitch and I hurt him so much –'

'How often did you see Jack?'

'Not often. Once a week at the most.'

'And how did he feel about you?'

'He felt nothing for me. It was just about sex. Nothing more.'

'How did he feel about Michael?'

She gasped for breath, as though a sharp spasm of pain had pierced her. She opened her eyes and the tears ran quicker. 'He thought Michael was boring. He looked down on him as a little man with a nothing life –'

'Did he ever threaten to harm him in any way?'

'Why should he?' she asked. 'Michael never harmed anybody. He was no threat to Jack or to anyone else.'

Vallance stood up and walked to the window. Jack's house was clearly visible, from the shiny black Mercedes parked in the front to the streamer of yellow ribbon that cordoned it all off. 'Do you remember anything of Jack's movements on the morning that Michael was killed?'

'No – You're not saying that Jack killed Michael, are you?'

'Mrs Cunliffe,' Vallance said, turning from the window to look at her directly, 'are you on medication right now?'

She nodded slowly. 'The doctor gave me some sleeping tablets and some anti–depressants.'

'Why aren't your parents here with you?'

'Because I want to be left alone,' she said quietly. 'I've got a lot to think about –'

For a second Vallance considered calling a halt. She was in a bad way. 'Can I get you some tea?' he suggested.

'No, I don't want anything – I want to get some sleep.'

He shook his head. 'Not yet,' he said. 'Tell me, did Michael know or suspect that you were having an affair with Jack?'

It took a long while for her to come to an answer. 'No. He didn't know about Jack – He had no idea, all he knew about was my fling with Trevor Watkins.'

'You're sure he didn't suspect?'

She laughed softly. 'That was the thing,' she explained, 'he always suspected but at the same time he didn't suspect – He was always paranoid that I was having an affair but at the same time it was so over the top that it was never focused. I don't know – He didn't suspect a thing about Jack – It just used to turn him on thinking that I was having sex with other men –'

'What?'

She looked up sharply. 'It turned Michael on,' she said. 'When he thought about me having another man's cock inside me it would make him so hard – It was the best sex we ever had –'

The drugs were probably loosening her tongue. Vallance didn't want to know. 'Michael must have been pretty good with money,' he said. 'The house must have been covered by some kind of endowment policy or insurance –'

'Michael was so good at that sort of thing,' she admitted. 'He was so obsessed with money, though – He could be so greedy – I'm a wealthy widow now –'

Vallance turned away as she began to sob quietly to herself. There was one more question to ask but the timing wasn't right. Would the time ever be right to ask her to provide an alibi?

'Mrs Cunliffe,' he said softly, 'Jenny, I'm going to call your parents. I can't leave you here like this.'

'I was such a bitch –' she wailed.

Desperately he sought the words that would assuage her

guilt, that would staunch the flow of tears and ease the pain. He tried in vain. There was nothing to say. He walked into the other room, flicked through her address book and dialled through to her mother.

THIRTEEN
Wednesday 11th December

Sarah looked at the screen on her desk. There were half a dozen messages on e-mail waiting to be looked at. Her diary was flagged as being updated, which meant that she had been booked for meetings in her absence. She glanced down at the phone by her computer and saw that the voice-mail light was flashing green to tell her that messages had been stored. So many things competing for her attention but she knew that they would all wait.

She turned from the computer back to her desk. Her notes from the morning were all laid out neatly side by side. Michael Cunliffe, Graham Scott, Patrick Collins and the final addition: Jack Thomas. They were all connected in some way that was meaningful and would provide the key to the entire case. The most obvious connection was Good Neighbours. Cunliffe had worked there, the poster for the parachute jump at Components International was evidence of some tenuous connection to Graham Scott. How did Good Neighbours link in to Jack Thomas?

The library department had been prompt, thankfully. Sarah had phoned in her request for information during the long drive back into London. The photocopied sheets had been on her desk by the time she had got back. It was slim pickings but better than nothing. The few articles on Thomas detailed his horrific attack on an innocent motorist. There was little doubt that Thomas was a notorious petty thug and at least one of the newspapers had dug a little deeper to mention his club and that he was a known associate of a number of well known gangsters.

Collins, Cunliffe, Scott and Thomas. It was an incongruous little group of men. What did they have in common apart from the obvious facts of biology? Collins was a fanatical Christian, Cunliffe a dull accountant, Scott a scheming and ambitious capitalist and Thomas a violent criminal.

Vallance had been right to ask for the link between Collins and Thomas. Damn him, he was right of course. Sarah still bristled at the way he had spoken to her. The police are always grateful to members of the public – How dare he? She was trying to help, trying to pin down the person responsible for two murders, and was he grateful? No. Not a bit of it.

Was it a coincidence that the Good Neighbours poster had been on display in Components International? Once she had found out about Collins and the motorbikes everything else had slipped. Now, viewing things more dispassionately she cursed herself. She had gone in with the intention of finding out more about Scott and his company and in the end she'd done neither.

Was there a connection between AlarmIC and Jack Thomas? That was a question worth asking too. She turned over to a clean sheet of paper and carefully wrote out the four names so that they formed a square. She drew a thick black line between Cunliffe's name and Scott's and labelled the connection 'AlarmIC'. A second connection, between Cunliffe and Collins, was inked in and labelled 'Good Neighbours'. The connection between Cunliffe and Thomas was a diagonal across the page and she drew it as a dotted line labelled 'victims'.

The next step was to fill in the missing connections that would complete the square. To do that she needed to link Collins to Thomas and then Scott to Thomas. The only other connection was another diagonal to link Scott and Collins. She inked that in as a dotted line also and labelled it 'Good Neighbours'. It was only a suspected link and it seemed important that it be confirmed as quickly as possible. She kept looking at the diagram, trying to see something else in the significance of the shape and the pattern of names and lines.

The idea came suddenly. She picked up the notes for Graham Scott and dialled the number for Components International. The call was picked up after only three rings. That was a good sign, she thought, she hated companies who let the phone ring forever.

'Can I speak to Mr Scott please?' she asked the receptionist.

'Yes, may I ask who's calling please?'

'Yes, my name's –,' she looked quickly around her office as she searched for a name, '– Antonia Vallance.'

'I'll just put you through.'

'Graham Scott, can I help you?'

Sarah smiled to herself. She remembered the spiel she had heard while waiting to see Patrick Collins. 'Hello, my name's Antonia Vallance and I'm calling on behalf of the National Association for the Welfare of the Blind,' she said, making up what she hoped was a plausible sounding charity. 'I do appreciate that you might be busy, Mr Scott, but I was hoping to have a few minutes to –'

Scott decided to end the conversation there. 'I'm sorry, but I am right in the middle of things.'

'I'll be brief, Mr Scott, I was just calling to talk to you about our Christmas –'

'You're too late,' Scott snapped impatiently.

'Our Christmas Appeal Fund,' she repeated, as though reading from a prepared script.

'You're too late. We've already made arrangements on that score.'

'In that case, Mr Scott, I'm so sorry to have troubled you and I would just like to ask with which charity you've made arrangements. It's just for our records, you see,' she added, 'it'll mean we won't trouble you again in the future.'

'Yes, OK. It's a local organisation called Good Neighbours.'

Sarah decided to push her luck. The worst he could do was to hang up. 'And can I ask how you came to decide on them?'

'One of my employees is married to someone who works there. Now, I am busy.'

'Thank you for your time, Mr Scott,' Sarah said. 'And a Merry Christmas to you.'

'Yes. Goodbye.'

It had been almost too easy. She smiled to herself and then inked in the connecting line in her diagram. Graham Scott was linked to Patrick Collins and the link was labelled 'Good Neighbours'. And in real life who was that link? The obvious candidate was Mrs Cunliffe. There was only one place to get an answer.

Getting through to Anthony Vallance was a good deal trickier than getting through to Graham Scott. It took a while but eventually she managed to convince one of his colleagues to call him and to let him know that she needed to talk to him urgently. The call came through a few minutes later, by which time she was beginning to despair.

'Sarah? What is it?' he asked. His voice was muffled and distorted by the crackle of static which suggested that he was calling from his car.

There was no point in beating about the bush. 'Does Jenny Cunliffe work for a company called Components International?'

'Yes.'

'Thank you.'

'Is that all you called me for?' he demanded.

'Yes.'

'I thought it was urgent. Look, Sarah, there's no —'

'Thank you and goodbye, Chief Inspector.'

She put the phone down and then stared at it. Why had she done that? She suddenly felt foolish for being so childish. It was the sort of behaviour that she expected of him. She could imagine his anger and the look in his dark brown eyes. The image was suddenly unsettling. His eyes always seemed to sparkle with good humour but she had seen the anger there before.

The diagram on her desk suddenly looked pointless. She screwed up the paper and stood up. There were too many unanswered questions and the diagram did nothing to clarify things. The only thing that could help was more information. And the only way to get that was to spend more time digging around rather than sitting in the safety of her air-conditioned office.

She looked at the computer once more. There was nothing for it but to cancel all her meetings for the next day. She couldn't afford to hang back any longer. Besides, after the way they'd handled her proposal for the Alibhai programme she was in no way inclined to play ball.

And what about Air Express Heathrow? Sarah had forgotten the courier company she had seen picking things up at Components International. At the time it had seemed highly significant but later it had slipped her mind. Was it significant? Instinctively she felt that the answer was yes. Graham Scott had appeared unrepentant at the end of the TV investigation, and he had wormed his way through the collapse of the company without any show of remorse. Why believe that he had changed?

The phone by the side of the computer looked at Sarah temptingly. She picked it up and dialled Components International once more. There was a risk that the receptionist would recognise Sarah's voice, but it was a risk she had to take.

'Hi,' she said, adding half an octave to her voice, 'I'm calling from Air Express about one of your export orders. Can I speak to whoever deals with it?'

The receptionist hesitated before answering. 'Didn't our order go out?' she asked.

'This morning's order went out OK,' Sarah said reassuringly. 'I've just got a query about the next one.'

The receptionist sounded more relaxed now that she knew the order had gone out. 'I'm sorry, love,' she said, 'but the person who deals with all of that is out for a few days. Can it wait or should I get Mr Scott to deal with it?'

So, not only did export orders really exist, they were a regular occurrence. There was time for one last question. 'I'll call back,' she said. 'When does Jenny come back?' she asked, guessing that it was Mrs Cunliffe who dealt with the export orders.

'I can't say. I don't know if you've seen the papers, but Jenny's husband was killed at the weekend.'

The woman had relayed the news in shocked tones. 'My goodness,' Sarah said, responding with the same hushed voice. 'How did it happen?'

'He was murdered. Shot in the head from what I've heard.'

'Poor Jenny,' Sarah whispered sympathetically. 'How's she coping?'

'I don't know, the poor woman's probably still in shock. Mr Scott's tried to call her but she's not answering the phone. Listen,' she added, 'what's your query and I'll see if I can sort it out for you.'

What to ask? Anything too general and it would give the game away, anything too detailed would be incorrect. 'It's just these customs forms,' Sarah said, aiming to buy time.

'Not again,' the woman sighed. 'What are they querying? The value of the goods?'

'Not this time. They're asking about the description of the goods.'

The receptionist did not sound too surprised. 'I don't know,' she exclaimed, 'no matter how many times we do this there's always something crops up.'

'So what should I put on the form?'

'Electronic circuit boards, the same as we always do.'

Sarah decided not to push her luck. She needed to know what type of circuit boards but if she went too far it might tip Scott off that he was being investigated again.

'Right, thanks,' Sarah said. 'Oh, and wish Jenny all the best from everyone here, won't you.'

'Yes, I will. Bye, love.'

Sarah sat back and smiled to herself. Progress. She already had a good idea of what kind of circuit boards Scott was manufacturing; the next thing was to prove it.

It was early evening before Isobel Thomas was hauled in for questioning. Dobson had insisted on keeping Simon Clark down in the cells until she had been safely lodged in one of the interview rooms. He left her there with nothing but a WPC and a cup of coffee for company and then headed down to the holding cells.

'Can I piss off, then?' Clark asked as soon as the door to

the cell was opened by the custody sergeant.

'You know the rules,' Dobson warned. 'Anyway, your girlfriend's upstairs,' he added. 'It'll be interesting to hear what she's got to say for herself, Clark.'

Clark took the news badly. He swore to himself and then looked warily at Dobson. 'Jack's not going to find out about this, is he?'

Dobson smiled. 'That's your look-out, Clark,' he said. 'I wouldn't want to be in your shoes when he does find out that you've been having it off with his wife.'

The thought clearly terrified Clark. 'Please, I've been bloody helpful, Inspector. I mean, it ain't as if I've buggered you about, is it?'

The custody sergeant was waiting. Dobson nodded finally, as though agreeing with the prisoner. 'All right, Clark,' he said quietly, 'I'm willing to give you the benefit of the doubt. You've been straight with us and we both know that your woman friend's going to give you an alibi. You're clean, you've got nothing to do with Michael Cunliffe's death. Now play straight again and tell us what you know about it.'

'But that's the thing,' Clark exclaimed irritably, 'I don't know anything about it. For God's sake, until you lot pulled me in I thought he'd done himself in.'

Dobson sighed and turned to the sergeant. 'He's free to go, Sergeant,' then he turned back to Clark. 'Have you got somewhere else to go?'

Clark looked perplexed by the question. 'What for?'

Dobson grinned. 'For when Jack Thomas decides he wants to talk to you man to man.'

Clark lunged forward suddenly. 'You fucking bastard!' he screamed. The custody sergeant was there to grab him. Clark fought hard, trying to lash out and Dobson grabbed hold of his arms and helped pin him to the wall. More officers rushed over and in moments Clark was pushed down onto the stone floor of the cell.

'Right, that's assault,' Dobson declared, straightening his tie carefully as he watched the uniformed officers holding Clark down. They'd got him at last.

'Do we charge him now, sir?' the sergeant asked, disentangling himself Clark.

'Yes,' Dobson decided, 'the bastard's not going to walk out of here so easily.'

For a second he considered breaking the news of Thomas's death to Clark but then he decided against. There was a chance that while he was being processed Clark would change his mind and tell them what he knew. In the mean time he would have more time in the cells to fret about the confrontation with Jack Thomas that would never come.

'You're a bastard, Dobson! A bastard! I know you're going to blab to Jack about this –,' Clark cried as Dobson turned away. His angry words echoed along the corridor and would no doubt attract even more attention. Words were all that Clark had left. He was firmly pinned against the wall by the sergeant and a couple of hefty PCs.

'You can swear all you like,' Dobson said, 'and if you shout loud enough Jack's going to hear you all by himself.'

'What the shit does that mean?' Clark demanded. 'It's all right,' he declared. 'I'm all right now, you can let me go.'

'Shall I, sir?' the sergeant asked.

Dobson nodded. There was nothing to fear from Clark. He was scared and the only thing left to him had been to vent his fear and frustration.

'Is Jack here as well?' Clark whispered.

'That's not the sort of information I can share with scum like you,' Dobson sneered. 'Now, be a good boy while the sergeant charges you with assaulting a police officer.'

As Dobson headed back up to the interview rooms he was certain of one thing: it wasn't what Vallance would have done. Vallance would have simply let Clark go. That was no way to behave, no way at all. Someone like Clark responded to harsh treatment the best, and if the only way to get information out of him was through fear, intimidation or blackmail than so be it. So long as no one laid a finger on him there was nothing that Clark could do to complain. Had Clark ever treated his victims any better?

Vallance was waiting outside the interview room. He needed a shave and a change of clothes. It was all right looking fashionably scruffy but by the end of the day he looked a mess.

He turned towards Dobson when he heard him approaching. 'What was all that downstairs?' he asked.

It was a direct question that deserved a direct answer. 'It was Clark,' Dobson said, 'he tried to attack me and Bill Patterson.'

'What gives?' Vallance asked. 'He's been as good as gold all day, why screw up just when he's going to be let free?'

Dobson grinned. 'I forgot to tell him that Jack Thomas is dead. He got it into his head that we were going to tell Jack all about his wife's sordid little affair.'

Vallance wasn't grinning. 'You mean *you* gave him that idea,' he said.

'The man knows more than he's letting on, sir,' Dobson insisted. 'It seems to me that he's more afraid of Thomas than he is of us, so I just made use of that.'

'No wonder he called you a bastard,' Vallance remarked. He was tired and if his comment was supposed to be disapproving that wasn't how it sounded. 'Anyway,' he added, 'I can tell you why he's been shit scared of Jack Thomas.'

Damn it! What else had come up? 'What have you heard, sir?'

'It's not so much what I've heard, it's more a case of what the scene of crime people found at his house. It looks like he was blown away by his own gun.'

'You've found the weapon?'

Vallance shook his head. 'If only. No, they found the place where he kept his gun and some ammo hidden. No sign of the gun but some of the ammo's still there. We're still waiting on ballistics but it's not going to be a major surprise when they tell us that it's the same weapon.'

'And the same one that killed Cunliffe?'

'Yep. So, where the hell does that leave us, do you think?'

It left them no better off, Dobson realised. Were they now faced with two murderers? 'That leaves us still with the possibility that Jack Thomas killed Michael Cunliffe,' he said.

'You've broken the news to the widow Thomas?'

Dobson had experienced no difficulty in breaking the

news to Isobel Thomas. She had accepted it with an equanimity that bordered on the ice cold. It was entirely what Dobson had expected of her. 'She took it well, sir,' he reported.

Vallance didn't look too surprised either. 'There was no wailing or gnashing of teeth from Jenny Cunliffe either. It looks like we're the only ones mourning Jack's departure.'

'You look tired, sir,' Dobson said. 'Do you want me to question her? I can get someone else to sit in.'

'Thanks for the offer,' he responded, 'I'm glad someone on my team's got my best interests at heart.'

The sarcasm was over-done, even for Vallance. 'Sir?' Dobson said, trying not to rise to the bait.

Vallance looked at Dobson sharply. 'The answer's no. We'll handle this one together.'

What was eating him? There seemed to be something other than exhaustion fuelling Vallance's irritation. After the slanging match earlier in the day Dobson decided not to push his luck. 'Yes, sir. She knows about Jack's murder but nothing else.'

'Not even the fact that lover boy's down in the cells?'

'No. She's just assumed that we've pulled her in because of Jack's murder.'

'All right, we might as well make a start now.'

Dobson pushed the door open and went in first. Isobel Thomas was still sitting at the table, her fingers curled around an empty coffee cup and her eyes full of boredom. She looked up at Dobson without emotion but when Vallance came in she shifted uneasily. The apparent interest was there on Vallance's part too. Dobson noted the way the dark scowl had been transformed into something approaching a smile.

'This is Chief Inspector Vallance,' Dobson said. 'He's heading the investigation into your husband's death.'

'You poor bastard,' she said. 'How many people do you think you're going to find who've wanted to kill Jack?'

Vallance sat down. 'You tell me,' he said.

She laughed. 'Hundreds probably. Do you want all this on tape?'

'Yes,' Vallance said. 'Give us a second to get it sorted. Do you want another coffee?'

Isobel nodded as Dobson worked the tape equipment. She was the epitome of the stereotypical Jack Thomas woman that the garrulous Mrs Grant had described. Her blonde hair had come from a bottle, her skirt was several inches too short for her long legs and her top was too tight around the chest. Cheap and slutty, just the way that Thomas had liked his women. Was it how Vallance liked his women too? He was certainly paying her enough attention.

Vallance despatched the WPC to fetch more coffee, much to Isobel's obvious approval judging by the smile she gave him.

'Ready, sir,' Dobson said, having set the tape up.

'Shall I start again?' Isobel asked.

Vallance shook his head. 'No, let's just carry on. You don't seem too surprised at the news that Jack's been shot dead.'

She shrugged. 'It's like an accident that's been waiting to happen,' she said. 'He's got on the wrong side of somebody he shouldn't have and they've decided they've had enough.'

'Any ideas who that somebody might be?'

She shrugged again. 'I don't know, it could be anybody. He never used to tell me what he was up to.'

'Never?' Vallance asked incredulously.

'Nope. He was always the lad, you know. He did what the fuck he wanted and that was all that counted. That's why I ditched him.'

Dobson smiled. 'You ditched him because he failed to keep you informed of his activities?'

Isobel ignored the question. Her attention was focused on Vallance. 'I just got sick of his screwing around. After he came out of prison it was even worse. I mean I've turned a blind eye before, but then he was really taking the piss. Rubbing my nose in it, you know?'

Vallance nodded sympathetically. 'We've heard all about his affairs,' he said. 'What was different this time? Why ditch him now when you've let it slide in the past?'

'Like I said, he was taking the piss. A one-night stand with some slag he's picked up at the wine bar is one thing, but —' she let the sentence trail to silence.

'But what?'

'He was having one-night stands and keeping a couple of regular girlfriends going at the same time.'

'Do you know who these regular girlfriends are?'

'One of them's Jenny Cunliffe,' she said. 'She's the one whose old man got killed last week.'

If it was meant to be a revelation then it showed how badly out of touch she was. 'And the other one?' Vallance asked.

She shrugged. 'Some slag who liked doing threesomes with Jenny Cunliffe and Jack.'

'You don't know her name?'

She shook her head. 'No, I just know she was a right dirty bitch who'd do anything to get Jack's hard-on inside her.'

Dobson winced. She looked cheap and she spoke like a slut. A perfect match for her thug of a boyfriend. 'This is on tape,' he said, pointing to the machine recording every word of the interview.

She laughed. 'I don't give a shit if it's on tape or not. Like I said, she was an even bigger slag then Jenny Cunliffe.'

Vallance obviously wanted her to continue in the same vein. 'You don't know this other woman's name?' he asked. 'What do you know about her?'

'I know that Jack was boasting to all the blokes at Cagney's about her. He'd say that she'd do anything he asked, anything. You know, threesomes, anything. He kept saying that she liked it in any position except the missionary position. He thought that was funny. Any position but missionary.'

She seemed incensed by the idea of group sex. As though she could forgive him for having a string of affairs so long as they happened serially. How could anyone make sense of a morality like that? Dobson gritted his teeth and decided to say nothing. What she was saying was clearly designed to shock, though judging by Vallance's expression he found nothing strange in it.

'Tell me about Jenny Cunliffe,' Vallance said, changing tack.

'What's there to say? She was bored with her nerdy little bloke and she went off with Jack whenever she could.'

'You knew about the affair?'

She nodded. 'Course I did. And I knew what a slag she was too.'

'You mean apart from the fact that she stole your husband?'

Isobel grinned. 'She didn't steal my husband,' she said. 'Screw it, I didn't give a shit about the two of them having it off.'

This time even Vallance looked perplexed. 'I don't understand,' he admitted.

'She was just a one-night stand that turned into something more,' she explained. 'But when he told me that she was game for the three of us — You know, the three of us together —'

'That's when you got pissed off,' Vallance concluded.

'I was his wife,' she stated vehemently. 'He should have thought more of me than to think I was going to share his hard-on with some slag.'

Dobson corrected her sentence mentally: share his hard-on with some *other* slag. Her outrage would have been more understandable if she had a view of the sanctity of marriage that was remotely normal.

The coffee arrived and there was a pause while the WPC handed the cups round. When they were ready to start again Isobel was smiling at Vallance.

'After you got pissed off,' Vallance said, 'what did you do about it?'

She grinned. 'I got myself a bloke,' she admitted. 'Someone who cares for me and doesn't treat me like dirt.'

'Can you tell us who?'

She shrugged. 'I don't suppose it matters now. Simon Clark.'

'When you ditched Jack did you then move in with Simon?'

'You've got to be sodding joking,' she said. 'Jack would have taken Simon's head off if he knew.'

'So where did you go?'

'I've been staying at my sister's for a while,' she said.

'What about Clark?'

She smiled. 'All right, I was there on Saturday night.'

'What time did you leave?'

'Late Sunday afternoon,' she said. 'I can't remember what time exactly.'

Vallance had been right all along. Clark's alibi was solid.

Not that it mattered. Clark was still a criminal and Dobson had made sure that he wasn't going to get off scot-free.

'Do you know where Jack was during your absence?' Vallance asked, continuing the interrogation.

'At home, with one of his women, at Cagney's — I don't — I mean didn't care.'

Her tone of voice painted a picture that her words didn't. Her relationship with Thomas was marked by a complete absence of emotional warmth.

'Just now you said that Jack would have taken Simon's head off,' Vallance said. 'Tell me about that.'

She smiled. 'Someone's just done it to him.'

'Did you know that he kept a firearm at home?'

She nodded, as though unconcerned by it. 'Yeah, that was all part of him being a villain. He kept a gun at home and made sure everybody knew about it.'

Vallance looked at Dobson and smiled. 'Not everybody,' he remarked. 'We didn't, did we?'

What the hell was Vallance doing talking like that in front of a witness? 'No, sir,' Dobson admitted, unable to think of anything else to say. The man sounded as though he were on her side. What was wrong with him?

'Did Jack ever ride a motorbike?' Vallance continued, turning his attention back to Isobel.

'No. Motors were what he liked. Fast cars that cost a fortune.'

'Did he ever talk to you about Michael Cunliffe?'

The interrogation was going all over the place but she seemed not to notice or not to care. 'He called him a sap. You know, he thought it was funny shafting his wife like that.'

'Did he ever make any threats about him?'

The question seemed to strike her as odd. 'Why should he? I mean the little nerd was hardly likely to come gunning for him, was he? I mean if Jack had got her to give him a blow job in front of her husband the poor bastard would have said thank you.'

This time there was no holding back. The way she spoke was deliberately offensive and if Vallance didn't care than Dobson did. 'This is all on tape,' he snapped. 'Tone down your language.'

She looked at him and laughed. 'What's eating you, you old bastard?'

'Come on, now,' Vallance said, 'let's just concentrate on the questions.'

'It's him,' Isobel responded. 'Anyway, how come he's only an Inspector when he's ten years older than you are? Does that mean he's crap at his job?'

Dobson's knuckles were white under the table. The bitch was deliberately being provocative, as though it would get her anywhere. She'd regret it. She'd regret every word of it. She didn't know that Clark was in the cells.

Vallance reacted mildly to her outburst. 'Listen,' he said softly, 'don't make this more difficult than it already is. We were talking about Michael Cunliffe,' he reminded everyone.

Dobson stared at her coldly. 'I know you think I'm some hard bitch,' she accused him. 'You probably think I should be on my hands and knees sobbing because Jack's dead, don't you?'

She was a hard bitch, she was right about that. 'My feelings are not an issue here,' he said coldly. 'Now, will you answer the question: what do you know about Michael Cunliffe?'

She turned back to Vallance to give her answer. 'Jack never made any threats about him because he never needed to,' she said.

'Do you know where he was on Sunday morning?'

'Nope. I was with Simon and I didn't give a toss where he was.'

'Going back to this other woman,' Vallance said, 'you can't tell us anything else about her?'

'I can't. Talk to some of his cronies at Cagney's, they might know. I do know she wasn't one of the regulars there.'

'Think carefully,' Vallance insisted. 'There's nothing you can tell us?'

'Talk to Jenny Cunliffe, she knows.'

'There's nothing else?'

She started to shake her head and then smiled. 'There is one thing. She was married.'

They were already aware of the fact but Vallance acted as

though it were news. 'Did he ever give the impression that he was afraid of her husband?'

'No. He liked married women, it turned him on screwing someone else's wife.'

'Nothing else?'

She was adamant. 'Nothing.'

'And there's nothing else you can tell us about Jenny Cunliffe?'

'Only that she's a right bitch.'

Dobson glared at her. She was sitting with her arms across her chest, a broad smile across her over-painted red lips. The interview was over and all he wanted to do was to wipe the self-satisfied grin from her face.

FOURTEEN
Thursday 12th December

The simplest and most obvious ideas are the best. It was a basic truth that Sarah often liked to remind herself of. She had written it neatly on the top of the page while the call rang through to Air Express Heathrow. Outside the sky was a dull, uniform grey without any sign of the sunshine which had transformed the previous day. It was December again and the temporary respite from the cold and miserable weather had been swept away during the night.

Sarah looked at her watch. It was only just eight in the morning but she was already dressed and had started breakfast. Now all she needed was to make one last call from home and then she was ready to set off for the suburbs again. Duncan was still in bed in the other room. He was still half asleep and it looked as though he was going to be late for work. Again.

The call was picked up at last. 'Air Express, how can I help you?' the receptionist sounded breathless and the words were spoken with a practised sincerity that meant nothing.

'Hello, I'm calling from Components International,' Sarah began. 'It's about our export order that went out yesterday.'

'I'll just put you through to Sue,' the woman said, 'she deals with all of that.'

There was a second's pause and then a new voice was on the line. 'Sue Grainger, can I help you?'

Sarah crossed her fingers. 'Hello, I wonder if you can help

191

me. I'm standing in for Jenny Cunliffe at Components International and I'm –'

'How is Jenny?' Sue cut in, clearly concerned.

'She's still off work,' Sarah said. 'From what I've heard people say she's not doing too well.'

'It's just so terrible, she's such a nice woman.'

'I know,' Sarah sighed sympathetically.

'How's Graham coping without her?'

Sarah lowered her voice. 'He's not, to be honest,' she whispered. 'I mean the whole place is a mess. I'm only temping but I can't find anything and he really doesn't know what Jenny was handling from what I can work out.'

'Isn't that how it is everywhere? So,' Sue said, 'what're you stuck on?'

It was time for the big lie. 'I know this is silly,' Sarah said, 'but I can't find all the details of yesterday's order. I've had Customs and Excise querying the order and there's no one in apart from me.'

Sue laughed. 'God, you're keen, it's only just gone eight.'

Sarah had anticipated the reaction. Sue worked for a courier company, they were used to working odd hours, but a company like Scott's was strictly a nine to five operation. Again she whispered her answer. 'I've got a bit behind,' she confessed. 'And the thing is, well, if Jenny doesn't come back there could be a permanent job here.'

'I understand,' Sue said, sounding satisfied by the explanation. 'So, what do C&E want?'

'It's these fire alarms that went out yesterday,' Sarah said, 'I need to know what to put down for the description. It says circuit boards but Customs and Excise want to know what kind of boards. Do I just say it's fire alarms or what?'

'No, we've had this conversation before,' Sue explained. 'Mr Scott doesn't want that mentioned for some reason. If circuit boards isn't good enough he wants us to say that they're gas detector devices.'

Sarah faithfully wrote the description down on her pad. 'Got it,' she said. 'Gas detector devices. And what about the quantity?'

'I'd have to look, do you want me to call you back?'

'No, I'll hang on,' Sarah told her.

Gas detector devices. She looked at the innocuous words on paper, marvelling at how much they concealed. Graham Scott was in the same game after all. Gas detector devices. Such a simple euphemism for fire alarms. There was no point asking whether the design faults had been fixed. The secrecy was proof enough that the devices were probably still potentially lethal.

Sue came back with the details. 'Four thousand circuit boards,' she read, 'destination Zimbabwe. Signed, sealed and delivered. They'd probably be on their way now if C&E weren't so nosy.'

'Thanks, Sue, you're a life saver,' Sarah said, her voice full of genuine gratitude.

'No problem, and give my love to Jenny if she comes back.'

'Will do,' Sarah promised.

Such a simple idea and it had yielded results worth having. Far from having been eliminated, the AlarmIC connection to the Cunliffe case was still going strong. All that Sarah needed to do was to tie in Jack Thomas to the other suspects. She glanced at her watch once more. Duncan was still in bed. He was probably expecting breakfast in bed before she disappeared off to the icy wasteland of the suburbs. Tough. He'd have to get up and get out all by himself.

She stood up and walked quietly to the kitchen. Her cup of tea had gone cold and the cereal floating in a layer of milk looked less than appetising. It wasn't the first time she'd let a breakfast go to waste and it wasn't going to be the last. She carefully drained the milk from the cereal bowl and then dumped the mushy remains into the bin. Duncan would have let it set to concrete. He always assumed that the dishwasher would clear anything, even caked-on muesli. She ran the empty bowl under the tap and then carefully placed it in the half-empty dishwasher.

With that all done she glanced at her watch once more. There were still no signs of life from Duncan. Instinct told her to leave him to it, she was sick to death of him depending on her to do things. Why couldn't he look after himself? She crept towards the bedroom door and peered inside. He was still wrapped up in the duvet, curled up in the fluffy white folds that contrasted with the fading tan of his bare back. He was turned over on his side, an arm under his head and the other thrown possessively across the duvet.

He turned over suddenly. 'Sarah?' he murmured, reaching out blindly across the bed.

She knew she could probably get away with creeping out of the house before he was fully awake. She'd be in the car and away before he had time to crawl out of bed and hunt around for trousers. But then she felt a sudden and very familiar pang of guilt. 'I'm on my way out,' she said, stepping into the room despite her misgivings.

He yawned expansively and sat up in bed as he rubbed the sleep from his clear blue eyes. 'Off to the wilds of Surrey already?' he remarked, arranging a semblance of a smile on his face. He wasn't bad-looking really. With his blue eyes, muscled body and wavy blond hair she knew that lots of women found him attractive.

'Yes, I want to be there reasonably early,' she said, making sure she didn't stray further into the room.

'Breakfast?'

'I've just had mine,' she said, and then, catching the look in his eye she added, 'and you were asleep when I made it.'

'Any tea left?'

'It's in the pot,' she said.

He yawned again and then stretched hard, pushing his arms as far apart as they would go. 'God, I just can't be bothered with work today. I just don't know where you get the energy from.'

She smiled. 'Look, I've got to get going. I'm not sure what time I'll be home tonight.'

'Again? Can't you just make the effort to get home on time? Please?'

She hated the wheedling tone of his voice. It was the same tone of voice he used with his mother when he wanted something. 'I can't, this is important.'

'It's always important,' he complained. 'What about me? What about us?'

They were good questions but not ones she wanted to

194

talk about. 'This isn't the time. I've got to go.'

She crossed the room quickly, kissed him once on the lips and then slipped from his fumbled grasp before he really knew what was happening. He looked disappointed, the childish sulk spread across his lips. 'Please try and be early,' he pleaded.

'All right,' she said, and they both knew that she didn't mean it.

She waved him a last goodbye from the bedroom door and then headed out. If only she hadn't been so stupid as to agree to marry him in the first place.

Dobson paced the room impatiently, glancing at his watch several times as the long minutes dragged by. Vallance was late. For a man in command of a team the example he set the lower ranks was not one to be proud of. If the man in command was always late, insolent, scruffy and disorganised then what hope was there for the rest of them? Trying to instil a sense of discipline in the junior officers often felt like fighting a losing battle. No matter how hard Dobson tried, all his good work would be undermined by Vallance's poor behaviour.

DC Chiltern came in. He was dressed neatly enough but there was something about him that wasn't quite right. What was it? Something about the eyes, something in the way he glanced at Dobson and then looked away. Had Vallance been saying anything to him?

He thought back to the previous evening's interview with Isobel Thomas. The bitch had touched a sore point. The offensive way she had pointed out the age difference between him and Vallance. It was a raw nerve all right, and it was typical that a cheap slut like her could home in on it. Somewhere along the line Vallance had had a lucky break and he'd sailed through the ranks to make it to DCI. But did he deserve it? The man was a walking disaster area who had more in common with people like her and Jack Thomas than with the people he was supposed to serve.

Vallance wandered in at last. He looked as though he'd suffered a sleepless night. There were dark bags under his eyes and his chin was covered with a wiry stubble that looked more than a day old. If he'd been a constable he would have been sent home and told to clean himself up, and even that would have been too lenient. Instead of walking directly to talk to Dobson he stopped first to say something to Chiltern.

'I just need some caffeine,' he explained, having despatched the detective constable to get some coffee.

Was he suffering from a hang-over too? Vallance was known to like a drop of the hard stuff. 'A heavy night, sir?' Dobson said, attempting small talk. It wasn't something that came easily but he needed Vallance in a good mood.

'No, not really,' Vallance replied. He sounded tired but not ill, so perhaps he wasn't hung-over after all.

'Can we talk things through?'

Vallance, sitting on the edge of a desk, nodded. 'You mean a case conference sort of talk?'

There he was again, making light of normal procedure. 'Yes, sir,' Dobson confirmed. 'I think that after what Isobel Thomas told us last night we need to review the case together.'

'All right, after I've had my caffeine fix,' he said.

'Yes, sir.'

'It's bloody freezing out there,' Vallance said, nodding towards the window. The sky was low overhead, a dense grey that threatened rain or snow.

More small talk? 'It looks like it could snow,' Dobson said.

Chiltern arrived back carrying a couple of polystyrene cups full of tepid coffee from the vending machine at the end of the corridor. 'The percolator in the canteen's broken, sir,' he explained apologetically.

Vallance took one of the cups and scowled. 'Talk about being under resourced,' he complained. 'Thanks. Right, I suppose it's time for our case conference, Inspector.'

Chiltern smirked until he saw the stony expression on Dobson's face. Then he straightened up nervously. It was good to see that hanging around with Vallance hadn't completely blinded him to the realities of the police force.

Vallance's desk was a graveyard for files and paper. It was piled high in apparent disarray and perched at convenient locations on the mounds of paper were discarded coffee cups, chocolate wrappers and the kind of litter that most people reserved for the bin.

'This is why I look so screwed,' Vallance said, taking his seat behind his desk.

Dobson tried not to wince at the profanity. There was no need to talk like that. It impressed no one except the stupid or the juvenile. 'You've gone back through all the statements,' Dobson said, picking gingerly through the files.

Vallance took a loud sip of coffee before answering. 'Every single one of them,' he confirmed. 'And do you know something? I still don't know who we're looking for now that Jack's ready to be parked six feet under.'

Where was the native intelligence that Vallance was famous for? He was supposed to be one of the best detectives in the force, but from what Dobson could see he was just another chancer who'd run out of ideas. 'You've come to no conclusions, sir?' he said.

'None,' Vallance agreed happily enough.

'What do you suggest now?'

Vallance shrugged. 'Right now I could do with some decent breakfast and a week in the sun. What about you?'

The poor attempt at humour was graced with a fixed smile from Dobson. He had plenty of ideas to go on, but the problem was whether to risk sharing them or not. 'Are you suggesting that we sit back for a while?'

'There's good old-fashioned police slog to look forward to,' Vallance said. 'Let's interview everyone in the district, let's file every bit of information on computer, and then let's interview everyone again for luck.'

'Have we not got anything useful from the house-to-house interviews at Fenton Close yesterday?'

Vallance waved a hand over the desk. 'They're in there somewhere,' he said. 'The only thing I got out of it was a desire to meet Jack's new girlfriend.'

Dobson failed to smile. No doubt Vallance felt a desire for Isobel Thomas too. 'Yes, sir,' he said, keeping any emotion from his voice.

Vallance looked at him and sighed. 'You're not exactly a laugh a minute, are you?' he said.

'No, sir,' Dobson replied. 'Some people fail to find murder a laughing matter.'

'In that case, Inspector, what do you suggest we do with this case?'

Vallance was totally bereft of ideas. The most obvious suspect had been all but ignored by him. 'I think your assessment is correct, sir,' he said, deciding to play things close to his chest. 'I think we just have to rely on footwork to give us the break we need.'

'And who exactly do you plan on planting your feet on?'

Dobson feigned innocence. 'Sir?'

'Come on, man, it's obvious you've still got a pet theory. Who or what is it?'

'Clark, sir.'

Vallance shook his head sadly. 'You've got it in for the poor bastard, haven't you?'

It was precisely the reaction that Dobson had hoped for. 'No, sir,' he said. 'I just think that he knows more than he's letting on.'

Vallance wasn't having any of it. 'You're forgetting that he was locked up here while Jack was removed from this earth.'

'I'm aware of that, but I still believe he has information that can lead us to the murderer.'

Vallance smiled. 'Murderer, singular?'

'Or murderers,' Dobson admitted.

'Are you asking permission to carry on that line of enquiry?'

'Yes, sir.'

Vallance shrugged. 'If that's what you want,' he agreed. 'No more messing him about though,' he added. 'You've got him for assault already. Any more of that kind of thing and I'll get the charges dropped.'

Typical. Vallance had more sympathy for Clark than for the real victims of crime. 'He attacked us,' Dobson said.

'After you'd wound him up,' Vallance countered. 'The man's a few brain cells short of stupid. You know that if you provoke him he explodes, and I bet you did more than a little of that yesterday.'

A slanging match would be pointless. 'He got nothing he

doesn't deserve, sir, but if you think it necessary to let him go again —'

Vallance leant forward and fished through the paperwork at the front of the desk. 'You ought to take another look at this,' he suggested.

Dobson took the loose sheets of paper that Vallance had retrieved from the bottom of the pile. It was a statement from one Eileen MacDuffy. 'What is it?'

'The statement from Isobel Thomas's sister. She backs Isobel up a hundred per cent.'

Damn it! How had Vallance known? It was the angle that Dobson had planned on chasing up. Simon Clark and Isobel Thomas were in it together. Clark had killed Cunliffe and then Isobel had conveniently killed her husband to shift suspicion away from her boyfriend. Dobson swallowed hard. 'I'll have to check up on Isobel Thomas too,' he said.

'It's a waste of time,' Vallance declared confidently. 'Clark's too stupid to plan the murder and he was terrified of Thomas. Isobel's cleverer than Clark but she was too busy trying to get away from Jack to have anything to do with Michael Cunliffe's murder.'

It was true that Clark was stupid, but he was vicious and he had cunning. And Isobel Thomas had a ruthless streak in her that would take great delight in arranging the murder of her Jenny's husband. Vallance was wrong. 'Are you saying I shouldn't follow this up?' he said.

Vallance seemed unconcerned. 'I'm going to go back to the beginning,' he said. 'So long as the rest of the troops are busy I don't care what you follow up. Like I said, I think you're barking up the wrong tree, but that's your look-out.'

It was an appalling way to run an investigation but Dobson nodded his agreement. If it meant that he had free rein to solve the case then it was all to the good in the end.

Sarah could easily picture the scene in the summer: the long, wide road lined with trees, the houses set well back from the pavement, grass verges alive with colour. Leafy suburbia, a place of quiet roads, passive temperament and tranquil lives. Even on a stark grey morning in December, with a dreary sky and trees stripped of colour, there was a certain serenity about the scene. She drove the car slowly along the street, looking from side to side, savouring the essence of it. A perfect opening shot to a programme: a calm facade of sturdy Victorian detached houses, tracking from one to the other, each different in detail but the same in execution. Execution. The word stood in stark contrast to the suburban ideal she saw before her.

She stopped the car and got out. It was getting cold again but she needed to walk back to get a better view of the grand house that Patrick and Rosemary called home. The street was deserted. Not a single other soul was out in the cold. It was the sort of street that was always deserted, pedestrians would be few and far between. People walked their dogs, but then the countryside was near enough for most people to drive their dogs out for a walk in the woods.

The Collins's house was no different to any of the neighbouring ones. Solidly built, with a sloping roof, bay windows, a heavy front door and bricks brown with age. How much did a house like that cost? A fortune probably. It was a detail that needed to be filled in. She pulled her pad from her bag and quickly scribbled a note to herself to ring the local estate agents'. The price of property was likely to be a major topic of conversation across garden fences. It had been when Sarah had been growing up in a street not very different from the one in which she stood.

The house featured a garage at the side but it was closed. Patrick and Rosemary were both at work, which meant that their identical cars would be parked side by side at Good Neighbours. Were the Collins's good neighbours? She smiled to herself and wrote the question down. The idea of knocking on doors and asking the question made her smile. Patrick Collins: the most uncharitable charity man in the world and the most un-neighbourly good neighbour too. The phrasing was clumsy but it was something that could be honed into a good line.

Did she need anything else? Her motivation had been to build up a library of images that would be useful for the TV programme, assuming it ever got that far, and which might trigger off ideas with regards to the investigation. As she turned back to head for the car she saw the flicker of movement in the front window of the house across the road. She smiled. In a street unused to strangers anyone new was treated with suspicion. Perhaps Patrick's paranoia was merely an extension of the paranoia implicit in the Neighbourhood Watch schemes which were deeply rooted in the area.

The relative warmth of the car was a relief after the blustery cold outside. The next thing to do, she decided, was to talk to Rosemary Collins. If Good Neighbours was such a good source of funds then it was down to her skills as head of fund-raising. As Sarah started the car she tried to picture a female Patrick Collins. It was not a pretty sight.

The car was facing the wrong direction but the road was wide enough to allow an about turn without any trouble. She kept the car slow as she cruised by the Collins's house for one last look. The nosy neighbour was at the window again. Did she think that Sarah was staking the house out? Sarah smiled at the idea. Perhaps the police would be called. They'd swoop on her and pull her in for questioning. She smiled at the thought of the hell she'd raise. And of course she'd make sure that Tony Vallance would bear the brunt of it.

The drive to Good Neighbours was punctuated by the first fall of snow. It started as a few specks on the windscreen and then turned into a sudden flurry of white. For a second the world was lost in the patterns of white that were driven by the wind but then she snapped out of it. It was pretty and everything, but it would cause havoc on the roads. She slowed the car marginally, enough to convince herself that she was taking care.

She arrived at the Coach and Horses in time to see a battered old transit van pulling into the Good Neighbours car park. It lurched across two parking spaces and came to a stop. The back of the van was covered in a thick layer of grime which all but obscured the Good Neighbours logo that had been badly painted onto the rear doors. Sarah cruised to a halt on the other side of the road and then backed up slowly to get a better look.

Patrick Collins emerged from the van. He was wearing

dark jeans, boots, a heavy coat and a scarf wrapped around his neck and lower face. If it wasn't for his size it could have been anybody. The man who'd killed Cunliffe and Jack Thomas could have been anybody too. Looking at him it was easy to picture him on a motorbike, dressed anonymously in black and carrying out each ruthless murder in turn. Sarah shuddered at the thought. Patrick Collins was dangerous, and the sooner she managed to convince Vallance to act the better.

She watched Collins dash into the Good Neighbours office and then come out a second later carrying a black bin liner full of stuff. He was followed by two of the young women who worked for him, each carrying a similar black sack which they handed to him to load into the van. There was nothing to say what the sacks contained but from the bulk Sarah guessed that they were filled with the Christmas parcels that Collins had been so proud of.

There were several trips in and out of the office until the van was full. Collins slammed the doors shut and then jumped back into the driver's seat. He swerved back quickly, executing a sharp turn before roaring out into the road. Instinctively Sarah ducked down in her seat as the van rushed past. When she sat up again her heart was pounding and her throat was dry.

'Don't be so silly,' she scolded herself loudly. Collins wasn't about to come after her. Why let him frighten her so much?

If anything his zooming past in the van was fortuitous. He was out of the way which meant that the coast was clear to contact Mrs Collins.

'Hello, this is Sarah Fairfax,' she announced to the person who took the call, 'I'd like to speak to Rosemary Collins please.'

The name obviously had not been forgotten. 'Hi,' came the reply, 'I'll just, er, see if Mrs Collins is free.'

There was no messing about, the call went through to her almost immediately. 'Rosemary Collins,' she said. 'Can I help you?'

She had a voice that was quiet, calm, and in no way did she sound as hostile as her husband. 'My name's Sarah Fairfax, I spoke to your husband earlier –'

'Patrick told me all about it,' Rosemary said.

Sarah waited but Rosemary was not going to say anything more than that. At least there was an apparent absence of judgement from her. 'Would it be possible for us to talk?' Sarah asked.

'Of course. When did you have in mind?'

'If it's convenient I'd like to come up and talk to you now.'

She sounded surprised. 'You're here already? Well, I suppose now is as good a time as any.'

'Thanks. I'll see you in about thirty seconds.'

It had been so easy. Far from being an ogre like her husband, Rosemary Collins sounded like sweet reason itself.

Rosemary's office was a neater, more human affair than her husband's. Sarah noted that the bookshelves boasted a dictionary, several directories, a number of paperbacks and not one single biblical tract or religious tome. The walls were decorated with pictures taken at various fund-raising events. They were pictures worth detailed scrutiny but unfortunately Rosemary had a chair ready by her desk.

She looked tired and her hair seemed to have been brushed back only half-heartedly, making her look a little untidy despite the fact that she was wearing a beautiful black cashmere sweater. 'Please,' she said, sitting down, 'let me start by apologising on Patrick's behalf.'

Sarah half smiled. 'Does that mean he told you exactly how our interview went?'

Rosemary smiled in return. It suited her, it lessened the effect of the lines around her eyes so that she seemed younger and more attractive. 'I know my husband well enough to read between the lines,' she admitted. 'Patrick's not an easy person to deal with sometimes.'

It was a nice line in understatement but Sarah let it pass. 'He seems to have a real problem with the media,' she said, 'which I would have thought would be counter-productive for a charity.'

Rosemary's smile suggested that she agreed. 'It's normally my job to deal with the media,' she said. 'I suppose our success in drawing donations is directly linked to our media profile.'

A polite knock at the door heralded tea and biscuits. Sarah

glanced at her watch. It was way before lunch-time so there was no problem scoffing a few biscuits. 'Did he tell you why I was here?' she asked, picking up her tea.

'He said you were digging up dirt on Michael. He also said that you were digging up scandal about us.'

'And do you believe him?'

Rosemary took a sip of her tea before answering. 'No, I don't think so,' she said finally. It sounded as though she had only just made up her mind and that there was an element of doubt still lingering.

'I merely pointed out that Good Neighbours seemed to be remarkably charitable to its staff. Company cars, good salaries and trips abroad, that kind of thing.'

Patrick's rage had exploded at that point but Rosemary listened calmly. 'Company cars? Do you imagine that Patrick and I have any life outside of Good Neighbours? It's so closely entwined with everything that we do that I couldn't tell you what is and what isn't work any more. Is it so awful that we have cars? We run up miles and miles every week and most of it is directly related to what we do here. Tell me, Sarah, is it so unreasonable to have a car?'

'Three cars? You, Patrick and Michael all had cars.'

'Three very basic family cars, nothing fancy, nothing expensive. I admit that Michael did very little business mileage compared to Patrick and myself, but he saw a car as an essential part of the package. We needed a good finance person and so we were willing to grant him that.'

Again she sounded entirely reasonable and reassuring. Sarah had no idea of what salaries were being paid out by the charity, but she'd seen Michael Cunliffe's house, which must have been mortgaged to the hilt. 'What about the trips abroad?' she asked, hoping to home in on another sore point.

'We've been on three trips abroad,' Rosemary admitted. 'On each occasion we raised more money than we spent, so in real terms they were a good thing to have done. More importantly, Sarah, it gave us the chance to learn from other similar organisations. Do you know how many other people there are in our situation?'

Sarah didn't and she wasn't interested. 'Patrick mentioned

the work you're doing. He was angry because I sounded less than impressed by a few dozen food parcels.'

For the first time it looked as though Rosemary was annoyed. 'I can assure you that there's more to our work than a warehouse full of food parcels,' she snapped. 'Did he mention the holidays we'd organised for young people? Or the house renovations for pensioners? Or the hospital taxi service we were setting up?'

Sarah shook her head. She put her tea down and picked up her notebook. 'A hundred and fifty food parcels, shoes, boots, blankets and clothes,' she said, reading back her notes. Somehow those few parcels now occupied a warehouse or else they'd given birth to several hundred progeny.

Rosemary sighed loudly. 'I'm afraid that Patrick doesn't always keep tabs on how well we're doing,' she explained. 'In that case, I can see why you were so suspicious.'

Sarah nodded. Rosemary was doing a good job in allaying that suspicion, however everything she said needed to be checked up on. 'Can I see verification of all of this?' she asked.

'Of course,' Rosemary agreed. 'Would you like me to call some of the old people so you can talk to them about the work we put into fixing up their houses for the winter? Or would you rather talk to someone at the hospital about the car service?'

Damn it! 'Both,' Sarah agreed. 'I'll take the details in a minute. Now, I was also interested in Michael Cunliffe.'

'You were one of the people involved in the film about AlarmIC,' Rosemary stated. 'Are you following it up with a new one?'

'I wasn't actually involved in the first film,' Sarah explained. 'But I'm interested in what happened for obvious reasons.'

'You believe that Michael's death was linked to the fire alarms?'

'It's possible,' was all that Sarah was prepared to say. She knew she sounded cagey, but it couldn't be helped.

'Inspector Dobson seemed to have the same idea,' Rosemary said. 'It sounds unlikely to me, but then the idea that Michael could be murdered would also have sounded far-fetched a few days ago.'

'Of course now that Jack Thomas has been killed, it sounds even crazier,' Sarah said.

'Jack Thomas? Is that someone local?'

'A small-time criminal,' Sarah explained. 'He was actually a neighbour of Michael's,' she added. 'You've never heard of him?'

'No, but it's awful nevertheless. You know, Sarah, there's so much evil in the world that what we do, in our own small way, is important. We aim to teach by example – to show by doing – that it is possible to care for others and to help one's friends and neighbours.'

Rosemary sounded sincere enough, and her little speech carried none of the bombast and rhetoric that Patrick's did. Sarah smiled. 'I'm sure it must mean a great deal to you,' she said.

'Not just to us,' Rosemary countered, 'but also to the people that we help.'

The conversation risked getting bogged down in homilies. 'Patrick didn't sound exactly enamoured of Michael Cunliffe,' she said.

'They didn't see eye to eye on a lot of things, but that's no surprise, is it? Michael had worked for a large and successful company, with his own staff, an expensive car and a salary that most people only dream about. Coming here was something of a shock to him. He never really got to grips with the fact that we weren't here to turn over a profit.'

'He wasn't religious, was he?'

Rosemary smiled. 'Not in the way that Patrick and I are,' she said. 'But that's not a pre-condition for working with us.'

'But why take someone on in such an important position if there was no sympathy between you?'

'Because he was the best candidate for the job,' Rosemary said simply. 'We saw lots of people and he was the most well qualified and had the most valuable experience.'

'Did you know about his AlarmIC connection?'

'Yes, he was quite candid about it. We believe in forgiveness,' she said, then hastened to add, 'not that he had done anything wrong personally.'

Sarah sighed inwardly. Rosemary Collins was plausible,

reasonable and her answers all had the ring of truth. Damn it! A female version of Patrick would have been preferable.

'I wish that your husband had been this helpful,' she said, starting to pack her notebook away.

'Is there anything else I can help you with?'

Sarah paused. 'Actually there is,' she said. 'I understand that Good Neighbours has some connection with a company called Components International, tell me about that.'

Rosemary seemed surprised by the question. 'That's the company that Jenny Cunliffe works for,' she said. 'Through her we got them to sponsor some of our activities and last year they even donated their old delivery van to us.'

It was another answer that was so mundane that it had to be true. 'Do you know about their connection to AlarmIC?'

Rosemary nodded. 'Yes, we are fully aware of that, but that's all dead now, Sarah. Graham Scott, the MD there, is a good man and he's got nothing to do with that kind of business now.'

It was the one untruth that Sarah had detected in the conversation, and even that was probably because it had emanated from Graham Scott and not from within Good Neighbours.

So far Rosemary had been helpfully direct, too helpful in fact. The interview was heading to a boring close and she had learned nothing of value. There had to be more to Good Neighbours than a series of good works that left everyone feeling warm inside.

'You're very different to Patrick,' Sarah remarked bluntly.

Rosemary smiled. 'Are you and your partner very similar?' she asked.

Sarah was not the one under discussion and she wasn't going to allow herself to be side-tracked into talking about her and Duncan. Especially not Duncan. 'Why did Patrick react so violently to my questions?'

'Perhaps it was the way you phrased them,' Rosemary suggested.

'I phrased them the way I did for you, you reacted calmly and he hit the roof. It made me feel that he had something to hide.'

Rosemary shook her head. 'Patrick's got nothing to hide,' she said.

'Is it true that he rides a motorbike?'

'Pardon?'

Sarah was glad to see that even Rosemary could be perturbed by an awkward question. 'I asked if he rode a motorcycle. As I understand it he's quite good on one.'

'He doesn't have a motorbike,' Rosemary said.

She was sounding edgy. 'I didn't actually ask if he owned a motorcycle, I was merely talking about his ability to ride one.'

For a second it seemed as though Rosemary were going to deny the truth but then she changed her mind. 'Yes,' she admitted, 'he can ride a motorbike, though I can't see how it's relevant to this discussion.'

'Can't you?' Sarah asked accusingly.

Again there was a pause before the reply. 'I know that the police are seeking a motorcyclist –'

'And it's true that Patrick has a violent temper, I've seen that for myself.'

'Stop!' Rosemary cried. 'This is ludicrous. You're not seriously suggesting that Patrick had anything to do with Michael's death?'

Sarah was not about to stop. 'And it's true that he and Michael didn't see eye to eye. You've both confirmed that.'

'No, Sarah, this is crazy.'

Was it? 'If it's so crazy then why do you look so worried?'

Rosemary shook her head. 'I'm not worried at all,' she insisted. 'I'm just very shocked that you could even think such a thing.'

'He can use a gun, can't he?'

'Stop it!'

She didn't want to answer the question but the answer was clearly going to be a resounding yes. 'Is it true or not? Can Patrick use a gun?'

'I'm not even going to answer that.'

'I know that the answer's yes,' Sarah lied. 'I know about his past.'

Rosemary looked appalled. 'He was in the army,' she said, 'of course he can use a gun. That doesn't –'

What if he returned suddenly? The idea hit Sarah with a jolt. 'Think about it, Rosemary,' she said quietly. 'Where was Patrick on the morning that Michael was killed?'

Rosemary closed her eyes. She wasn't going to answer. She wasn't going to sink deeper into the mess. Had she suspected all along?

'I'm going to go now,' Sarah said. 'But please, think about what I said and talk to the police if you have to.'

'You've jumped to the wrong conclusions,' Rosemary whispered but her voice no longer carried much conviction.

'Talk to Chief Inspector Vallance,' Sarah advised as she stood up.

FIFTEEN
Thursday 12th December

Vallance shifted uncomfortably as the car pulled into Fenton Close. Going back to the beginning of the case meant going back to Jenny Cunliffe. There was no other place to go. Her husband's death could only be explicable if there was a motive, without that there was nothing. And, looking at things dispassionately, she had plenty of motive. Without him she was suddenly a whole lot richer. Without him she was free to carry on with her affairs. Sex and money. Money and sex. What more potent forces were there in most people's lives?

'Stop here,' Vallance said, deciding that he needed more time to think things through.

DC Chiltern stopped the car just at the entrance to Fenton Close. The entire estate was spread before them: a series of detached houses that could only be reached by a single narrow road. An enclosed world of expensive houses for people who worked hard to pay back mortgages with too many noughts on the end. It was the sort of place that gave Vallance the creeps.

'What do you reckon Michael Cunliffe was like?' he asked suddenly.

The question made Chiltern pull a face as he tried hard to picture the man whose body had been found lying in a bed of blood-soaked mud and gravel. 'A hard-working sort of bloke,' he suggested tentatively. 'Probably fretting about his missus all the time.'

It wasn't enough. 'No,' Vallance said, 'I mean what was he really like. Was he a good laugh? Was he the sort of bloke that liked a beer and a curry, or was he more the sort of bloke who'd want to put his feet up and watch the TV every night?'

'I don't know, sir,' Chiltern said, as though he were answering an exam question and Vallance had the right answer.

'He doesn't sound like a popular sort of bloke,' Vallance said. 'I mean no one seems that cut up about him being killed. Apart from his wife.'

'Do you believe all of that, sir? I mean she might be making it all up.'

Vallance knew what the statistics showed and it made Jenny Cunliffe the most likely suspect. 'I don't know whether it's real or not,' he said, 'but when she cries like that it seems real enough to me.'

'But she could be putting it all on,' Chiltern insisted.

He was right and Vallance nodded his agreement. Emotion could be faked, but whether that explained Jenny Cunliffe's tears or not he could not tell.

Now that he was so close to her home he felt reluctant to face her again. He had learned so much about her and it made him feel uncomfortable. Each time he thought of her he remembered Jack boasting of having her suck his cock. Images reared up in his head of Jenny and another woman sharing a hard cock, their naked bodies entwined erotically as they gave pleasure with their mouths. It felt wrong to be excited by such thoughts but there was no way he could stop himself.

'Shall we go, sir?' Chiltern asked after a few moments. He was young and eager, motivated by the desire to get on with it, to solve the crime regardless of its complexities.

Vallance sighed. There was no use in putting things off any longer. 'All right,' he agreed, 'let's get this over with.'

Chiltern started the car immediately, just as a call came through. He left the car idling and took the call.

'It's Sarah Fairfax, sir,' he said, handing over.

At any other time he would have been furious, but given

the situation Vallance was glad of the distraction. As usual Sarah wasted no time on social pleasantries.

'I've just spoken with Rosemary Collins,' she said, 'and I'm convinced now that you need to pull Patrick in.'

Vallance looked at Chiltern and raised his eyes to heaven. She was still convinced by her pet theory. 'What's his motive?' he asked.

The question seemed not to be the one she had been expecting. 'Greed, probably,' she said. 'Anyway, that's not significant, you can get that later.'

'Evidence?'

This was obviously what she had been waiting for. 'His violent temper,' she began, sounding as though she were reading back from a list. 'He rides a motorbike, he can use a gun and he's got no alibi for the Sunday morning.'

It was all circumstantial but still she'd dug up more on him that anyone else had. 'All right,' Vallance agreed, 'we'll make sure that he's interviewed.'

'What? That's just not good enough! Please, Chief Inspector, don't let the results of my investigation get in the way of your own –'

She was in good form. Again. 'What do you want?' he asked wearily. 'That we should drop everything and grab Collins off the street?'

'He's dangerous.'

'And I've said that he'll be interviewed by us. You made an allegation and we're going to investigate –'

'An allegation?' she echoed angrily. 'Mr Vallance, I'm telling you in all honesty that I think Patrick Collins is capable of murder. I would have thought you knew me well enough by now to know that I don't make allegations lightly.'

Vallance realised that Chiltern was keenly awaiting a riposte, the entire conversation had him riveted. 'Miss Fairfax,' Vallance said, 'if you're unhappy with the conduct of this investigation then you've every right to complain to my superior officers. Now, I've already said that we're going to talk to Mr Collins, what more do you want?'

There was a lengthy pause before she answered and Vallance could easily imagine her cold fury. 'I just hope you manage to talk to him before he kills again,' she said.

'Are you suggesting that he's about to do that? Who's the intended victim?'

'Ask him when you see him,' she snapped and closed the call.

'That's one pushy woman,' Chiltern remarked, driving the car forward into Fenton Close.

'She's pushy,' Vallance agreed, 'but she's smart. While I'm talking to Jenny Cunliffe I want you to get on the phone and see what you can dig up on this Collins bloke.'

'You think she might be right, sir?'

Chiltern sounded disappointed at the prospect. 'If she's right she's never going to let us forget it,' Vallance said.

'What about Mrs Cunliffe, sir? She hasn't provided an alibi yet.'

She hadn't provided an alibi because she hadn't been asked for one. 'She was at home when Thomas was blasted. There's no way she could have killed him. And it looks like the same MO in both cases, which means if she didn't kill lover boy she didn't kill her dearly departed either.'

'But we don't know that for sure, do we, sir?'

Chiltern phrased his questions carefully. He wasn't the fastest copper on the team and he was always slow and methodical in putting two and two together.

'You're right,' Vallance agreed, 'and we need to prove that. Jenny Cunliffe knows who Jack's second girlfriend is, and she's the one who can provide him with an alibi for the morning of Cunliffe's murder. I just hope that Jack's covered, that's all, then we can eliminate him from the enquiry in the same way he's been eliminated from the planet.'

Chiltern stopped the car outside the Cunliffe house. Nothing had changed from the outside. The same neat house sat squarely in front of them, the bricks and mortar unchanged by the earthquake within. Across the other side of the estate the Thomas house stared back at them, it's features similarly unchanged by the violent events that had taken place inside it.

'I'll handle this alone,' Vallance told Chiltern. 'You start checking up on Collins.'

'Should I arrange to have him picked up?'

It was what Sarah Fairfax had demanded. Hell, if she'd asked nicely it wouldn't have been so bad, but to call up and make demands like that – 'Not yet,' Vallance decided. 'Let's see what you come up with first.'

A sharp wind nipped at Vallance as he stepped out of the car. Instinctively he wrapped his leather jacket tightly around him and pushed his hands deep into his pockets. The snow shower had been brief but it was still freezing. He shivered and dashed from the car to the front door. He rang the doorbell and waited and then rang again. At last he heard footsteps and then saw a hazy and indistinct figure walk slowly to the door.

Jenny looked even more exhausted than before. Her face was pallid, her eyes lifeless and she looked thinner. The stuff her doctor was prescribing was turning her into a zombie.

'I need to ask you a few more questions,' Vallance said, forcing a smile.

She nodded and made way for him. The house was warm, stifling compared to the icy cold outside. He knew the way and headed straight for the front room.

'How are you feeling?' he asked, unable to find anything else to open the conversation with.

She walked slowly to her chair, moving across the room like an old lady and not the thirtyish woman that she was. 'What more do you need to ask?' she said, not bothering to answer his question.

He sat down too. 'I need to ask you about your relationship with Jack Thomas,' he said. He glanced away from her, unable to look her in the eyes because he was afraid that she'd see through to the images in his head.

'You know about that already,' she said, her voice flat and emotionless.

'We've been informed that Jack had another – another regular girlfriend apart from you,' he said. 'We need to find out who she is.'

'It's not true,' she replied simply.

'Jack himself told us that he was having an affair with another woman,' Vallance declared pointedly. 'Who was she?'

'It's not true,' she maintained. 'Jack was always boasting, always exaggerating – There were one-night stands, more than a few probably, but I was the only woman he saw regularly.'

Why was she lying? It didn't make any sense. 'Jack told us and so did his wife. Who was it, Jenny?'

Despite the drugs she refused to admit the truth. 'He was lying,' she insisted, 'there was just me.'

Why the hell wouldn't she admit the truth? 'I've had enough of this!' he snapped angrily. 'I want answers and I want them now, understood?'

Her eyes seemed to fix on him as though they'd only just regained the ability to focus. 'I'm not lying,' she said quietly.

'We know that you and this other woman used to screw him at the same time,' he stated coldly. 'We know that you were even willing to share him with Isobel Thomas. We know everything, Jenny, everything but her name. Who was she?'

The tears came predictably enough, and with it the self-pity and the guilt. 'I was such a bitch – I hurt Michael so badly –'

Vallance swore under his breath. The last thing he needed was to have her hysterical. 'Listen, Jenny, you've got to tell the truth. We need to know who she is so that she can provide Jack with an alibi. He claimed he was in bed with her during Michael's murder.'

'It's not true –' she sobbed. 'It was just me – Me – There was no one else –'

'What's her name?' he repeated, unable to stop desperation creeping into his voice.

'There was no other woman –'

'Who are you protecting? That's why you're lying, isn't it? To protect someone.'

She didn't answer, instead she leant forward and buried her face in her hands as the sobs ran through her. Vallance looked up in frustration. Nothing had worked. He stood up, realising finally that Jenny Cunliffe was the only real suspect in her husband's murder.

'Where were you on Sunday morning?' he asked.

She stopped crying for a second and looked at him

strangely. Her eyes were wet with tears but he could still see the fear in them.

'Where were you?' he repeated, his voice harder and colder.

'You don't – No, no –'

'If you don't come up with some answers I'm going to have no option but to arrest you, understand?'

'I was at home,' she said, forcing the words through ragged breath.

'Can you prove that?'

'Why are you doing this?' she sobbed. 'Why are you tormenting me?'

'You're doing this,' he countered. 'If you told the bloody truth then I wouldn't need to do this.'

'I have been telling –'

'I don't want to hear your lies,' he snapped.

She was trembling bodily and she looked as though she were about to be sick. Vallance knew that if a doctor were present he or she would sedate her completely.

'I'll be back later today,' he said, finally conceding defeat. 'Call your parents or get a solicitor,' he added.

'I loved Michael,' she whispered as he walked out of the room.

How could Tony Vallance ignore the patently obvious? Sarah knew all about male pride but that was no excuse. Patrick Collins was a danger to the public and the sooner he was taken in for questioning the better. Having a stubborn streak was one thing, but Vallance was taking risks. Of course there was no way she'd talk to his superior officers, even if she did think that he was letting things slide. Damn it, just for once she wished he'd listen to her properly.

In the mean time there were other angles to the case to be investigated. Graham Scott was her primary target. A man who'd export lethal devices to the third world would have little in the way of conscience. How many people had been killed or maimed because of him? The murder of Michael Cunliffe and Jack Thomas was no different, at base, to the murder of innocent children burned to death because his products failed to trigger.

Trigger. It was a good link word: alarms that failed to trigger; guns that always triggered. She wrote the phrases down in her pad and then sat forward in her car. Across the way she could see that Patrick Collins had yet to return to Good Neighbours. The thought of him returning to find her waiting in her car was more than a little unnerving. With his violent temper and total paranoia she was afraid that he'd try to attack her. She didn't think he'd pull a gun out but he was a big man and he'd have no problem beating hell out of her.

After glancing quickly over her shoulder she pulled out into the road and accelerated away in one swift movement. She needed to visit Components International one more time, to see for herself if there was anything else that could be gleaned from the place. What it needed was an outside surveillance unit to get a closer look. If Scott was using the place to manufacture the alarm units then it followed that there had to be machinery and production lines installed. A concealed camera or a number of remote listening devices would be sure to pick it all up. It wasn't her department, though she knew enough about how it worked to scout things out.

The fall of snow had left patches of white here and there but on the whole the world looked as grey and miserable as it had first thing in the morning. The important thing was that the road was clear and she could speed along without having to worry. That was the thing about the suburbs. Everything was spaced apart, spread out diffusely and only a car connected one place to the next. It wasn't quite downtown LA, but by its very nature suburbia demanded a car culture to make sense of things.

Her first impression of the industrial estate had stuck. Components International lived on a grubby patch of concrete that was enclosed by a high perimeter wall that protected the vandals and graffiti artists whose work marked every available surface. Even the TO LET signs advertising the vacant units were covered in vivid swirls of indecipherable spray. Driving onto the industrial estate was like driving into a piece of low-rent, run-down London that had been transplanted into the leafy outskirts of the city.

As usual the only vehicles on the estate seemed clustered at the far end, close to Scott's company. Driving up the empty car park was an experience worth recording, she decided. The camera could pan low, capturing the vacant units as they rolled by one at a time before coming to a stop outside Components International. What did that show? That in the midst of dereliction and abandon something immoral had taken root? Or that Scott's organisation was as empty at heart as the vacant units in which it nestled?

It was as she drew closer to the end of the estate that she saw the white van. Her heart skipped a beat and she felt the adrenalin flood through her system. Patrick Collins was on the estate. The discovery brought a rush of fear but there was also an excitement that made her drive forward rather than reversing away. Here at last she was going to prove a direct connection between Graham Scott and Patrick Collins.

Of course! It made sense, suddenly. She had seen the picture of Collins in Africa on the wall in his office; he and Rosemary were there at some sort of conference, from what she could tell. And Scott's alarms were being delivered to Africa, to Zimbabwe in fact. The pieces were falling neatly into place. Collins could easily use his contacts abroad to sell Scott's murderous devices. What better way of convincing someone to buy them than by having the products marketed by such an obviously charitable and committed individual as Patrick Collins? And what better way for the Collins's to make some extra money?

She slowed the car to a crawl, keeping one hand on the gear stick in case she needed to go into reverse. Her heart was pounding but she needed to go on, she needed to get proof once and for all. There might not be a second chance. Her camera was stashed in the glove compartment, all she needed were a couple of shots and that would be enough.

Her car was almost parallel with the van when she saw Collins and Scott emerging from one of the other units. Damn it! What the hell were they doing – She stopped the car instantly and started to reach for her camera. Common sense said it was time for her to retreat but then she'd miss the chance. She ducked down and pulled the camera from its hiding place. It wasn't much but the compact little 35mm had served her well before. As always it was packed and primed and ready to shoot.

When she sat up again she saw that Scott and Collins were standing by the transit van. They were looking at her. She swallowed hard and snapped the first picture even as they watched. Collins reacted instantly. He lunged forward angrily but Scott held him back, holding him by the arm and saying something that Sarah could not hear. There was no mistaking the rage on Collins's face. He looked ready to kill.

She took a second shot and threw the camera on the passenger seat beside her. Now was the time to bail out. She tried to slam the car into reverse but the gears grated noisily. Shit! She tried again but it wouldn't budge. Collins brushed Scott's arm away and then jumped into the driver's seat of the van. She released the clutch and then tried again. This time it slipped into reverse first time. She looked over her shoulder quickly and then started to swing the car back in a wide arc. The van's engine roared to life and she turned to see Collins turn the wheel towards her.

He was mad. She twisted the wheel round sharply so that the car was facing the exit. The van accelerated towards her, the engine belching fumes as it pushed the heavy vehicle forward with a squeal of tyres. She gripped the wheel, her fingers white against black, her eyes fixed on Collins as he headed directly towards her.

Death. It was heading right at her and there was nothing she could do to get away. Her strength was gone and her fingers could not turn the wheel and her feet were frozen into place above the gas pedal. She closed her eyes for the impact, screaming so loud that it drowned out the noise of the vehicle rushing towards her. She was still screaming a second later when the roar of the van shot by and the protests of its tyres filled the air.

She was shaking when she looked. The bastard had swerved at the last minute. He turned back in a tight circle and moved towards her slowly. Her hands were still refusing to work and all she could do was sit and watch and shake.

He slowed to a stop beside her and leaned across the

passenger seat to shout at her. 'Leave us alone you dirty bitch!' he cried, his face an ugly sneer of violent rage.

She looked into his eyes and turned away. Fear. She had never known it, she'd never felt something so raw and animal inside her before. Paralysis. She could do nothing but sit and wait for whatever he decided to do.

He swore at her once more and then accelerated away, driving the van forward with the same naked aggression.

She was still shaking a minute later when she realised at last that he had gone. The anger flooded through her but the fear fought it back. He could have killed her. He wanted to kill her. She could have been dead. Dead.

Graham Scott was watching. She saw him and realised that he had witnessed everything. He had tried to stop Collins. She had seen him trying to hold the maniac back.

The engine was dead. She'd stalled the bloody thing in her blind panic.

She closed her eyes for a second and breathed deeply, trying to calm herself down as best she could. If only Vallance had listened to her – But then there was no way that anyone could have guessed that Collins would be meeting with Scott. It was just a coincidence, lucky or unlucky depending on how you viewed it.

When she looked again Scott was still staring at her. He'd tried to stop Collins, did that mean that he wasn't the monster that she'd imagined? She started the car again, slightly embarrassed at herself for having stalled it in the first place. It was a detail that she wouldn't be passing on to Vallance.

As the fear receded her mind started to function properly. Scott and Collins had emerged from one of the other units on the estate, one that looked vacant and abandoned. Rosemary had said that the food parcels were stored in a warehouse. It was obvious now that she had been talking about one of the units next to Components International. Did the unit actually belong to Graham Scott and was it another example of his close liaison with Patrick Collins?

She locked the doors of the car and then drove forward slowly towards Scott, who continued to stare at her impassively. There was no point in pretending, he obviously knew who she was. She stopped the car beside him and opened the window a fraction to talk to him.

'What the fuck do you want?' were his first words, delivered with a cold venom that contrasted with Patrick's fiery violence.

'He tried to kill me,' she said, unable to keep her voice calm, 'you saw that. You're a witness.'

He shook his head. 'I saw nothing,' he said.

'But you tried to stop him. He's dangerous, you saw that, you saw how he tried to kill me.'

Scott laughed. 'If he'd wanted to kill you he'd have done it properly, you stupid bitch. Haven't you done enough? Why don't you frigging leave us alone.'

'What do you mean, done it properly?' she demanded. 'What do you know?'

He spat at the ground in front of him. 'I'm not talking to you,' he said. 'Now, get out of here, go on.'

Sarah looked at him. He wasn't going to do or say anything to help her. He had as much to hide as Collins did. She revved the engine hard and then let go of the clutch so that the car roared forward with a scream of rubber.

The burst of speed took her to the exit from the estate and then she swerved out onto the road. She felt anger surging through her, building on the fear that still lurked beneath the surface. A motorcycle courier hurtled towards her from the opposite direction, heading at speed for the estate. Another piece of the puzzle fell into place.

What better place to hide a motorcycle then in one of the units on the estate? No one would notice another black-clad motorcyclist coming in and out, they'd just assume that it was one more manic courier doing a delivery. And certainly the police would have no reason to search through the units, especially not one that looked vacant. She was certain that in amongst the Christmas parcels, possibly buried under the mounds of food and clothing for the poor, a search would turn up the murder weapon, the black leathers and the motorbike that Collins had used when carrying out the murders.

She pulled the car sharply off the road, almost colliding

with the kerb. There was no more time to waste. She'd done enough already, it was time for Vallance to get things moving. Quickly she replaced her camera in the glove compartment and then grabbed the phone from her bag. The phone number was already imprinted on her memory and she tapped the keys urgently.

Vallance looked at the crime scene once more. The table in the kitchen was still marked with blood, now caked black, an ugly stain that gave no clue that it once pumped through a human body. There was more of it on the walls and some on the floor.

'This is how we think it happened, sir.'

Vallance had only been half listening to the neatly dressed scene of crime officer who'd been overseeing the crime scene investigations. Although, like most of his colleagues, he was a civilian, constant contact with police officers had given him all the mannerisms of a serving copper.

'We think the suspect came in through the back door,' the man explained, pointing to the glass-panelled door. 'The key's on the inside but we think that it was usually kept unlocked. In any case there's no evidence of forced entry at any point within the house. From the blood dispersal pattern and the position of the body,' he continued, walking across the kitchen to the door to the hallway, 'we believe that the suspect was waiting behind this door and that the victim walked into the room unaware that the assailant was waiting for him. He turned towards the door and that's when the first shot was fired. Most of the blast missed him but it caused significant injury to his right shoulder and neck. The impact sent him reeling backwards where he fell across the table.'

Vallance looked down and saw the deep scuff marks on the floor where the table had been pushed back roughly. He tried to picture the look of shock and fear on Jack's face but his imagination failed him. The only picture of Jack that he could conjure up had him laughing, bragging and acting the big-time gangster.

'The assailant then walked towards the victim and fired the second shot which effectively killed the victim,' the man paused. 'We believe that the assailant then got away using the back door again. There are very faint tyre marks near the back garden which closely match those found at the other crime scene.'

'Fingerprints? Fibres?'

The man shrugged. 'It's too early to identify any fingerprints but we're not holding out much hope, sir. On a professional job like this you'd expect the assailant to be wearing gloves. We're still trying to see if we can get a decent footprint but that wouldn't give us much to point to a suspect, sir.'

Vallance thanked the man and then walked back through the house to the front. He stood in the doorway and looked out across the estate to Jenny Cunliffe's house. Who was she protecting? He had given her clear warning, his options were limited and, like it or not, he was going to have to arrest her if she didn't tell the truth.

DC Chiltern was still in the car parked outside Jenny's house. Vallance had walked to Jack's house because he needed the time and the space to clear his head. Had it done him any good? No. Nor had viewing the second crime scene. In spite of what he had just heard, there was still a question mark over Jack's involvement in the first murder. Cunliffe's murder had clearly been a well planned and professional contract killing. In comparison Jack's murder was a mess. A contract killer would not have needed two shots at such close range. And why kill Jack in his own home? Surely it would have been safer to get him somewhere more secluded, somewhere isolated and without the danger of eye witnesses.

The police car parked in Jenny's drive suddenly reversed, turned and started to head towards Jack's house. Had Chiltern grown impatient with all the waiting, or had he merely spotted Vallance and decided to come and pick him up?

Chiltern opened his door before the car had even come to a stop. 'Sir, there's an urgent call for you,' he called.

'Who is it?'

Chiltern sounded almost apologetic. 'It's Sarah Fairfax, sir,' he reported. 'But it sounds urgent, sir,' he add, trying to justify himself.

Not again. Vallance was in no mood to be lectured by her. There was nothing for it but to put her straight. He was running the case. He was the police officer. She was a journalist. She didn't investigate murders. Damn it! What was wrong with her?

'I'll call her right back,' he said. It was going to be a difficult call and the last thing he needed was Chiltern listening in.

He walked back into the house looking for a phone. The front room was the obvious place to look but two of the forensics people were tucking into sandwiches and a third was reading a newspaper. He looked at them wearily but decided not to commend them on their good work. The phone in the kitchen would have to do, he decided. The sight of blood on the walls was probably appropriate given Sarah's temper.

The phone was on the wall, next to a cork notice-board that sported half a dozen postcards from the South of France and Spain. He dialled the number and Sarah picked it up even before the first ring had finished.

'Patrick Collins has just tried to kill me,' she announced calmly. 'I know you think I've been over-stating the case, Mr Vallance, but this is serious now. Please, will you act now before he succeeds in killing me or someone else?'

She was telling the truth, of course. 'What happened?' he asked. 'Where are you?'

'I'm safe, now. He tried to run me down in his van. I hate to say it but he scared the life out of me. You've got to listen to me this time, he's dangerous.'

'Where are you now?' Vallance repeated.

'I'm OK now,' she said. 'I'm parked about five minutes from where Components International are. He was there to see Graham Scott about something, I turned up looking for him as well and that's when Collins went mad.'

'Did you manage to get his number plate?'

'Shit! No, I didn't and it was stupid of me not to,' she said. 'He's driving a battered white transit van. It's even got Good Neighbours painted on the rear door.'

'What about Scott? How was he involved?'

'He saw the whole thing but afterwards he denied it. Good

Neighbours have got an industrial unit that they're using to store the stuff they're collecting for Christmas. I'd say it was a good place to start looking for that motorbike.'

Vallance smiled to himself. Having the fear of God put into her certainly made a difference. He couldn't remember her ever being so free and easy with the information she'd collected. 'I'll make sure that Collins is picked up immediately,' he promised. 'The best thing for you to do now is to get out of the area.'

'What? Do you really think I've done all this just so that you can wrap it all up?'

'Fair enough,' he sighed. 'Get to Area headquarters and wait there for me. You can make a statement while we wait for Collins to be arrested.'

He knew instinctively that it wasn't going to be good enough for her. 'No, Mr Vallance,' she said, proving him right, 'I think I want to be there when Collins is arrested. After what he did to me I want the satisfaction of seeing him caught.'

'In that case I'll meet you at headquarters,' he suggested.

'You're lying,' she snapped. 'You'll have me waiting there for hours before you arrive. I know you're at Fenton Close, I'll meet you there.'

'But –'

But nothing. She'd put the phone down. There was only one way she could have known that he was at Fenton Close: DC Chiltern. What was it about junior officers that they needed to gab constantly?

He put the phone down and looked at his watch. It wouldn't take Sarah more than twenty minutes to arrive. It sounded like Collins was a headcase, but did that make him the murderer? The killings looked like the work of someone cool and calculating, not someone prone to violent rages and impulsive acts. Chiltern was supposed to have been checking up on the man –

Vallance was just about to go when he spotted the telephone bill tacked neatly into the corner of the notice-board. He smiled. Even gangsters needed to pay the phone bill. What was more, he realised as he pulled it from the board, even gangsters received itemised bills.

He checked through the list of numbers quickly. The same numbers occurred repeatedly, and two numbers in particular appeared more than any others. Isobel Thomas had been right. Jack was taking the piss, he didn't care what she knew and had made no attempt to hide his love affairs from her. The dialling code of the first number was local and Vallance guessed that it belonged to Jenny Cunliffe. Which meant, he hoped, that the second number belonged to Jack's mysterious other woman.

It was a lot to hope for, but Vallance needed the break. He dialled the number and waited. It rang again and again before, finally, an answer-phone kicked in. A male voice.

'Hi, there's no one here to take your call,' it said, 'but if you want to leave a message for Patrick or Rosemary we'll get back to you as soon as possible. Bye, and have a good day.'

Vallance was still listening as the message ended and the machine beeped into record mode.

SIXTEEN
Thursday 12th December

Chiltern was in the front room of the house, chatting amiably with the forensics people. He stopped as soon as he saw the look on Vallance's face.

'Trouble, sir?' he said, though it seemed fairly obvious from the urgency of the call that it had to be trouble.

'Outside,' Vallance said.

'Where are we going?' Chiltern asked, following Vallance towards the car.

'Nowhere, yet. Now, what the hell did you get on Collins?'

'Not a lot, sir. He's pretty clean, no criminal record, no outstanding summonses or anything. He sounds like a bit of a religious nut though. Aside from working for the charity he runs a Sunday afternoon class after church. There's been a couple of complaints from parents about him in the past. He's smacked a few of the kids, nothing serious, just a belt across the ear and no one's ever pressed charges. That's a real turn-up for the books, though, a Sunday school murderer.'

Vallance nodded. It sounded like Collins had real problems with his temper. And if he had found out about his wife having an affair – Perhaps that was what Jack had been afraid of after all. It looked as though Sarah had been right about him all along.

'I want him arrested on sight,' he said. 'He's driving around in a white transit van. Number unknown but do a computer check on him. While you're at it I want Graham Scott of Components International nicked as well. He should be at work, so get whoever's back at base round there pronto.'

Chiltern was excited by the sudden flurry of activity. 'Who're we going after, sir?'

'No one,' came the reply, 'we're staying put for the moment.'

Chiltern was clearly disappointed. 'Does that mean that Jenny Cunliffe's in the clear?'

Vallance shrugged. 'Have you got money on it being her?'

Chiltern nodded sheepishly. 'I stand to lose a packet if it's not her,' he admitted.

'You should have said, then we could have framed the poor cow.'

'I'll get back on the radio to base then,' Chiltern said, obviously deciding he preferred the police radio to any more of Vallance's sarcastic comments.

Vallance headed back to the house. Now he knew why Jenny was being so secretive about the identity of Jack's other woman. Was she afraid of Patrick Collins too? Why had no one other than Sarah picked up on the man? It had been Dobson's job to investigate the Good Neighbours connection, and what had he come up with? Nothing. And where was Dobson now? Chasing up his obsession with Clark and Isobel Thomas. Vallance knew that Dobson needed to be informed about the latest developments in the case, but given all of Dobson's underhand dealings with Riley he decided to hold off. The case was going to be solved without him, and if it caused Riley to hit the roof then so much the better.

He walked back into the front room to find that the forensics people had taken root. They stopped talking as soon as he entered the room. 'Don't you people have work to do?'

There were mumbled apologies and one by one they vacated the room. They'd be slagging him off behind his back but Vallance didn't care. He needed to sit down more than they did. The questions kept coming back to him. Why had Jenny Cunliffe gone out with Trevor Watkins? He was certain that she had some ulterior motive other than sexual pleasure. Before Sarah had called he had been certain that Jenny had gone out with him so that she could, perhaps, learn to ride a motorbike. Or else she wanted access to a bike.

He slumped onto the sofa and put his feet up. His boots were caked in mud but he was too knackered to care about it. Jenny Cunliffe was still hiding something. Gut instinct told him that she knew more than she was letting on. More than just the fact that Rosemary Collins had also been having an affair with Jack. Was it possible that she had suspected Patrick and had been too afraid to admit it?

Vallance stood up again. He was tired but jumpy, he needed to do more than just sit and wait for Sarah Fairfax to arrive. God, if only he had a detective half as good on his team – She was stubborn, bad-tempered and refused to take advice. And she looked good.

From the window he looked across the Close to Jenny's house once more. Had Michael Cunliffe ever looked across to the Thomas house with suspicion? From what Jenny had said the man was terribly jealous and constantly suspected her of being unfaithful without once pointing to Jack Thomas. The idea of his wife with another man had also excited him in some way. Vallance remembered her describing how her husband had been turned on by the idea.

He turned slightly and looked at Mrs Grant's house. Vallance smiled. She hadn't suspected Rosemary Collins either. Vallance realised that the woman Mrs Grant had described as Jack's sister was actually Rosemary. She was older than Jack and so she hadn't imagined that he'd be interested in her. More than that, Vallance realised, it meant that Jack's alibi for the Cunliffe murder was likely to be confirmed. It meant that Jack was probably out of the picture once and for all.

He glanced at his watch. Why the hell couldn't she drive faster? Vallance felt impatience surge powerfully through his chest. It was only concern for Sarah that stopped him rushing out with Chiltern to arrest Scott or Collins. The problem was that alongside the concern he felt for her he also felt irritation and anger. If she'd kept out of the way then – Then what? It looked as though she had been proved right and it rankled. He was the cop, he was the one who should have made the connection to Patrick Collins, not Sarah. He had been as blinded by his theory as Dobson had been with his.

He sat down again. What if Collins got to Sarah before she managed to make it to safety? The idea made his blood run cold. If he'd killed twice there'd be nothing to stop him doing it a third time. And if he had an idea that the game was up there'd be nothing for him to lose. A man with his violent temperament would want to take revenge on Sarah while he still could.

The minutes dragged on. At last, unable to stand the wait, he dialled through to headquarters. There was no point in calling anyone on the team, he hoped they were all out looking for Collins and Scott. The only other person he felt able to trust was Anne Quinn.

She recognised his voice instantly. 'Yes, sir?' she responded.

There was something odd about her voice. She didn't sound at all pleased to be hearing from him. 'Listen, Anne,' he said, 'I need to know what's going on –'

'I'm sorry, sir,' she said, 'but as I'm not on the case I –'

'Is Riley looking over your shoulder?' he said, hazarding a guess as to why she was being so cold.

'No, sir. The superintendent's not here, I'm on my own at the moment.'

It was lunch-time, the rest of CID were probably out at a pub somewhere. If she was on her own then why the formality? 'What's the problem?'

'Nothing, sir,' she replied stiffly. 'I'm just obeying orders. I've not been assigned to the case and –'

'That's crap, come on, Anne, I need to know what the hell's happening? Has Patrick Collins been nicked yet?'

She hesitated. 'No, sir,' she said, finally. 'But from what I've heard Graham Scott's under arrest and is on his way here.'

'So, there's no news at all on Collins?'

She hesitated again. 'No. But this isn't my case,' she added. 'I'm sorry, sir, but –'

'What the hell is it?' he demanded angrily. He was used to taking crap from people like Dobson and Riley but why was Anne Quinn joining in?

'Nothing.'

'Something's eating you,' he said. 'Has Riley been giving you a hard time or something?'

She snorted indignantly. 'No, sir. Superintendent Riley has been absolutely straight with me. Now, if there's nothing else —'

He heard a car braking sharply and realised that Sarah had arrived. 'We'll talk later,' he promised and closed the call.

Sarah came rushing into the house immediately. She looked pale but otherwise no worse for wear. As she entered the room Vallance breathed a sigh of relief. She was safe.

'Have you arrested him yet?' she demanded.

He was pleased to see her but he couldn't tell her so, it wasn't what she wanted to hear. 'No, there's no sign of him,' he admitted. 'Scott's under arrest though, he's being taken to headquarters for questioning right now.'

'Ask him about the export of his non-functioning fire alarms to the third world,' she said. 'That's what he's doing. The fire alarms that he can't sell in this country any more he's manufacturing and selling abroad to countries like Zimbabwe. Presumably he feels it's OK to burn and maim people abroad now that he can't get away with it over here.'

Vallance listened impatiently. 'How's that linked to this case?' he asked.

'Collins is acting as his export agent. They're using the charity as a cover.'

'And you think that Cunliffe knew about it?'

She shrugged. 'I've got no proof, yet, but that's what I'm assuming.'

'What about you? Do you feel OK?'

'Of course I do,' she snapped. 'I'm ready to give a full statement as soon as possible.'

Vallance sat down again. The mere suggestion that she might be human enough to be shaken by her experience had been enough to annoy her. 'What happened when he tried to run you down?'

She sat down too, though she appeared too agitated to sit still for long. 'I was in my car when he jumped into his —'

'What?'

She stopped and looked at him calmly. 'I said I was in my car and he was —'

He shook his head. 'That's not how it sounded earlier. How could it be attempted murder if you were in your car and he was in his van?'

She looked at him angrily. 'You weren't there, you didn't see the murderous look in his eyes.'

'He was trying to frighten you,' he said. The colour was starting to come back to her. It was probably the anger exploding inside her. Collins wasn't the only one with a temper.

'Look at my car,' she said, standing up to point through the window. 'Go on, Mr Vallance, take a good look at it. Do you really think that it would stand an impact from a transit van going full throttle? And if you've got an imagination, which I sincerely doubt sometimes, then try to imagine what it would be like to be sitting there with a two-ton vehicle heading directly for you.'

Vallance glanced through the window. Something caught his eye. A car. Not Sarah's sporty little number but the dark-coloured Astra that was parked outside Jenny Cunliffe's house. Jenny's father had an Astra, he remembered seeing it when her parents had arrived after the murder. But Cunliffe himself had the same type of car.

'It's Patrick Collins,' Sarah stated quietly.

Vallance turned to her. 'You think he's dumped the white transit?'

She nodded. 'I wouldn't put it past him. It's the obvious thing to do.'

'There's only one way to find out,' he said. She didn't need to say it, he knew that she'd be coming with him. They raced out of the room, through the house and out onto the driveway.

One of the forensics people was on her hands and knees, carefully going over a patch of grass with her white gloves and sample bag. 'When did that car arrive?' Vallance demanded urgently.

The woman looked up at the car and shrugged. 'Can't have been more than a couple of minutes ago,' she said. 'It wasn't there when I started this.'

Chiltern stuck his head out of the car. He was still on the radio but he covered up the mouthpiece. 'What is it?'

'Did you see who got out of that car?'

Chiltern looked over his shoulder. It was obvious he hadn't even seen the car arrive. 'No, sir. Shall I go and check?'

Sarah was at the car before Vallance. She slid into the back seat while Vallance jumped into the front passenger seat. 'Go on!' he urged as Chiltern started the car.

The tyres screamed as Chiltern spun the car round. He put his foot down hard and sped furiously down the length of the Close, easily dodging the few parked cars along the way. He pulled up sharply, making the tyres protest again and jerking everyone in the car forward.

Vallance was out first and he went straight for the window of the front room. No one. No sign of Jenny and no sign of anyone else.

'It's his car all right,' Sarah called. 'It's got a 'Jesus Saves' sticker in the back window.'

There wasn't time to reflect on the irony. Vallance moved quickly, tried the front door and found that it was locked. 'The back door,' he said, jogging round the side of the house. He hoped for Jenny's sake that she was as trusting as Jack Thomas had been.

There was no one in the kitchen either but, thankfully, the back door was unlocked. Vallance went in first and, only a step away, he was followed by Sarah and Chiltern. They moved quietly, heading through the house into the dining room and then checking the front room once more. Nothing.

'She's crying,' Sarah whispered. They stood at the foot of the stairs and listened to the stifled sobs coming from one of the rooms upstairs.

'What if he's got a gun?' Chiltern whispered cautiously.

It was a good question to which Vallance had no answer. 'Wait here,' he said, 'and call for back-up.'

He didn't wait for an answer. He took a deep breath and raced up the stairs. His footsteps seemed to boom throughout the house but they were nothing compared to the pounding of his heart. What room? There were three doors leading off from the landing at the top of the stairs. Which door? The door at the end. He took the gamble and launched himself forward just as Sarah reached the top of the stairs.

He crashed through the door and fell forward. He ducked down, half afraid of the shotgun blast he expected to take full face. Jenny was in bed, sitting up, crying softly. A second woman was on the bed, sitting on the edge beside her. No sign of an enraged Patrick Collins.

Vallance straightened up quickly. He was shaking but that was nothing compared to how stupid he felt.

'Rosemary? What are you doing here?' Sarah asked. She too seemed very shaken.

Rosemary Collins. Jack Thomas's elusive girlfriend. It was hard to picture anyone less like one of Jack's women as described by Mrs Grant. She was older than Jack was, with greying hair that looked a mess and tired eyes that radiated compassion.

'Jenny needed help,' she said softly, handing Jenny a number of pills and a glass of water. 'She called me earlier,' she added. 'She was afraid that she was going to be arrested.'

Vallance looked at Rosemary and then at Jenny. He tried not to picture the two of them in bed together with Jack Thomas. 'Do you know where your husband is, Mrs Collins?' he asked.

'He was delivering a stock of parcels to the warehouse,' she said. 'Come on, Jen, you need these, you know what the doctor said.'

Jenny shakily took the handful of pills. She looked exhausted, on the edge of collapse. Vallance felt sorry for her. Damn it, if she hadn't been so cagey –

'He tried to kill me,' Sarah said. 'Come on, Rosemary, why not admit the truth now? There's no need to cover up for him.'

Rosemary shook her head. 'There must have been some misunderstanding. Patrick can fly off the handle but he's not a murderer.'

Jenny was studying the pills in her hand, looking through the tears that poured copiously down her face. She took the glass of water and started to lift the pills to her mouth.

'No!' Vallance sprang forward and grabbed Jenny's wrist.

She dropped the glass and the water went everywhere, splashing Vallance as well as staining the pristine white sheet and the pillow cases. She looked up at him fearfully, shrinking back as though expecting a blow to the face.

'What is it?' Sarah asked as he carefully prised the pills from Jenny's hand.

Vallance looked at the pills and then reached for the bottles of tablets on the bedside cabinet. He opened the anti-depressants first but they didn't match the ones she was about to take. The sleeping pills did, there were only a couple of the dark blue capsules left in the bottle. Jenny had been about to take seven of them in one shot.

'How did you guess?' Rosemary asked.

Chiltern picked the glass up from the floor and sniffed it tentatively. 'It smells like vodka, sir.'

'You mean it wasn't Patrick after all?' Sarah said, sounding more surprised than anything else.

Rosemary looked at Jenny and then back at Vallance. 'Did you know?'

'I saw how many pills she was about to take,' he said. 'Each time I've seen her she's been more out of it than before. I'd just put it down to the normal effects of the drugs she's been given, but now I realise you've been helping her along.'

'What is it?' Jenny asked, her voice barely audible.

'It's nothing,' Rosemary reassured. 'Mr Vallance just wants to talk to me for a while.'

Jenny wasn't completely gone. 'Does he know?' she asked.

Rosemary sighed and nodded. 'Yes, he knows.'

Jenny began to cry again. 'It was his own fault,' she gasped. 'If he hadn't been so greedy – I loved him, but he was just so greedy and – He ruined everything –'

'Look after her,' Vallance told Chiltern. 'And for God's sake make sure she doesn't take anything else.'

'You'll have to call a doctor,' Rosemary said. 'She's already had six of the pills.'

'I'll call an ambulance,' Chiltern said.

'Sarah, stay with DC Chiltern and try and keep Jenny talking. For God's sake don't let her sleep.'

Sarah nodded. 'Come on, we need to get her on her feet,'

she said, instantly taking command of the situation.

Rosemary stood up. She smiled at Jenny and then kissed her softly on the cheek. 'I'm so sorry it turned out like this,' she whispered.

Jenny looked as though she were about to drop off. Whether she heard Rosemary or not was unclear, but she nodded vaguely. Sarah grabbed her under the arms and started to pull her out of bed.

'Shall we talk now, Mr Vallance?'

He looked at Rosemary. Her face was deeply lined and her sad eyes carried the same fatalism as her voice. For some reason that he couldn't quite fathom, he felt immensely sorry for her. At first sight he could hardly imagine her as a ruthless and calculating killer, but clearly that was what she was.

She walked down first, going straight for the kitchen. 'Do you mind if I make some tea?' she asked as Vallance followed her in.

'No, go ahead.'

'Would you like a cup?'

He had just caught her trying to poison Jenny. 'No thanks,' he said, 'I've just had one.'

She smiled, as though she recognised that he was lying and understood why. 'I didn't want Jenny to suffer,' she said, filling the kettle. 'That's why I didn't let her take all the pills in one go. She's been taking more and more all week, I'm surprised she's managed to keep going for so long.'

He sat down at the kitchen table. 'You'll probably still be charged with her attempted murder,' he said. 'You were more successful with her husband and with Jack.'

She put the kettle down and switched it on before turning to face him. There was no sign of nerves about her, she was completely calm as she spoke. 'How much do you know already?'

It was time for him to trust his instincts. 'I know that you didn't act alone. I know that Jenny's deeply implicated.'

'She regrets it now, but it was her idea to begin with. Michael told her about the money that was being – siphoned I think is the word he used. I've put more years of my life and more energy than I dare think about into Good Neighbours.

I've sacrificed everything to help people and then, when things got tough with the mortgage and everything I – That's how it started.'

She stopped to make herself a cup of tea, pouring the steaming water straight onto a tea bag in a bright blue mug. It was as though she were in her own home, she knew where everything was kept and she was clearly at ease.

'I didn't take much, at first. But then when I saw how easy it was – I didn't take vast sums, just small amounts to buy the occasional present for myself. God knows I wasn't getting any attention from Patrick and it didn't seem such a crime – And then when I went out with Jenny a few times I saw that things could be different.'

'She introduced you to Jack Thomas,' Vallance guessed

'He wasn't the first,' she said, her face reddening slightly. 'But he was the first I really felt something for – By then I was taking more and more money. Patrick had no idea of course, he still doesn't,' she said. 'He cares more for the scriptures and spreading the bloody word than he does about me,' she added vehemently. 'If Patrick hadn't been so bloody-minded then I'm sure that Michael would never have looked so deeply into things. When he discovered what I'd been doing he threatened to tell Patrick about it unless he got a share. Poor Michael Cunliffe, that poor victim was a blackmailer, Mr Vallance.'

'That's why Jenny said he was so greedy,' Vallance guessed.

'Yes. He wanted more than I was taking, he said it would be easy to cover up. And then when he found out about Jack Thomas –'

'Did he know about Jenny?'

Rosemary smiled sadly. 'No, he just thought it was me. He had no idea what she was up to – I told her, of course, I told her about the blackmail and that he knew about me and Jack and that it would only be a matter of time before he found out about her and Jack – That's when she suggested we get rid of him. It sounds awful, doesn't it? But she said it would be so easy – Jack had already killed a man before. We asked him and he refused. He thought it was funny –'

It sounded so unreal. 'But it was such a professional job,' he exclaimed.

'It was, in a way. Jack had told us in detail how he'd killed a man and how the police had pinned the blame on Simon Clark. Jack called him a loser, he laughed at the idea that the police saw Clark as a hit man. All we did was to plan the murder in the same way. I know how to use a gun, I learned how to shoot when Patrick was in the forces. And Jenny went out with a motorbike courier to learn more about bikes because I already knew how to ride one. It was easy to steal Jack's gun, and the bike he'd used when he'd killed someone. And it was easy to hide them in the warehouse for when we needed them.'

'So who killed Michael?'

Rosemary sighed regretfully. 'We both did. She pulled the trigger but we were there together. Once we'd done it she was filled with remorse – All that emotion was real, Mr Vallance. But then Jack realised exactly what we'd done. He guessed what had happened immediately. That's when he got greedy too. He hadn't known about the money, but once I told him he decided that he needed a cut too.'

'Is that why you killed him?'

'The money? No, I didn't care about that, I would have handed him every penny. No, it's just that he threatened to tell you about the murder. Another blackmailer, Mr Vallance. I'm afraid that I killed Jack on my own, Jenny was in no fit state to help me by then.'

'But she knew about it?'

She nodded. 'We trust each other completely.'

'Does that trust include poisoning her?'

Rosemary looked hurt by the suggestion. 'No, she wanted to kill herself. I was just helping her, it was what she wanted.'

He became aware of the distant siren of the ambulance. 'What about Graham Scott and your husband? How do they fit in?'

'They don't, not really. Patrick thinks I don't know about the alarms thing –'

'So Sarah's right about that?'

Rosemary nodded. 'The last couple of times we've been abroad Patrick's fixed up a few orders for Graham. He's convinced himself that the alarms are safe and that the whole thing was cooked up by evil people in the media. I don't know if he really believes that or whether he's doing it to make money –'

The banging on the door could only be the ambulance people come to save Jenny Cunliffe.

'Wait here,' Vallance said.

Rosemary took a sip from her tea and smiled. 'I've no where to go, Mr Vallance,' she said. 'Oh, and you'll find the gun under Jenny's bed. We agreed that she'd take the blame, posthumously of course.'

'That was good of her,' he said. 'You know, I can't ever remember meeting such a considerate pair of murderers before.'

EPILOGUE
Friday 13th December

Vallance looked at the date at the top of the charge sheet. Friday 13th, unlucky for some. Unlucky for Jenny Cunliffe, still recovering in hospital, and for Rosemary Collins, remanded in custody. It looked as though Rosemary had been telling the truth about Jenny wanting to kill herself. Even after having her stomach pumped Jenny had refused to say anything bad about her friend and had not tried to shift the blame at all.

The end of the case had a few consolations. Dobson had been livid at the outcome. Not only had his favoured suspect been comprehensively cleared, but Vallance was pushing for the assault charge against Simon Clark to be dropped. Jack Thomas had been a shrewd judge of character and his description of Clark as a loser was spot on. In fact it now seemed that the murder which Clark had been suspected of had been down to Jack Thomas all along.

It was also something of a consolation that Sarah Fairfax had not been proved right about Patrick Collins. She'd been right on lots of things but in the end she'd been picking on the wrong Collins. Sure, Patrick and Graham Scott were involved in some deeply suspect activities but outright murder was not part of that. Morally they stunk to high heaven, but then that wasn't a police matter.

Vallance had been right about Jenny Cunliffe, even though

he'd blown hot and cold about the idea. It was the emotion that had fooled him. He'd been convinced by the tears of grief, which were real though they were mixed with tears of remorse. However he hadn't suspected Rosemary. Even when he'd found out that she was Jack's other woman he hadn't suspected her.

The gun and the motorbike were there in the warehouse, just as Sarah had suggested. Forensics were going through the motions of course, but with two outright confessions there was no hurry in what they were doing.

After all the excitement and the adrenalin in the case Vallance felt oddly deflated. Two serious crimes had been cleared up and evidence on other crimes also unearthed, but he could feel no satisfaction. He'd uncovered a whole web of lies and deceit that left a nasty taste in the mouth.

The phone buzzed just as he was about to get up for some coffee. He dropped the charge sheet on the desk and lazily reached for the phone.

'Mr Vallance?' Sarah's voice came through loud and clear.

'Yes, Miss Fairfax,' he replied, adopting the same formal language and tone that she did.

'Now that we've cleared up the Cunliffe case,' she began, 'there is one other matter we need to discuss.'

He noted the use of 'we' in clearing up the case. She was probably right, she'd done more than most of the people in his team in getting to the bottom of the case. 'And what's that?'

'The case of Malik Alibhai,' she said, reminding him of the case she'd talked about previously.

'But I've explained that,' he said, 'it's out of my area —'

'You're a senior policeman,' she snapped. 'Please, will you just see what you can find out for me?'

'But —'

'It's important to me.'

What the hell? 'I'll see what I can dig up,' he promised. He knew that there wasn't much he could do, but if it helped —

'Thanks. I'll be discreet of course.'

'Of course. Perhaps we can discuss this over dinner?'

There was a long pause while she considered her answer. 'What about lunch?'

He smiled. It wasn't much in the way of progress but the promise of lunch was better than the flat refusal he'd got the first time he'd asked her out. 'When?' he asked, trying not to sound too pleased.

'When you've got something to report,' she said. 'I'll talk to you then.'

He put the phone down. OK, she saw it as a business lunch, but that was still better than nothing. He knew that they'd argue before the start of the first course. Hell, they'd probably argue *about* the first course.

'Yep!' he called cheerfully when there was a sharp knock on the door.

He smiled as DC Quinn came into the office. 'The Chief wants to see you, sir,' she said.

He looked at her. She was still acting strangely. Gone were the friendly smiles, the banter and the undercurrent of desire that they felt for each other. 'What is it, Anne?' he asked.

'I don't know what you mean, sir,' she lied.

'Look at me and say that again,' he challenged angrily.

She looked away. 'He wants to see you now, sir,' she repeated.

'Shit! He can wait. What's going on, why won't you tell me?'

She leaned back against the door, afraid that someone would overhear. 'I thought you were different,' she said quietly. 'Now I know that you're not. I just feel so stupid for trusting you in the first place.'

'What the hell are you talking about?' he demanded, this time keeping his voice low.

'Don't you know?'

'Would I be going through this if I knew what the hell you were talking about?'

'I thought you understood the difference between what we did in bed and what goes on in real life. Just because I get off on being told what to do – Just because I liked calling you "sir" and all of that – Well, that's just sex, it's what turns me on.'

What was she talking about? He knew that it was sex; he understood that it was a fantasy that she had and which had turned him on too. 'I know all of that,' he said emphatically. 'So what's the problem?'

'Superintendent Riley told me all about you needing me to provide a woman's touch on the house-to-house enquiries at Fenton Close. You needed a little woman to collect all the gossip, isn't that what you said? You're just like the rest of them,' she said bitterly.

Riley, the devious bastard, had played his cards just right. 'I was just talking bullshit to see if I could get you on my team,' Vallance protested.

She looked unconvinced. 'All I know is that you used that sexist crap instead of asking for my help properly.'

'I know it's crap,' he insisted angrily. 'I was just using his language to get the better of him, that's all.'

She shrugged. 'It doesn't matter now. Shall I tell the Chief that you're otherwise occupied?'

Vallance accepted defeat. 'I'm sorry this ever happened,' he said, standing up. 'You're a good copper, Anne, and I just wish that you could see how Riley's manipulated this whole thing.'

'I'm sorry too. But what went on between us is over now.'

'If you say so,' he said quietly. He wanted to touch her, to just stroke her face softly and to kiss her on the lips but he knew she'd push him away as soon as he touched her. 'Do you know what the Chief wants?'

She nodded. 'He and Superintendent Riley want to discuss your relationship with Sarah Fairfax.'

Vallance closed his eyes. There were lots of things that left a nasty taste in the mouth, and not all of them were down to the lies and deceits of villains.

CRIME & PASSION

DEADLY AFFAIRS
by
Juliet Hastings
ISBN: 0 7535 0029 9
Publication date: 17 April 1997

Eddie Drax is a playboy businessman with a short fuse and taste for blondes. A lot of people don't like him: ex-girlfriends, business rivals, even his colleagues. He's not an easy man to like. When Eddie is found asphyxiated at the wheel of his car, DCI John Anderson delves beneath the golf-clubbing, tree-lined respectability of suburban Surrey and uncovers the secret – and often complex – sex-lives of Drax's colleagues and associates.

He soon finds that Drax was murdered – and there are more killings to come. In the course of his investigations, Anderson becomes personally involved in Drax's circle of passionate women, jealous husbands and people who can't be trusted. He also has plenty of opportunities to find out more about his own sexual nature.

This is the first in the series of John Anderson mysteries.

CRIME & PASSION

A MOMENT OF MADNESS
by
Pan Pantziarka
ISBN: 0 7535 0024 8
Publication date: 17 April 1997

Tom Ryder is the charismatic head of the Ryder Forum —
an organisation teaching slick management techniques to
business people. Sarah Fairfax is investigating current
management theories for a television programme called
Insight and is attending a course at Ryder Hall. All the women
on the course think Ryder is dynamic, powerful and
extremely attractive. Sarah agrees, but this doesn't mean that
she's won over by his evangelical spiel; in fact, she's rather
cynical about the whole thing.

When one of the course attendees — a high-ranking civil
servant — is found dead in his room from a drugs overdose,
Detective Chief Inspector Anthony Vallance is called in to
investigate. Everyone has something to hide, except for Sarah
Fairfax who is also keen to find out the truth about this
suspicious death. As the mystery deepens and another death
occurs, Fairfax and Vallance compete to unearth the truth.
They discover dark, erotic secrets, lethal dangers and, to their
mutual irritation, each other.

This is the first in a series of Fairfax and Vallance mysteries.

CRIME & PASSION

INTIMATE ENEMIES
by
Juliet Hastings
ISBN: 0 7535 0155 4
Publication date: 15 May 1997

Francesca Lyons is found dead in her art gallery. The cause of death isn't obvious but her bound hands suggest foul play. The previous evening she had an argument with her husband, she had sex with someone, and two men left messages on the gallery's answering machine. Detective Chief Inspector Anderson has plenty of suspects but can't find anyone with a motive.

When Stephanie Pinkney, an art researcher, is found dead in similar circumstances, Anderson's colleagues are sure the culprit is a serial killer. But Anderson is convinced that the murders are connected with something else entirely. Unravelling the threads leads him to Andrea Maguire, a vulnerable, sensuous art dealer with a quick-tempered husband and unsatisfied desires. Anderson can prove Andrea isn't the killer and finds himself strongly attracted to her. Is he making an untypical and dangerous mistake?

Intimate Enemies **is the second in the series
of John Anderson mysteries.**

A TANGLED WEB
by
Pan Pantziarka
ISBN: 0 7535 0156 2
Publication date: 19 June 1997

Michael Cunliffe was ordinary. He was an accountant for a small charity. He had a pretty wife and an executive home in a leafy estate. Now he's been found dead: shot in the back of the head at close range. The murder bears the hallmark of a gangland execution.

DCI Vallance soon discovers Cunliffe wasn't ordinary at all. The police investigation lifts the veneer of suburban respectability to reveal blackmail, extortion, embezzlement, and a network of sexual intrigue. One of Cunliffe's businesses has been the subject of an investigation by the television programme, *Insight*, which means that Vallance has an excuse to get in touch again with Sarah Fairfax. Soon they're getting on each other's nerves and in each other's way, but they cannot help working well together.

A Tangled Web **is the second in the series
of Fairfax and Vallance mysteries.**

HOW TO ORDER BOOKS

Please send orders to: **Cash Sales Department, Virgin Publishing Ltd, 332 Ladbroke Grove, London W10 5AH**.

Be sure to include with your order the title, ISBN number, author and price of the book(s) of your choice. With the order, please enclose payment (remembering to include postage and packing) in the form of a cheque or postal order, made payable to **Virgin Publishing Ltd**.

POSTAGE AND PACKING CHARGES

UK and BFPO: £4.99 paperbacks: £1.00 for the first book, 50p for each additional book.
Overseas (including Republic of Ireland): £2.00 for the first book, £1.00 each subsequent book.

You can pay by VISA or ACCESS/MASTERCARD: please write your card number and the expiry date of your card on your order.

Please don't forget to include your **name, address and daytime telephone number,** *so that we can contact you if there is a query with the order. And don't forget to enclose your payment or your credit card details.*

Please allow up to 28 days for delivery.

A Blakes Cottage for Only £5* per person, per night when you buy any two Crime & Passion books

Offer is open to UK residents aged 18 and over. Offer closes 12th December 1997.

Booking your Blakes Cottage is easy. Just follow the step–by–step instructions listed below:

1. To book your Blakes Cottage for only £5* per person, per night, simply call 01282 445056, quote the Crime & Passion £5 per person, per night offer and reference MPJ702.

2. The Blakes Holiday Adviser will ask you for the following:
   * the number of adults and children in the party
   * your preferred holiday dates (the duration must be a minimum of one week)
   * your preferred holiday area

3. You will then be offered a choice of selected properties and provided with details of price, location, facilities and accommodation.

4. To confirm the booking you will be asked for full payment by credit card or cheque.

5. Send the completed application form shown below, together with two Blakes Cottages/Crime & Passion tokens and a till receipt highlighting your purchase to: Blakes Cottages, The Crime & Passion Offer, Stoney Bank Road, Earby, Colne, Lancs BB8 6PR.

Application Form

Title   Mr/Mrs/Ms ....

First Name(s) ....

Surname ....

Address ....

....

....

Postcode ....

Telephone Number ....

C & P

One Token

A Tangled Web

If you do not wish to receive further information and special offers from Virgin Publishing or Blakes Cottages you should write to Blakes Cottages, Dept. DPA, Stoney Bank Road, Earby, Colne, Lancs, BB8 6PR

Terms and Conditions

1. Each property must be booked at maximum occupancy (i.e. four people cannot occupy a property which sleeps seven).

2. Holidays must start and finish between the following dates: 5 April–23 May; 13 September–17 October; 1 November–19 December 1997 inclusive.

3. All holidays and properties are subject to availability.

4. * Blakes Cottages standard booking terms and conditions apply. These are published in the Blakes Cottages Brochure and are available on request. This offer applies to new bookings only. Blakes Cottages, the name of which is used under licence from Blakes Holidays Limited, is a trading division of Holiday Cottages Group Limited. Prices do not include Blakes' compulsory cancellation protection insurance cover ($£17$ for a family of 4 staying in a $£5$ per person, per night property). There are additional charges for pets, linen, credit card payments and additional insurance if required. Details of the relevant amounts are given in Blakes Cottages Brochure or at the time of booking.

5. No cash alternative is available.

6. Closing date for bookings is 12 December 1997.

7. The offer is available only to people over 18 and resident within the UK. The offer is not open to employees or their families or agents of Holiday Cottages Group Ltd or Virgin Publishing Ltd. All holidays are subject to Blakes Cottages standard Booking Conditions. These are published in the Blakes Cottages Brochure which is available upon request from Blakes Cottages or through any travel agent. Properties are available throughout England, Scotland and Wales.

Blakes Cottages, the name of which is used under licence from Blakes Holidays Limited, is a trading division of Holiday Cottages Group Limited.

Promoters: Virgin Publishing Ltd., 332 Ladbroke Grove, London W10 5AH; TLC Ltd., 48 Harley Street, London W1N 1AD and Blakes Cottages, Stoney Bank Road, Earby, Colne, Lancs BB8 6PR